TICK TOCK

A Detective Shakespeare Mystery

By
J. Robert Kennedy

Detective Shakespeare Mysteries

Depraved Difference

Tick Tock

The Redeemer

James Acton Thrillers

The Protocol

Brass Monkey

Broken Dove

The Templar's Relic

Zander Varga, Vampire Detective

The Turned

TICK TOCK

A Detective Shakespeare Mystery

J. ROBERT KENNEDY

CreateSpace

ISBN: 146814295X
ISBN-13: 978-1468142952

10 9 8 7 6 5 4 3 2

For my mom, the most avid reader, and mystery lover, I know. Thanks for always being there, for always caring, and for always being a mom when I needed it, and a friend when I didn't.

TICK TOCK

A Detective Shakespeare Mystery

FORWARD

The events in this book occur almost immediately after those in *Depraved Difference*, Book #1 in the Detective Shakespeare Mysteries series. Reading *Depraved Difference* is not necessary to enjoy *Tick Tock* as it is a wholly self-contained novel, however it is recommended to fully understand how many of the characters met, and to understand some of the references made to previous events. Should you choose to read *Tick Tock* first, effort has been made to not reveal too many of the secrets of *Depraved Difference*, allowing you to still enjoy it in the future.

ONE

Today she felt pretty.

Usually she didn't. She was about twenty pounds overweight, okay, twenty-five, but this morning's ritual visit to the scale had shown her down two pounds, adding to the three she had already lost this week since her latest diet had begun. Five pounds was a huge psychological boost, and today she had put on an extra couple of splashes of Estée Lauder Sensuous Nude to celebrate. She always tried to keep herself presentable. Smart outfits, nice faux jewelry as accents, with a couple of real pieces she had managed to buy herself over the years—18 karat gold bangles and a gold-by-the-yard chain from the one trip she had done to Vegas. Her hair was coiffed nicely, her makeup subtle, and she always tried to have a smile on her face, which she found the most difficult part of her effort.

I just want to be given a chance.

She knew she was chubby; there was no hiding or denying that. But didn't she deserve to be happy too? She was like any other young woman. She wanted to *be* loved. She wanted *to* love. She wanted to be happy. She had never had a boyfriend. In high school a few boys had gone on dates with her thinking she'd be an easy lay since she'd obviously be desperate, but they had left disappointed. She had been too shy to show her body, and now the opportunities had disappeared.

She had friends, and they sometimes set her up on blind dates, but they never worked out. Either they weren't interested in the fat girl, or she would do something to sabotage things from going further. She seemed to be her own worst enemy when it came to rectifying that situation.

Do I want to be alone?

No, she didn't. But it was Friday evening. And she was going home alone. Again.

The elevator chimed and the doors opened. Frank Brata, one of the techno geeks at the lab stepped on. He smiled at her.

He's so cute!

"Hey, Sarah. Working late?"

She knew she blushed. She couldn't help it. Frank was about the only good looking guy that paid any attention to her. She knew he was way out of her league, but he never seemed to judge her. "No rest for the wicked."

He chuckled. "Tell me about it. Vinny has me working on the final cleanup from the Eldridge case." His face clouded over, as if the memory of those events were about to overwhelm him.

"I know, none of us can believe it."

He nodded. "Shakes is taking it really hard."

"I can imagine."

Suddenly Frank turned to face her. "He was such a great guy!" His voice cracked. "He was about the only guy who treated me like I was normal!"

Her chest felt tight. *He thinks he's not normal?* She reached out and touched his arm. He looked down at her hand and she was about to withdraw it when he clasped his other hand over it and gave it a squeeze then let go. She wanted to leave her hand there, to feel the warmth of his touch, the warmth of his arm, but she knew she had to let go.

The bell chimed and the door opened for the lobby. They both stepped off and Frank turned to her. "Listen, there's a place I go every Friday after work for coffee. Would you like to join me?"

She had to stop herself from yelping 'yes'. She made a show of looking at her watch. "Yes, I suppose I've got time."

Right, you've got until Monday 8 a.m.

Frank smiled, as if happy with her response. *Well, why wouldn't he be, he invited you, didn't he?* She knew she had to stop the negativity. Frank was a nice guy. She deserved a nice guy. *And by the sounds of it, he may be just as insecure as you.* "So, how're the ribs?"

"Huh?"

"Your ribs. From being shot."

"Oh! Pretty good now. It's been a couple of weeks. Still a little tender when I try to work out. I find I can't take deep breaths without gasping. Doc says it'll be weeks before I'm completely back to normal."

"How'd it happen?"

"You haven't heard? I thought everyone had by now."

She'd heard it a dozen times. But never from him. "Just the rumor mill, and you know how accurate that is. I'd rather hear it from the source."

Frank nodded and recounted the incident as they walked to the coffee shop that turned out to be about ten minutes away. By the time they reached there, she had made enough physical contact with him, touching his arm, patting his back, his chest, and any other part she could find an excuse to touch without it seeming creepy, to feel a connection forming. Or was it just her getting her hopes up again? She didn't know. All she knew was she was having the best time she had had in years.

As they approached, he took her hand and held open the door. She smiled up at him and he returned the smile. A genuine, heartfelt smile.

And she melted inside.

Frank woke, his head pounding. *What the hell happened last night?* He tried to think back. *I left the office. Where did I go? Sarah!* And then he remembered. They went for coffee, were having a great time, then nothing.

But there was something.

He had the vague memory of kissing. It must have been Sarah. *But why don't I remember?* He opened his eyes and sucked in a breath. He was in a bedroom, but not his, the only light coming through the partially closed drapes. *Where the hell am I?* He checked the bed and was alone. He looked around and found a lamp on a nightstand. He flicked it on. *Definitely a chick's place.* He lifted the covers. *Naked.* He looked on the floor and spotted his clothes lying in a bundle. He grabbed them and headed toward what he guessed was the bathroom. He flicked the light on and squeezed his eyes shut, the sudden change blinding. He tossed his clothes on the counter, found his boxers and yanked them up. He pulled his dress shirt from under his pants and shoved one arm in then the other. Looking in the mirror to button it up, he gasped.

He was covered in blood.

His face and neck were splattered with it, his chest clean, but his shirt was stained near the neck, with drops of blood covering most of the front and shoulders. He ripped off the shirt, threw it into the bathtub and jumped back in shock.

Sarah's blood-soaked body sat in the tub, half submerged in the dark red water, her lifeless head laying on the tap, facing the wall away from him, the finger of her right hand resting on the edge of the tub, near the wall. Near the wall that had "Frank Brata" written in blood.

He leaned over the toilet and vomited.

It was a quiet funeral. Detective Justin Shakespeare wasn't sure what he was expecting. Obviously the customary funeral afforded a dead cop was out of the question, and he didn't begrudge the city that. The people he expected to see were there for the most part, including that bastard Vincent Fantino, who had, he had to admit, been a little bit friendlier toward him over the past week. He was shocked to see Aynslee Kai there. *I wonder if she's here in an official capacity.* He looked for a camera crew, but there was none. *Huh, back to a brunette.* He walked over to her.

"Miss Kai."

She looked up from behind a handkerchief. "Detective Shakespeare, how are you?"

He looked at the casket containing his partner of three years. "About as good as can be expected, I guess."

She glanced around. "Not much of a turnout."

"Nope. He had no family except the department, and most of them just don't know what to do, so most 'had plans'," replied Shakespeare with air quotes.

"I can understand that," said Aynslee. "In fact, I don't even know why I'm here. I feel ridiculous."

"Sometimes you need closure. Perhaps this is it for you."

She looked up at him then at the casket. "Yes," she whispered. "Closure."

The priest cleared his throat and the few in attendance turned to pay their final respects to Detective Hayden Eldridge.

Shakespeare looked around at those assembled.

Where's the kid? And Trace? I thought they said they were going to be here?

Frank sat in a chair in the kitchen of the small apartment, shirtless, pulling at his hair. *What am I going to do?* Working as a tech in the NYPD, he knew what he should do. He should call it in, and let the system do its job. But the evidence against him was overwhelming, and worse, he couldn't even say himself whether or not he was innocent. He had no memory after the coffee shop. Had they been attacked, had he been hit over the head? He reached up and checked his skull for bumps, for any evidence of a hit to the head that might explain his memory loss. Nothing. *Then I must have been drugged.* But if drugged, why? And by who? So they could kill Sarah and have someone to blame seemed the logical explanation.

And they've definitely done their job.

He looked about him, at the perfectly appointed small apartment. Everything neat, everything in its place, and everything screamed no struggle. Had the struggle occurred in the bathroom? The kitchen and bedroom were immaculate except for the bed and floor, indicating sex had most likely taken place.

Man, I finally get laid and I can't remember it.

He smacked his forehead with his palm, disgusted at what he had just thought. *Sarah's dead, and you're disappointed you don't remember having sex with her? Just before you probably killed her?*

And that's when it hit him. His chest tightened, his ears filled with the rush of blood as the room narrowed around him. *I killed her. My life is over.* His head dropped into his hands and he sobbed. *But I'm only twenty-six!* He opened his eyes and watched a tear roll off his nose and onto the pristine floor below. It hit, almost as if in slow motion, the perfect circle it formed immediately marred by the splash radiating outward, as if a flower suddenly opened its petals.

What am I going to do?

He grabbed a tissue from a nearby box and blew his nose. He wiped his eyes clear with the back of his hand, and rose.

There's no way I'm going to prison.

Shakespeare made the sign of the cross, said "Amen", and turned to Aynslee.

"Can I give you a lift somewhere?"

"No, that's okay, the station gave me a driver." She smirked. "I guess they don't trust me to drive just yet."

"Perfectly understandable."

"Well, it's been over a week. I'm going back on the air Sunday." She squared her shoulders, took one final look at the casket resting in the ground, and began to walk toward the too empty parking lot. "How are you doing?"

Shakespeare shrugged his shoulders. "Okay, I guess. I still can't believe the first person in my career I shoot is my partner." Vinny walked up and joined them. Shakespeare jerked a thumb at him. "I always figured if I was going to shoot someone, it would be him."

Aynslee leaned ahead of Shakespeare and gave Vinny a slight smile, which he returned.

"I'll give you that one, Shakes."

Shakes. I haven't heard that in years. It had been his nickname throughout his career until the incident five years ago where his diabetes had got the better of him, and he had lost evidence, and in the disgrace that followed Vinny had publicly shamed him, and most of the department shunned him. To this day no one knew his diabetes had driven him to seek food before his blood sugar fell too low, it was his diabetes that had caused him to not think straight and leave important evidence, a murder weapon no less, in the front seat of his car with the window down. Since then, the collegial nickname Shakes had been replaced with things far worse.

"Fat bastard," muttered Shakespeare.

"Huh?" Aynslee looked at him, then at Vinny.

Vinny seemed to trip over his words. "Uh, yeah, well, I'll see you back at the station, Shakes, I mean, Justin." He scurried away, leaving Shakespeare and Aynslee alone in the parking lot.

"What was that all about?"

Shakespeare watched Vinny's car pull away. He turned to Aynslee. "Perhaps I'll tell you some day." *God knows I need to tell someone.*

She smiled and squeezed his arm, then pointed at a man standing near a corporate limo, the door held open. "That's my ride. Don't be a stranger." She pushed herself up on her tiptoes and gave Shakespeare a peck on the cheek, then strode toward the waiting car.

Shakespeare watched her climb in, her stunning beauty not lost on him. *You're old enough to be her father.* He hit the fob for his car, the alarm giving a double chirp in recognition. He opened the door then fished his cellphone from his pocket.

Where the hell is Trace?

Frank had made a decision—an easy one. He wasn't going to prison. Which meant he wasn't going to turn himself in. But his decision had consequences. If he rid the crime scene of any evidence that may incriminate him, any evidence that may clear him and lead to the real killer would be destroyed as well. He stood up and paced back and forth, from the kitchen to the bedroom, but never the bathroom, trying to decide what to do. He knew he was in the system. Everyone who worked for the NYPD was in the system so their prints and DNA could be excluded from crime scenes they accidentally contaminated. His problem was there was no good reason for him to be on the call. When the murder was discovered, the scene would be locked down and there would be no reason for him to be there. There was a computer, but they'd just bag it, tag it, and bring it to him. He could think of no possible reason for him to gain access so his DNA, his fingerprints, could be chalked up to accidental contamination.

Could he process the scene himself?

Yes, he knew enough to do it since he had taken some basic training to be a Crime Scene Tech before returning to his original love, computers. But he didn't have the equipment with him to dust for prints, or take samples.

Think!

He stopped and looked about. There were no signs of a struggle. The killing must have happened in the bathroom, and from what he remembered of the few moments he spent in there, *in* the bathtub. If he wasn't the killer, which is an assumption he had to make otherwise he deserved anything that happened to him, the killer had gone to a lot of trouble to frame him. *Gloves!* Anybody who went to this amount of trouble, would surely use gloves. That meant there would be no prints from the killer. He could confidently wipe the place down to make sure his prints wouldn't be found.

One hurdle down.

DNA. What are the sources of DNA? Blood, saliva, hair, skin. And semen. *Oh my God! How do I deal with that?* He pulled at his hair then let go, removing his hands slowly and looking for any he might have just yanked free. *Idiot!* He looked about. He had to stop spreading even more of himself about the scene. He returned to the kitchen and looked under the sink, finding a pair of rubber gloves. He slipped them on.

Okay, no more fingerprints.

He headed toward the bathroom and nearly jumped out of his skin when his phone rang. He fished it out of his pocket and looked at the call display. *Fantino, Vincent.* It rang again, his trembling hand almost dropping it. He knew there would be no way to control his voice. It rang a third time, then went to voicemail. *You're off duty.* He knew there was no reason for them to expect to reach him today; it was Saturday.

His heart suddenly thumped in his chest as he realized he had missed the one event scheduled for his entire weekend. The one event scheduled where cops would be. The one event he didn't have a reasonable excuse for missing.

The funeral!

Vinny flipped his cellphone closed without leaving a message. *The kid probably just couldn't face it.* He had lost enough friends over the years to know funerals were hard, especially this one. He and Eldridge had been close, he considered him one of his best friends, and now he was gone, and in such a shocking manner. *Give him the weekend.*

He left the funeral heading in no particular direction and soon found himself at the Detective Bureau. He parked and sat behind the wheel for a few minutes, staring at nothing, his mind filled with images from that night, the night his friend had died. *Hayden, why?*

He pulled the keys from the ignition and headed inside. *Work will help take my mind off of it.* He bounded up the stairs to the fifth floor where the detectives were and strode into the squad room, for what reason, he had no idea. There was a full complement on duty, no rest for the NYPD on a weekend, but as he walked in, the entire squad room went quiet and turned to look at him.

And no one made eye contact.

Lieutenant Gene Phillips looked up from his desk behind the glass separating him from his squad, and motioned for Vinny to join him. Vinny stepped through the maze of desks and poked his head in the LT's office. "You wanted to see me?"

Phillips beckoned him with two fingers. "Close the door."

Vinny closed the door behind him and took a seat in front of the desk.

"So, how was it?"

Vinny shrugged his shoulders. "About what you'd expect."

Phillips nodded. "Turnout?"

"Not many. Me, Shakes, the reporter Aynslee Kai, a few of the guys he went through the academy with, a couple of army buddies."

"Nobody else from here?"

"Brata and Trace said they'd be there, but were no shows."

Phillips leaned back in his chair, the ancient contraption squeaking in protest. "Frank doesn't surprise me, he's young. Trace was on her way but I had to call her back in. You probably passed her on your way up, she just left on a possible homicide."

"Possible?"

"Anonymous tip."

"You should've called me."

Phillips shook his head. "No, not today. You needed to be there and your team can handle it themselves."

He's right. I needed to be there.

"Well, I'm here now. Idle hands, you know."

Phillips frowned for a moment, then sighed. "It's your crew, so knock yourself out. I'm sure they'll love having their boss hanging over their shoulders on a weekend." He smiled and Vinny chuckled. "Dispatch has the address."

A commotion on the other side of the glass caused them both to spin in their chairs. A perp was being led in, screaming at the top of his lungs, "It ain't no stealin' if the keys is in the ignishun!"

Detective John "Johnny" Walker pushed the teenager into a seat and handcuffed him to the desk as Vinny and Phillips joined the gathering throng, Walker's hand beckoning them. "Okay, gents, here's one for the record books. Anyone got the number for Guinness?"

"What've you got, Detective?" asked Phillips.

"Hey, LT, get this, genius boy here"—Walker jerked his thumb at the perp—"decides he's gonna steal a car."

"I di'int steal it!"

"In front of a cop no less."

"I di'int knows you wuz no cop!"

Walker smacked him on the back of the head. "Shut up! So, I'm walking out with my coffee from Eddie's, and I see this Jag sitting there with the door open, engine lights flashing, you know, typical Jag."

"Broken down?" offered Vinny.

"Of course."

"How's I supposed tuh know?"

"Because you're a freakin' car thief!" Walker raised the back of his hand at the perp but didn't strike him, instead turning back to the squad.

"So, bold as brass, this punk walks up to the car as if it were his own, climbs in, and pulls away."

"How'd you end up with the collar?" asked Phillips

"I chased him."

"In your car?"

"Nope, foot pursuit."

Vinny's eyes narrowed. "Huh?"

"Yup, car engine was so fucked it was in safety mode and would only do about five miles per hour. I just trotted up alongside, put my coffee"—he held up his cup—"on the roof, held up my badge, and after a couple of blocks he finally gave up."

"So you're telling me—"

"That you are looking at the first ever successful foot pursuit of a high performance sports car."

Walker bowed several times as the squad room erupted in laughter and clapping.

"Next time I won't steal no damned Jag!"

Walker looked at him. "Next time? You aren't too bright, are you?"

Vinny shook his head, smiling, and headed to his office to grab his gear.

Never try to make a getaway in a Jag.

Frank, now sporting a shower cap duct taped to his head, his shoes bagged and taped to socks his pant legs were stuffed into, sprayed and wiped every surface outside of the bathroom he may have touched with a bleach solution to destroy any DNA he might miss. And he was dripping in sweat. He had his shirt collar buttoned up tight, anything that might let a stray hair free was taped, his poor man's crime scene bunny suit crude, but effective. He knew enough from his forensics training to get the areas people didn't think to wipe down, like door jambs, cutlery, coffee machines (inside and out), entranceway walls where one might put their hand to balance when putting on a shoe, light switches, bulbs, anything.

He cleaned like he had never cleaned before, and with each wipe, his shame grew. But he had no choice. He couldn't go to prison. Not for something he was sure he hadn't done. At least he was pretty sure. He wiped the door frame to the bathroom, and turned to survey the living room and kitchen with a satisfied nod. Done. Wiped down from top to bottom, the floor and every seating surface vacuumed twice, spotless. If there was any DNA left that was his, he'd be stunned.

And now for the gruesome part.

He turned to face the bathroom and stepped toward the vanity, starting at the topmost surface he may have touched, and began to work his way down.

He saw a hair.

Too long to be his, and the wrong color. Sarah was a blonde, and this was brown or black. Could it be a friend of hers? Could he take that risk, to actually destroy a real piece of evidence? He knew the killer had to have worn gloves, so his cleaning up the living area had most likely not destroyed anything. But here he was, at the scene of the crime. If anything unexpected had happened, it would be here. Here would be where the mistakes were made.

He put down the cloth and headed to the kitchen. Opening the drawers, he soon found what he was looking for—a box of Ziploc bags. He returned to the bathroom, bagged the hair, and looked about for any others, but found none. He resumed wiping down the vanity and spotted a drop of blood on the top of the faucet. One lone drop. Could it be his? No, he was sure it wasn't. Before putting on his homemade bunny suit, he had stripped and checked himself for any cuts, anything that might have left blood evidence, and found none. This meant if he found any he could leave it as is with confidence.

But it could be Sarah's. He looked at it. *I have to know!* It was the only drop. Every other spot of blood in the bathroom was in the bathtub enclosure. There appeared to be nothing else anywhere, except this one lone drop. If he took a sample, perhaps with a cotton swab, he might be able to sneak in a test of his own at the lab, and…

And prove what? He stopped. He knew it wasn't his. It was Sarah's or the killer's. *Leave it; it might be the only thing that leads them to the real killer.*

He looked at the bag with the hair. *What are you doing?* He unzipped the bag and returned the hair to where he had found it. It wasn't his. The blood drop wasn't his. He had to give the CSU guys every chance he could to let them solve the case and find the real murderer.

Turning to the tub, he knew there was one piece of evidence he couldn't leave.

He leaned over Sarah's body and sprayed the wall where she had written his name, silently apologizing to her. As he scrubbed at the dried blood, he began to think about this vital connection to him. *Did she think I did it? Or* am *I the killer?* He shuddered. *Or did the* real *killer write this?* He paused. Should he leave it? Could the handwriting experts tell whose handwriting it was?

They wouldn't need to! It's your *name! You might have been seen leaving with her! Case closed!*

He sprayed some more and wiped, this time with a little more vigor.

Vinny pulled up in front of the apartment building Trace's crime scene was supposed to be at, and was surprised to find his team milling about outside. He parked behind a squad car and climbed out. Constance "CC" Cruz, one of his senior investigators, walked up to him.

"Hey, boss, wasn't expecting you here today."

"Felt like keeping busy."

She nodded, a slight smile showing she understood why. They all did. All week he knew they had been walking on eggshells, not sure what to say around him, and when he'd enter a room, conversations would suddenly stop and people would busy themselves without making eye contact. Hopefully now with the funeral over, things could start to get back to normal.

"What've we got? Why are you all out here?"

"Haven't got a scene to process."

"Tip didn't pan out?"

"No, they just haven't found it yet."

"Huh?"

"Tip was this building. No apartment was specified."

Vinny rolled his eyes as he looked up at the towering apartment complex. "How many units?"

"Almost five hundred."

"When did they start?"

"Not even an hour ago. Trace is in there with some uniforms going door to door. More are on the way, but it could take a while."

Vinny sighed, then raised his voice so they could all hear. "Okay, let's put everything away, then get in there and help find this scene."

Frank stood back and surveyed his handiwork, not with a feeling of pride in a job well done, but with a sickness in his stomach, and an overwhelming shame at what he had just finished. He stepped toward the bathtub, held out the bottle of bleach, and poured what was left, almost half a bottle, into the water, unable to look at Sarah's body. This was a long shot. If he did have sex with her, then his semen would almost definitely be found. This was more of a Hail Mary pass, a last ditch effort he hoped would work if he was right about yet another assumption of his. He had found no evidence of a condom anywhere, and in his inspection of himself, he had found no evidence he had had sex, with a condom or otherwise. He was sure he hadn't had a shower, he could tell from his hair and just his general feeling of grunginess. And if he hadn't had a shower, and hadn't had sex, then the worst he had to worry about was saliva, which would be on the surface, and which the bleach should destroy. He looked down at Sarah, her hair and blood matted together, the rest of her head submerged under the water, and poured the last of the bleach directly on her head.

I'm so sorry.

He stepped back and out of the bathroom, turning off the light and closing the door. He put the now empty bottle of bleach in a large garbage bag, and backed himself toward the apartment door, all the while scanning the room for anything he may have missed, but found nothing. The vacuum cleaner was in a suitcase he had discovered under the bed, along with his blood stained shirt. He wore a sweater he had found on the top shelf of her closet, an oversized sweater with I Love New York emblazoned across it, a one-size fits all that fortunately for him, didn't look too ridiculous with his casual-Friday pants.

He picked up the suitcase and garbage bag. All that remained was for him to toss the garbage bag down the garbage chute, go down the stairs a couple of floors, then take the elevator the rest of the way out. With luck he'd make it off the floor unseen, and with even greater luck, he'd make it out of the building. He stepped toward the door and spotted a baseball cap. He grabbed it and pulled it low over his eyes.

He reached for the lock when he heard three rapid knocks on the door.

"NYPD, open up!"

Detective Amber Trace knocked on the umpteenth door of the day. In fact it was the seventy-third according to her list. Luckily it was a Saturday morning, and most people were still home. This had made it easier to strike units off the list. Those who wouldn't let them in were threatened with a possible warrant, and the door always opened. A quick search of each apartment had turned up nothing.

And none probably will.

She hated these calls. They were almost always pranks, but they couldn't be ignored. If someone had been murdered, then they had to find out. And the tip was rather specific according to the 9-1-1 call she had listened to. A young, twenty-something female had been raped and murdered in her apartment at this address. The voice had been disguised electronically, which was why this call was taken seriously. Usually the punks pranking the system didn't go to that much trouble.

She was on the fourth floor, working up with two uniforms in case there was trouble, and more were on the way to start from the top. They could hit the jackpot on this very door, or it could be the 484th door. And what particularly pissed her off about this call was she had missed Eldridge's funeral. She wasn't sure she had wanted to go until she wasn't able to. It was closure to a horrible night she would now never get. *Somebody better have died!* She mentally kicked herself for that one and knocked again.

Still nothing.

She put her ear to the door and listened for a moment. She stepped back and marked a star on the list of apartments.

"We'll come back to this one."

Frank hadn't moved in inch, had barely breathed, for what felt like hours, but had only been minutes. The voice was unmistakable, he had heard it enough over the years to know it was Detective Trace. He heard her say something after the second knock, then moments later, heard more knocking, but this time further down the hall. He slowly let out a sigh of relief, and put the suitcase and garbage bag down.

What now?

He walked over to the window and opened the drapes for the first time and gasped. The view was one he had seen a thousand times before, probably ten thousand times before. It was the same view he enjoyed from his own apartment, only lower. He looked down at the street below. There was no doubt; he was in his own apartment building, just on a lower floor.

His phone vibrated in his pocket with a text message. He flipped open the display and his eyes shot open then looked out the window, searching, but finding nothing. He looked back down at the message.

TICK TOCK
LITTLE TIME ON THE CLOCK
IF YOU DO NOT LEAVE SOON
YOU WON'T SURVIVE PAST NOON

Frank grabbed the curtains and yanked them shut. *I'm being watched.* He held his thumb over the power button, but hesitated. *I'm in my own building. I just need to get to my apartment. How hard can that be?*

But who had sent him the text message? And why? It had to be the killer. And for a brief instant he felt a huge weight lift off his shoulders. *I'm innocent! I must be! There's a third person involved!* It must be whoever drugged him—but that could wait. Regardless of whether or not they were in fact helping him now, he knew he needed to get to his apartment on the eighth floor, with the garbage bag and suitcase. But there was a problem. He knew they had cameras in the elevators. If he were seen getting on at this floor, how could he explain that? But he also knew they didn't have cameras in the stairwells. From the view, he figured he was three, maybe four floors up. Could he make it up four or five flights of stairs without being seen? Would they have uniforms in the stairwells?

He took another quick peak out the window to the street below. He could see only one squad car, but two more pulled up as he looked. *If they don't have people in the stairwells now, they will soon.*

The phone vibrated again.

TICK TOCK
LITTLE TIME ON THE CLOCK
DON'T WASTE YOUR CHANCE
ON ONE LAST GLANCE.

This was advice he decided to take. He ran to the door, opened it slowly and looked out. Seeing no one, he stuffed his hand in the sleeve of the sweater and cleaned the doorframe along with the door handle on either side. He grabbed the garbage bag and the suit case, then walked with purpose toward the garbage chute, which he now knew the exact location of. He opened the door to the small room and was about to shove the bag down the chute, when he thought better of it. He reached in and pulled out the empty bleach containers and other items he wouldn't be able to flush upstairs in his own apartment, and shoved them down the chute, all the while careful to keep his hands in the sleeves to protect against fingerprints. Finished, a check out the door found the hallway still clear, and he walked quickly toward the stairwell.

He opened the door and stepped halfway in, listening for footfalls. Nothing. He stepped inside and took the stairs two at a time. *Fifth floor.* He raced past, grabbing the rails as needed, not worrying about leaving prints here, since he could honestly claim he occasionally took them to keep in shape. *Sixth floor.* He heard the door open one floor below. He couldn't risk it; he kept racing up the steps. *Seventh floor.*

"Hey, you there, police! Stop!"

It was Trace. He hesitated, but for only a moment. He knew they couldn't see him, as long as he kept away from the railing, and kept at least a double-flight of steps ahead of them. He moved to the outside edge of the stairwell and continued to run.

"Stop!"

The urgency in Trace's voice told him he was no longer a curiosity, but a suspect. He raced up the steps, the echo of several sets of boots below him echoing through the stairwell, and he knew they were gaining, as they could hug the inside, and didn't have a suitcase hampering their ascent. *Eighth floor.* He grabbed the handle and pushed, spilling out into his hallway. He raced toward his apartment, fishing the keys out of his pocket as he did so. He skidded to a halt in front of the door, stuck the key in the lock and turned. He shoved himself against the door as the doors at the end of the hallway burst open. He thrust himself inside and closed the door behind him as quietly as he could, bolting it. He heard the pounding of footsteps down the hall halt near his door.

Think fast.

He raced into his bedroom, shoved the suitcase and garbage bag under his bed, stripped out of his clothes, throwing them all in the hamper, then wrapped a towel around his waist. Somebody hammered on a door, but it wasn't his. *They don't know which apartment it was!* He took a deep breath, checked himself in the mirror, and walked toward the door just as the sound of a fist hammering on it thundered through the apartment.

"NYPD, open up!"

He counted to five then opened the door.

"Detective Trace! What're you doing here?"

TWO

Trace tried not to let her jaw drop. "Frank? What the hell are *you* doing here?" Frank's face flushed a little more than it already was.

"Um, living?"

"Huh?"

"I live here."

Trace eyed him for a moment as she processed the information. Her eye wandered down involuntarily, taking in the young, firm body standing in front of her, the bruises from the shooting still evident, but a pale yellowish brown now. *Not bad, kid.* She chuckled inside. *You're old enough to be his—*. Her eyes flew back up as she realized she was staring at the towel around his waist. *Older sister.*

"Were you just in the hall?"

He shook his head. "No, why?"

"We had a murder reported here."

"Here"—he swept his hand inside—"in this apartment?"

A little dramatic, aren't we kid?

"No, in this building." She pointed at the towel. "Weren't you supposed to be at the funeral?"

"Weren't you?"

Trace raised her eyebrows and opened her hands, palms upward, trying to convey the idiocy of his question without saying it. "I got called to a possible murder?"

He blushed. "Oh, yeah, well, ummm, I guess that's as good an excuse as any."

"And yours?"

He paused, as if thinking up one. *Take it easy kid, nobody blames you for not going.*

"I guess I just couldn't face it, you know, the body and all, the—" His voice cracked.

The big sister in her wanted to reach out and give him a hug, but she resisted.

"Don't worry about it, I understand." She squared her shoulders, bringing the situation back to business. "Did you hear anybody run past here a few minutes ago, or a door open?"

He shrugged his shoulders. "Can't say I did, but then again, it's not the kind of thing you listen for—doors are opening and closing all the time in an apartment building."

Trace nodded.

"Okay, Frank. You take it easy, we'll see you Monday."

He gave a weak smile and closed the door.

Trace turned to the two uniforms.

"Did either of you see which door the guy went into?"

The first, an Officer Richards, shook his head. "No, ma'am, can't say as I saw anyone. Could have gone out the other stairwell door for all we know."

Trace nodded.

"Possible, but I didn't think he had that much of a head start." She pointed at Richards. "You stay here; detain anyone who tries to leave." She turned to the other. "And you come with me, we'll continue where we left off."

She walked toward the stairwell and pushed open the door.

There's no way the guy got this far.

Frank leaned with his back against the door, listening to his heart hammer in his chest, and Trace talking to the two officers. He forced himself to take slow, deep breaths, each one sounding so loud he feared they would be heard on the other side of the door. He heard the stairwell door open, then close.

They're gone.

He pushed himself off the door then looked through the peephole and nearly swallowed his heart as it leapt from his chest. One of the uniforms was standing directly in front of his door. He quickly stepped back, then tiptoed deeper into the apartment. He turned the television on to make some background noise, then went into his bedroom, sitting on the edge of the bed.

He closed his eyes, and breathed in through his nose, out through his mouth, trying to calm himself. After a few minutes the pounding in his chest had eased, and he was able to focus. He moved his heels back and felt them touch the suitcase from Sarah's apartment. He had to get rid of the evidence there, he knew, but for now, there was no way to get it out of the building. As if to reinforce the point, he heard another siren out on the street.

His phone vibrated. He searched for where he had tossed it in his mad rush to get undressed, and found it still in his pants pocket, in the hamper. He flipped it open and hit the button to read the newly arrived text message.

TICK TOCK
LITTLE TIME ON THE CLOCK
WHAT WILL YOUR POLICE FRIENDS THINK
WHEN THEY DISCOVER YOUR DRINK?

What does it mean?

Then he knew. They would retrace Sarah's last movements, and he would be seen on the security cameras leaving with her, to go get the coffee.

Frank's mouth filled with bile as he rushed to the bathroom.

Trace stood impatiently waiting for the building maintenance man to open the apartment. It had taken hours of knocking door to door fruitlessly, and then hours more waiting for the warrants to search the apartments they hadn't gained access to. The warrants were specific. Enter, search for a body of a woman meeting the description, then exit, leaving the place exactly as it had been found, even if they found a different body. She'd done this before, and hated the part where she couldn't act on what they saw. They almost always found something in any building they did this type of search. But the law was the law.

No matter how flawed.

The super unlocked the door and she motioned him aside.

"NYPD, executing a search warrant!" she yelled at the door, then turned the handle and pushed. The door opened into a darkened apartment, the lights all out, the drapes closed shut. She reached a gloved hand out and flicked the light switch nearest the door. The light in the entranceway blazed, and Trace quickly found a panel of several light switches. She flipped them all on, lighting the open concept kitchen and living room.

The incredibly clean, nearly gleaming, kitchen and living room.

And reeking from bleach.

The hairs on the back of Trace's neck stood up and she motioned to the two uniforms to follow her in. She cautiously stepped across the threshold and into the entranceway. She quickly glanced behind the door to make sure no one was there, then slid the closet door aside. Empty, save for a few jackets and other expected items.

She cleared the kitchen, then living room, and stepped into the bedroom. She motioned to the uniforms to check the closets and under the bed, while she stepped out and entered the bathroom. She flicked the light switch, and frowned.

In the tub lay their victim.

And sitting on the bathroom vanity, a photo showing two naked people lying under bed sheets together, two circular swirling patterns obscuring their faces, as if someone had stuck their thumb in wet paint and twisted.

Vinny grabbed the last of the gear from the back of the Crime Scene Unit truck and headed for the lobby. By now a large crowd had gathered, the flickering lights of the squad cars drawing them like moths to a flame. Yellow police tape cordoned off the area, and pedestrians were redirected to the other side of the street unless they lived in the building. He turned to use his shoulder against the glass door when he saw Shakespeare's distinctive mint condition 1959 Cadillac Eldorado Seville pull up, its bright red with white soft top screaming to be noticed. *For a fat guy, he doesn't seem to mind drawing attention to himself.* He made momentary eye contact and nodded, then pushed the door open and entered the lobby.

As he waited for the elevator to arrive, Shakespeare waddled through the door and walked up to him, slightly out of breath. *How the hell can you be out of breath from just two minutes of walking?*

"Hi, Shakes." He eyed his severely overweight colleague. "You okay?"

He nodded. "Fine, but I'm definitely going to start hitting the treadmill. This is getting ridiculous."

Maybe if you lay off the damned Krispy Kreme's, you wouldn't be in such shit shape.

An elevator chimed and they climbed aboard along with several other members of his team. They rode to the fourth floor in silence. Shakespeare held the door open for Vinny's team, then took up the rear. An officer noted down their badge numbers and let them enter the apartment. Shakespeare immediately headed toward Trace, who didn't look happy to see him. Vinny didn't blame her. He didn't like Shakespeare. As a matter of fact, for years he had despised the fat bastard, but he had to admit the past couple of weeks Shakespeare seemed to be back to his old self, if not form. *Maybe some good can come from Hayden's death.*

"In the bathroom, Vinny!" Trace thumbed at a room to the left as she turned back to Shakespeare. He entered the bathroom as he heard her say, "Jesus Christ, how am I ever going to get my gold shield if the LT keeps handing off my cases?"

Vinny looked at the tub and whistled. *Is this place ever clean!*

He looked at the photo on the vanity and pointed at it.

"CC, dust and bag that. It'll be key, I'm sure." He leaned in and looked at the two swirls over the faces. "And you better call Frank. I think we may need his computer talents on this one."

Shakespeare splayed his hands, palms up. "Sorry, Trace, but the LT wanted more experience on this." Trace wasn't making eye contact, and

Shakespeare knew she was biting her tongue. He wouldn't want to give up a case to him either. Not with the reputation he'd managed to garner for himself over the past few years. Lazy. Sloth. Pig. Unreliable. Incompetent. And those were the polite words he had heard said about him. But he was determined to change people's opinions of him, to get his reputation back. There was a time when he was considered the best detective in the Bureau. People *wanted* to work with him. People *wanted* his opinion.

Not anymore.

"Listen, Trace, you're still on the case, I'm just lead."

She nodded her head, still not making eye contact.

If she bites that lip any harder she'll draw blood.

He looked around. "Okay, tell me what you've got."

This seemed to snap Trace out of her funk, and to her credit she became all business.

"At 9:32 this morning we received an anonymous tip with a computer distorted voice, phoned in from a throwaway cell phone, that the body of a young female would be found in this building, but no apartment number was given."

"Distorted, eh? That's unusual."

Trace nodded. "We went door to door, narrowed it down to a couple of dozen units, got warrants, and started executing. We found the vic in the bathroom about an hour ago."

Shakespeare slowly spun on his heel, taking in the living room and kitchen area. "This place is spotless." He sniffed. "Bleach?"

"It was really strong when we first arrived. I don't think they're going to find anything except maybe in the bathroom. This place has been cleaned top to bottom, by a pro."

Shakespeare's right eyebrow shot up at the conclusion. "A pro? What do we know about the vic?"

"Nothing yet. White female, mid-twenties, blonde, dead less than a day I'd say. ME can tell us more when he gets here."

"No ID?"

"Nothing that I've found."

"Name?"

"According to building management, Larissa Channing."

Frank stood over the toilet, flushing wad after wad of paper towel and Kleenex he had taken from Sarah's apartment. He couldn't risk putting anything in the trash disposal as that would certainly be searched. As he waited for the tank to fill again, his cellphone rang. He pulled it from his pocket. *Cruz*. He knew he had to answer it now that Trace knew he was here. He pressed *Talk*.

"Hello?"

"Hey, Frank, it's Connie Cruz, how are yah?"

"Fine."

"Listen, we need you at a crime scene."

He knew CC would be the primary CSU criminalist today since Vinny would have taken the day off for the funeral. That meant she was almost definitely in the building. *Should I play dumb?*

"The one in my building?"

"Huh?"

"Trace was here earlier, going door to door."

"You live here?"

"Yeah, eighth floor. What apartment number?"

"Four-oh-four."

"Okay, I'll be down in a few minutes."

Best not to play dumb.

He hid everything away in the suitcase again, got dressed, and took the same stairwell he had used earlier to the fourth floor, making certain he touched everything he could reasonably touch, just in case they decided to dust it for prints.

He pushed open the door and slammed it shut, making certain the officer manning the crime scene entrance saw him exit the stairwell. Now he had established a witness. He took a deep breath as he approached the apartment. He hadn't even realized Sarah lived in his building. In fact, he found it nearly impossible to believe they hadn't bumped into each other, but maybe she was new, maybe she had just moved in. He showed his ID to the officer and entered the apartment. It was eerie. Almost as if in a movie. He had been here only hours before, cleaning like a mad man, after a night of God only knows what, and now, here he was on the job, the apartment filled with his colleagues, hell bent on capturing him. He wanted to cry out he didn't do it. To tell them everything he knew. To tell them how ashamed he felt at what he had done. And how terrified he was.

Trace nodded at him.

Shakespeare turned to him. "What are you doing here?"

Frank gulped and he was sure he had turned several shades paler. "CC called me to look at something."

Shakespeare's eyebrow shot up.

That can't be good.

Trace pointed to the left. "Hey, Frank. CC's in the bathroom."

He hurried toward the bathroom before the conversation could continue, and stepped inside to find Vinny and CC leaning over Sarah's body. He looked away. "You needed me for something?"

Vinny looked over his shoulder at him. "What's wrong with you, you look like you've seen a ghost?"

Frank wasn't sure what to say.

"Hey, give the kid a break, last time he was at a crime scene he got shot."

Vinny grinned at him and jerked a thumb at Sarah. "Don't worry, kid, she's unarmed."

CC shook her head. "You've got no couth, boss."

Frank stayed quiet, wondering why they needed a computer tech at a crime scene. "Ummm, you, ah, wanted me for something?"

CC pointed at the vanity counter. "Check out that photo."

Frank's eyes darted to the counter and he gasped. *That wasn't there when I left!* He stared at the photo, the two bodies entwined, their faces obscured with a Photoshop Swirl he instantly recognized. He felt the world start to close in on him. His heart hammered in his chest, his ears filled with the rush of panic, his vision began to lose focus, and go dark. He felt himself collapse to his knees, and Vinny's concerned voice, as if thousands of miles away, too faint to understand. Something gripped his arm, and he tried to pull away, but it wouldn't let go.

Then everything went black.

Shakespeare spun toward the commotion in the bathroom and covered the distance in three quick steps. What he found shocked him. The kid was lying on the floor, blood coming from a small gash in his forehead, Vinny was holding him by the wrist, and CC had one hand over her mouth, another hand stuck in the water with the victim.

"What the hell is going on in here?"

"The kid fainted!" Vinny let go of Frank's wrist and glared at Shakespeare. "What's he doing here anyway?"

Shakespeare returned the glare. "Don't look at me, I didn't call him. He's a computer geek, not Crime Scene."

"I'm amazed you know the difference."

"Blow it out your—"

"I called him."

They both turned to look at CC.

"You told me to call him to process the photo."

Vinny sighed. "In the lab, not here."

"But he lives in the building, so—"

"He lives in the building?" interrupted Shakespeare.

Trace poked her head in the crowded bathroom. "Yeah, I ran into him today. We chased someone earlier that refused to stop in the stairwell. Could've sworn he went into the kid's apartment, but obviously not."

Shakespeare looked down at the kid who began to stir. "Obviously." He looked around. "So, where's this photo?"

"On the—" Vinny stopped as he looked at the counter. "It was on the counter here a minute ago."

Shakespeare bent over and pulled the kid's other hand out from under him.

In its tight grip was the evidence bag containing the now crumpled photograph.

At first he heard murmured voices, then light followed by blurred images. *What happened?* As things slowly came into focus, he realized he was lying down, and his head was killing him. He reached up to touch the source of the pain.

"He's coming around."

He saw a shadow fill his vision, and someone touch his shoulder.

"You okay, kid?"

It was Vinny. *The bathroom! The photo!* Reality rushed back, and the room snapped into focus. Vinny was leaning over him, CC was perched on the side of the tub, and Shakespeare's huge frame filled the doorway.

And he was holding the photograph in his hand.

"Are you okay to stand?"

Frank looked at Vinny and nodded. "Yeah, I think so."

Vinny hauled him to his feet then held him by both arms. "You sure?"

Frank took a deep breath and nodded. "Yeah. What happened?"

"You fainted," said CC.

Frank felt himself flush.

"Don't worry about it, kid," said Vinny. "First time you've seen a body up close?"

They don't know why I fainted! Run with it!

He nodded, making sure to avoid looking at the tub.

"How about you give me that?" said Shakespeare, pointing at the photo. Frank nodded and handed it over. "Now, get yourself a drink of water in the kitchen," said Shakespeare, stepping from the doorframe.

Frank stepped out and headed to the kitchen. He opened the cupboard and removed a glass, filling it with water from the tap. He took a few sips, then turned to face the room. All eyes were on him. *Do they know?*

"Feeling better?"

"Yes, Detective, I'm okay now."

Shakespeare nodded, then held up the photograph. "Any reason why you grabbed this?"

Frank's heart pounded and he screamed inside his head. *Keep it together!* He shook his head. "No, I guess I just reached out for something to grab onto, and it was on the counter, so, you know…"

"Hmmm."

If Frank didn't know better, he almost had the impression Shakespeare wasn't buying it.

"What do you make of it?" Shakespeare held the photo out for Frank. He took it, and looked at the two people, obviously in the heat of passion, the computer generated swirl obscuring their faces. "Do you think you can do anything with it?"

Should I lie? He knew he could reverse the swirl. It had been done before, and with the right algorithms, and some trial and error, he'd be able to show the faces of the two lovers. The face of Sarah. And himself. He would be the investigator to prove he committed the crime. *You deserve it.*

"Listen, kid, if you don't think you're up to it, I can assign it to someone else."

"No!" Frank yelped. "Sorry, I'm okay, I can do it. It'll just take a few days."

Shakespeare frowned. "Okay, make sure you sign your name to it. I don't want some damned lawyer claiming a chain of evidence violation. This just might be our only clue."

Yeah, to my guilt.

"Work on the guy first; we're pretty sure we know who the girl is."

Frank gulped. "Wh-who's the girl?"

"We think it's the occupant, Larissa Channing."

"What?" exclaimed Frank. "Who?"

Shakespeare's eyes narrowed. "Larissa Channing. Did you know her?"

"N-no. No I didn't." He took a deep breath. "I guess I'm just still messed up from earlier." He held up the photo. "I'll go get to work."

"You do that."

Frank went to find Vinny to update the evidence log, his mind racing.

If that's not Sarah, then how the hell did I get here last night?

And where's Sarah?

Shakespeare watched the kid as he walked toward the bathroom. *Seems awfully excitable.* He knew they were all upset over Eldridge's death, but this was something else. *There's something he's not telling us.* Could he have known the girl? Perhaps. Even likely since they lived in the same building. Then again, he lived in an apartment building for years and never knew any of his neighbors. This was modern day New York. Who wanted to know their neighbors? If you did, they're liable to start coming over and visit. And he valued his privacy. Too much at times. It had kept him mostly single for decades, until he had met Louise several years ago. Her and her son Tommy had filled a void inside him he hadn't realized was there. It had restored his will to live, to be the man he once was, rather than the pathetic excuse he had allowed himself to become.

It had taken years, but he now realized he had used his diabetes as an excuse, rather than a crutch. At least a crutch was used to get somewhere—an excuse used to get out of going to that same place. He had spent many nights feeling sorry for himself, even crying in his pillow, asking a God he had long stopped believing in why it had to happen to him. His form of acceptance finally came, but in the ugly veil of self-loathing, of a desire to commit suicide through neglect, to give the finger to the world, and to die on his own terms, with nothing to live for, and nothing to leave behind. No family. No legacy. No pride. No self-respect.

But Louise changed that. Why she had ever taken an interest in him he'd never know. She was a waitress at a thirties style diner he frequented, one of those retro style ones with more chrome and glass block on the outside and stainless steel with checkered tiles on the inside, than the genuine article. *The Chrome Worx Diner*. He went for breakfast every Sunday and ordered the same thing. Three eggs over easy, brown toast buttered, sausage and bacon, side of home fries, coffee and orange juice. *Heart attack special.* She'd been his regular waitress, and loved to chit-chat to whoever would listen. And he would listen. Especially over the past couple of years when he had really withdrawn from the world. He had no one to talk to at work, he didn't want to worry his folks as they were getting up there in years, and he had no friends—his loner lifestyle and living the job had taken care of that. Once he was disgraced, he had lost the few work friends he had had.

So he listened.

And she fell in love with him for it.

She would talk about her son, and the problems she was having raising him as a single mother. He would listen, and occasionally venture some advice. Over the months the conversations became more and more two way, and she had asked him out. She said she wasn't going to wait for him to ask her, because she knew he never would. He was stunned to hear the answer come out of his mouth.

Yes.

One word, to save a life. His own.

The next week it was two eggs, poached, ham and brown toast, with a side of sliced tomatoes.

She had smiled at him. And he knew she understood what he was trying to tell her.

I care.

They were inseparable ever since.

He watched Frank scramble out of the apartment, seeming to avoid eye contact with everyone.

Definitely something up there.

"Hey, Shakes, whadaya got for me?"

Shakespeare smiled at Miles Jenkins, one of the city's Medical Examiners, and one of the few who had never given him a hard time over the stolen evidence. He would almost consider him a friend, but for the fact they did nothing together beyond work. He sometimes caught Jenkins eyeing him, as if assessing him medically, and wondered if he had figured out the truth he was hiding, that he was an out of control diabetic. If he had, then he would have seen right through the "I was hungry" explanation to the stolen evidence, and cut him the very slack he had shown.

"DB in the bathroom. See if you can give us an approximate TOD and preliminary COD as well."

Jenkins nodded and headed to the bathroom Shakespeare was pointing to. "I'll see what I can do." Stepping inside, Shakespeare heard him yell, "Okay, everybody out! I need some room to move."

CC and Vinny appeared a moment later.

"Anything?"

Vinny shook his head. "Not much. The whole place has been wiped down and bleached. We're not finding prints on anything. We found one strand of hair, doesn't look like the vic's, and one drop of blood we're hoping to get some DNA off of, but other than that photo and the body itself, we've got nothing. Once MJ is finished with the body, we can take a look in the tub, see if we find anything, then of course we'll go over the body with a fine-toothed comb back at the lab, so maybe we'll find something."

Shakespeare held up his hand. Vinny was rambling, most likely because he was uncomfortable not spitting insults at him. "Okay, I'm going to try and run down the background on the tenant. You get back to me if you find anything, and if you get a positive ID."

Vinny and CC nodded as Shakespeare leaned into the bathroom. "Hey, MJ, call me with time and cause as soon as you have it."

Jenkins was leaning over the victim and didn't turn. "Will do!"

Shakespeare strode from the apartment, nodded to the scene officer who logged him out, and pressed the button to call an elevator. He leaned against the wall, taking a deep breath and wiping his dripping hairline with a handkerchief. He knew his blood sugar was acting up again. And he was so out of shape just standing for the past hour had exhausted him.

His stomach growled.

He patted it.

Time to feed the beast.

Frank stared at the crumpled photograph. He hadn't grabbed it on purpose; he had genuinely passed out and was just reaching for something to hold onto. Unfortunately, if anything, this made him look more guilty. Because guilty was exactly how he was going to look once the photo was enhanced and the swirl reversed. He knew he could do it; it would just take some time, but not enough time. This time tomorrow his face would be there for all to see.

Unless he stalled.

Or…

No, he couldn't do that. Or could he? Could he live with lying? No one would know if he said the swirls couldn't be reversed. But then they might just send it to the FBI, and it would all be over.

What if…?

He could reverse one of the swirls, and then blur the one of him, saying the image was too degraded. That, they would buy, that they would be—

No!

No, he wasn't that type of person. He would have to face up to what he had done. *Or hadn't done.* And that was what was driving him crazy. He was sure he hadn't committed the murder, especially now that he knew the victim might not even be Sarah. He looked up, as if through the many floors of concrete and steel, through the clouds and into Heaven, and prayed Sarah would show up for work Monday as if nothing had happened.

Maybe she knows what happened last night?

He was tempted to look up her number and call.

But what if something did happen to her? What if I did it?

"Aaargh!"

He slammed his fists against the elevator wall.

What if she's in trouble?

He looked at the photo. It was clearly two people, in bed, covered to their necks by a white sheet that clung tightly to their intertwined bodies. But other than that, he couldn't even be sure it was him or Sarah under the sheets. It could be a photo of anyone for all he knew.

He had to know.

The elevator doors opened to a lobby filled with police.

Soon they'll be coming here to arrest me.

His cell phone vibrated with a text message.

TICK TOCK
LITTLE TIME ON THE CLOCK
WHAT WILL YOUR FRIENDS SAY
WHEN IT'S YOUR TIME TO PAY?

He stood frozen in the elevator, staring at the message, as the doors closed.

Shakespeare descended on the elevator and exited into the bustling lobby. To his right was a door with "Tenant Services" written on the brass nameplate. He strode over and opened the door. Inside were two women, sitting behind their desks, their chairs turned toward each other, speaking in hushed but excited tones. They both turned their heads to look at him as he entered.

"NYPD, Detective Shakespeare"—he held up his badge—"I have a few questions about the tenant of apartment four-oh-four."

One of the women nodded and pushed her tiny frame up from her chair. "What do you need to know, Detective?"

"And you are?"

"Marlene Morrison. I work for Bridlewood Property Management."

"I need anything you've got on her, previous addresses, next of kin, anything."

Morrison nodded and held her hand out to the other woman who passed her a folder. "We pulled the file, figuring somebody would eventually come down here. This is everything we've got on her." She handed the file to Shakespeare who flipped it open.

He frowned and pointed at the folder. "*This* is the tenant in four-oh-four?"

Morrison nodded. "Yes."

"You're sure?"

"Absolutely."

"Does she live alone?"

"Yes."

Shakespeare flipped open his phone and dialed.

"Yes," answered a shaky voice.

"Frank? This is Shakespeare. Forget what I said before. Concentrate on the woman in the photo."

"Wh-why?"

"Our ID just went to shit. Unless the woman in the bathtub was drowned in Botox, there's no way she's seventy-two years old."

THREE

Samantha Alders checked her makeup in the vanity mirror then flipped it back up. Stepping out of her Mercedes SL350, a gift from her sugar daddy, she nodded to the valet and strode into the Waldorf Astoria, the doorman rushing to hold his charge open lest it interrupt her glide down the runway. She didn't head to the front desk—there was no need. Richard would already be here, he would already have the champagne chilling, and he'd have already popped his little blue pill.

They think I'm a tramp.

Her large sunglasses and the high collar of her Versace jacket hid the shame she felt from those gawking at her model good looks. *Or maybe a gold digger.* Was that any better? She didn't care, she had her own reasons. It was an arrangement, made over the Internet on one of the many sites designed to hook up young girls with older, rich men. Someone she trusted convinced her to register herself on one of the sites, and she had figured, why not? A real relationship wasn't possible at this time, and she didn't know when she might have another chance at taking advantage of her current situation. Richard's profile had arrived in her inbox within hours of registering. He sounded intriguing, so she forwarded it to her confidant, and was urged to go for it. She had heard of these sugar daddy websites, and knew most of the men turned out not to be rich, just wannabes who rented a hot car, blew their week's pay on a fancy restaurant, then expected sex in a cheap hotel room.

But not Richard.

Definitely not Richard.

He was the real deal. Real estate mogul, worth tens if not hundreds of millions, and married to a shrew of a woman (if he was to be believed), who withheld sex every time he did something wrong, which, again according to him, he'd done nothing but for many years. They had lost interest in each other, and she refused a divorce since she knew she'd lose the glamour and lifestyle she had become accustomed to. Yes, she'd probably milk him for half, but she would no longer be the wife of Richard Tate, wealthy developer, patron of the arts, philanthropist extraordinaire. She wanted the limelight.

Samantha had thought Richard was adorable when they first met. He was early fifties, in good shape from all Savile Row clad appearances, was a good conversationalist, had exceptional taste in food and wine, and his story had touched her. They had come to an arrangement. He would pay her two thousand dollars a week, provide her with a car, and she would be available whenever he *needed* her. She convinced herself it wasn't prostitution. Yes, money was exchanged, but there were no pimps involved, no multiple partners, nothing kinky. Just straight sex, and not all that great sex, in exchange for some cash she used to pay off her student loans and enjoy a lifestyle she hadn't imagined possible. It was a symbiotic relationship. Besides, his wife cost him far more than two thousand a week, and really, wasn't dating just legalized prostitution anyway? Men take girls out for dinner and a Broadway show, and expect something in return. What, nice conversation? No, they expected a roll in the hay for the three hundred bucks they just shelled out. Hell, a prostitute was cheaper, so if they knew they would never get anything out of it, why bother dating?

What have you become that you are so cynical?

She sighed as the elevator doors opened to the 42nd floor.

I am *a tramp. But a tramp with a purpose.*

"What's up?"

"Huh?"

"You look like you've seen a ghost. Bad news?"

Frank shook his head and looked in the side view mirror, avoiding eye contact with the officer who was driving him to the lab. "No, just the victim isn't who we thought it was."

"No shit? Man, you detectives have the life. As soon as I'm eligible, I'm taking the exam." He stuck out his hand. "Scaramell. Call me Steve."

Frank eyed the hand and shook it weakly. "Frank Brata."

"Nice to meet you, Frank. How long've you been a detective?"

"I'm not. I'm a computer tech. I investigate the electronic side of things, set up electronic surveillance, stuff like that."

"You're the one who got shot a couple of weeks ago, aren't you?"

Frank's ribs winced in remembrance. "Yes."

Scaramell nodded. "Man, that must have been something. Haven't been shot yet, hope never to be obviously, haven't even had to fire my weapon yet." Scaramell cranked the steering wheel and descended into the underground parking at the lab. "Here you go, Frank. Good luck!"

Frank nodded and rushed from the squad car and into the stairwell, racing up the few flights of stairs and into the sanctuary of his deserted lab. He sat at his computer and logged in, quickly scanning the photo. His fingers hammered away at the keyboard as he configured the software to try and reverse the swirl. He selected the swirl obscuring the face of the woman with his mouse and clicked, beginning the process.

Soon he would know just who was hidden in the photo.

And he prayed it wasn't Sarah.

Or him.

Shakespeare knew he had to eat, and he wasn't far from the diner in Hell's Kitchen where Louise was working. He had barely seen her the past few weeks since he had recommitted to the job, and missed her. They didn't live together, she had said she didn't feel right living in sin with a teenage son, and she wasn't ready to remarry. Hell, marriage had been a four letter word to him until recently. But now he found himself considering it. Not anytime soon, but at least it was something he could see for himself before he met his maker.

Remember to visit the Father.

He had promised to drop in after the funeral and visit Father O'Neil who had just been released from hospital. He secretly felt it was the Father's way of trying to get him back to church on a regular basis, but what had happened two weeks ago was just too fresh, too raw, too evil, to rekindle any type of belief in God at this moment.

Then why do you pray to him nightly?

He didn't know why. But he found himself doing more and more praying. Not hands and knees praying, just silent prayers to himself, more than anything else. His diabetes and its myriad of related health problems were a constant source for prayers along the lines of repeated "God help me" pleas when climbing stairs, or getting off the couch and feeling a tightening in his chest.

I have to start taking better care of myself.

He pulled his Caddy up in front of the diner and climbed out, his hand caressing the driver side fin as he walked around it and into the diner. He loved that car. It had been his dad's, and he had "pre-inherited" it, as his dad called it, when macular degeneration had claimed his father's eyesight a few years ago. He had grown up with that car, and now it was his. Mint condition, and he had sworn to keep it that way. Blind or not, he knew his dad would tear him a new asshole if he let anything happen to it.

He stepped into the diner and waved at Louise behind the counter.

"Hey, hon!"

"Shakey!"

He blushed slightly at the nickname as she pushed herself over the counter to give him a kiss, her feet no longer touching the ground. He returned the kiss and sat down at a stool near the cash register. It was nearly five, too early for the dinner rush, so the place was fairly quiet, with only the regulars who spent the better part of their lives here drinking coffee and arguing politics or the news of the day. Lately it was nothing but solutions to the financial crisis.

"How's business?"

"Quiet now, but steady all day. Good thing you didn't come in here earlier, it was hoppin'. And my puppies are barkin' right now."

"That's cuz you wear those damned high heels. You should wear comfortable shoes in your line of work."

She swatted him on the arm. "You know very well that every inch of heel adds five percent to the tip, especially with these dirty old men!" She raised her voice so a table of half a dozen vets could hear.

"Don't you dare stop wearin' them, darlin'!" yelled Phillip "Flip" Johnson, a World War Two vet who had landed on Utah beach on D-Day. "If you do, I'm goin' across the street for my coffee."

"Oh you know very well you don't like their coffee," replied Louise. She returned her attention to Shakespeare. "So, what can I get yah?"

"The usual."

"Right away, darlin'." She turned around and yelled into the kitchen. "One Philly with the runs, easy on the wax!"

"Comin' up!" yelled the chef and owner Mitch. He leaned through the opening where he plated the food. "That you, Shakey?"

"Hey, Mitch, how's it goin'?"

"Can't complain!"

"Cuz' no one will listen!" yelled Flip.

The table of old timers roared with laughter, then surrendered in a spate of coughing.

Louise lowered her voice and leaned in as she poured him a cup of coffee. "So, how was it?"

Shakespeare knew what she meant. *The funeral.* "About as good as you could expect, I guess. Not a very good turnout, but at least a few of us were there." He shrugged his shoulders and took a sip of the bitter brew. "I don't know, hon, it was just strange. He was my partner for three years, but I never really got to know him until those last few days, then—" He stopped. He had relived the shooting enough over the past two weeks, what with Internal Affairs grilling him, and non-stop questioning and whispers among his fellow officers.

She patted him on the hand, as if she knew what he was thinking. "It's okay, dear. It's over now." She forced a smile. "So what's going on? I expected you earlier."

"Caught a new case. Weird one. Woman found dead in a bath tub, but it wasn't her apartment. No ID yet, but we're working on it."

"Sounds kind of routine. What's weird about it?"

"Well, someone left a photograph of two people bumpin' uglies, but hid the faces with some computer tricks."

"That is weird. Sounds more serial killer to me than a regular crime of passion or drug hit."

Shakespeare smiled. "We'll make a cop of you yet!"

She grinned. "Tell me more."

That was one of the many things he loved about her. She loved reading mysteries, watching mystery TV shows, and hearing about his cases. She acted as a sounding board to his ideas, and he loved talking shop with someone who genuinely found it interesting. "Well, remember Frank?"

"The one who got shot?"

"Yup. Well, he lives in the building."

"Quite the coincidence."

"Yeah." Shakespeare took another sip.

"You don't sound convinced."

"Well, there's something I can't quite put my finger on." He counted off with his fingers. "One, Trace says she chased somebody onto his floor. Two, he was very jumpy, even passed out when he saw the body. And three, he never showed up for the funeral when he said he would."

"Well, there's your answer, isn't it?"

"What?"

"Order up!" yelled Mitch.

Louise turned around and grabbed the plate Mitch had pushed through. She placed the Philly melt sandwich in front of him, and removed the small bowl of au jus gravy and placed it beside the plate. "Bon appetite."

Shakespeare smiled and sliced into the sandwich, taking a bite. His stomach rumbled in appreciation. He motioned with his knife. "You were saying?"

"Well, you said it yourself. He was supposed to go to the funeral. He was probably embarrassed about not going, he's pretty green from what I remember you telling me, not a crime scene guy, probably saw his first body, and coming off of the shooting and Eldridge's death, it all just caught up to him."

Shakespeare swallowed another bite. "Maybe."

"Humph. I know that tone. You think he's involved somehow."

"Perhaps, but how for the life of me I don't know. I just can't see the kid being a murderer."

Then again, did you ever see the past two weeks happening?

"I'm sure you'll figure it out, dear."

"Hey, sweet cheeks, howsabout some more coffee over here?" yelled Flip.

"Excuse me for a minute while I teach an old timer some manners."

Shakespeare smiled and turned to watch the show.

"Oh, darling, how I've missed you."

Samantha threw her arms around Richard and kissed him passionately. She had to admit, though the sex wasn't the greatest, the man knew how to kiss. For several minutes they just stood in the entrance, their hands exploring each other's bodies, their mouths expressing the growing passion, then he pushed her up against the door, grinding his hips into hers, and she knew what he wanted. She gave herself to him, completely, shutting her eyes, imagining someone else, but careful to call Richard's name, and when she felt him release, she faked her own, and spent, Richard let her go, leaving her on the entrance floor as he left to clean up in the bathroom.

I am *a tramp.*

She picked herself up, straightened her clothes, kicked off her heels and looked about the suite. It was huge. The light yellow and gold wallpaper on the walls was offset by floor to ceiling royal blue curtains, trimmed in gold, the light sheers covering the nearly suite-wide windows letting plenty of light in from this height. A checkered royal blue and white wall to wall carpet was wonderful to the touch, her bare feet enjoying the extra underlay. She perched herself in one of the regal looking chairs scattered about what could easily be mistaken for some millionaire's living room.

This is the life.

A life she knew she wasn't really living. Once or twice a week she'd live like this, occasionally, like today, she'd get a weekend of luxury—trapped in a palatial room, hiding from the servants, as he couldn't risk being seen with someone other than his wife. She was sure the help knew what was going on, but as long as he had his "plausible deniability" as he called it, he was okay.

But she did live a decent life beyond that of a monogamous whore. The money he paid her allowed her to live in a good apartment in a good building. He showered her with gifts, which meant she was able to deck out the apartment with beautiful fashions, and if she needed anything, the mere mention of it usually had delivery men showing up within a week. Last week it was a new Panasonic 65" 3D television she had heard about and mentioned in their idle chitchat over dinner.

I wonder what I'll ask for tonight.

She disgusted herself. But was what she was doing really wrong? There were no pimps, no drugs, no disease, no children. She was sleeping with one man, who treated her extremely well. Yes he was married, yes he was paying her, but who was getting hurt?

The wife?

From every indication she had, the wife had brought it upon herself, and what she didn't know couldn't hurt her, right?

She shook her head. She didn't want to think about the wife. Every time she did, she felt queasy. Which is what told her, deep down, what she was doing was wrong, but also that she was a good person. Surely a bad person wouldn't feel guilty?

Richard walked into the room in a housecoat, slightly flushed, with a huge smile on his face. He leaned over and gave her a peck on the forehead. "Thanks, Darling, I needed that." He sat down in a chair across from her and put his feet up on a table worth more than the annual salary of some.

She smiled at him. It was a genuine smile. She did actually like him. She did actually care for him. She felt sorry for him in some ways, and realized she was not only filling a sexual need that went unanswered at home, but also one of companionship. He needed a friend that wasn't involved in his work. And she was happy to be it. "Tough day?"

"Tough week."

"Drink?"

He nodded. "Scotch on the rocks, please."

She got up and went to the fully stocked liquor cabinet. She tossed a few ice cubes in the crystal glass and poured him an eighteen year old Dalmore scotch, the lush liquid surging over the ice, turning them into a golden kaleidoscope of relief. She poured herself a vodka on ice and brought the two drinks over to where Richard sat, his head leaned back, his eyes closed. She shook the glass slightly, the ice chiming against the sides. He opened his eyes and smiled, taking the proffered glass. She sat down beside him and crossed her legs under her as he took a long drink followed by a satisfied sigh.

She drained half her own glass, put it down on the table, and stretched. "I'm going to get out of these clothes and into something more comfortable."

He nodded as she grabbed her bag and headed into the bathroom. She quickly stripped, then put on a simple Victoria's Secret pushup bra and high-cut lace panties. Lifting one of the bathrobes from the hook behind the door, she pulled it on and wrapped it around her, the rich, soft terrycloth enveloping her near naked body.

This is what I should ask for.

It was small, but it would be wonderful. A nice little luxury for the evenings alone in her apartment. She tied up the robe then thought better of it. Better to leave it open so he could get a glimpse of what he was paying for. She untied the belt, and let the robe slip open, revealing her taught, tanned body.

I may be a tramp, but he's one lucky bastard.

She flicked off the light and returned to the living area where she found Richard struggling to keep his eyes open, his nearly empty glass perched on the arm of this chair, gripped lightly by his hand. She smiled and sat down beside him, curling her legs up. Yawning, she picked up her glass and took a sip as Richard's head lolled over to the side, looking at her.

"Tired, dear?"

"Something's wrong," he whispered, as the glass fell from his hand, bouncing lightly on the carpeted floor.

Shakespeare pulled into a vacant spot in the lab parking lot and spun his legs out the door, then pushed-pulled himself upright. Slamming the door shut behind him, he pressed the fob to activate the alarm, the only aftermarket piece of equipment he dared add to the vehicle. And one he never told his dad about, his naïve argument that no one would dare steal a work of art like a 1959 Cadillac perhaps applying to days gone by, but definitely not modern New York City.

He took the elevator down to the basement where Vinny's crew lurked, and made his way to the morgue. He found MJ at the autopsy table, hosing what looked like their victim from earlier. He looked up when Shakespeare stepped through the double swinging doors. "Hey, Shakes, what's shakin'?"

"Two cheeks too many. You heard about the ID?"

"Yup. She doesn't look seventy-two to me."

Shakespeare nodded as he approached the table. Clearly a young woman, maybe mid-twenties, slightly overweight, blonde. "Anything yet from your end?

MJ shook his head. "I've got her prints running now. I'll get dental x-rays and a photo once I've cleaned her up." He pointed at her fingernails. "This is no drug addict. She's clean, well groomed, manicure, pedicure, good teeth. Someone will notice her missing."

Shakespeare nodded. "Cause of death?"

MJ pointed at her skull, deformed at the back from some sort of impact. "Looks like a blow to the head, or more likely, repeated blows to the head from behind, incapacitated her, then"—he motioned for Shakespeare to help him flip her over onto her back—"they slit her throat from ear to ear."

"Jesus. TOD?"

"The bathtub didn't help—no way of knowing how hot or cold the water was. I give it anywhere from twelve to twenty-four hours before my initial examination."

"Okay, keep me posted."

MJ nodded and started spraying the body again. "Will do."

Shakespeare headed to the door when MJ stopped the spray.

"Forgot. Vinny wants to see you."

Shakespeare's shoulders slumped. "Ugh, what does *he* want?"

MJ shrugged his shoulders in an exaggerated manner and turned his palms upward. "The pleasure of your company?"

"The day that bastard enjoys my company is the day I do my first triathlon."

"Never say never!"

Shakespeare chuckled and walked down the hall to Vinny's lab, knocking on the door frame. Vinny looked up and waved him in, a momentary frown replaced by a slight smile.

"Hi, Detective, I see you got my message."

Shakespeare nodded. "What've you got for me?"

"Not much." He held up an evidence bag. "One hair, not belonging to the victim"—he held up a vial with a swab inside—"and one drop of blood, not belonging to the victim."

"So they could belong to our killer."

"Or the old lady who's supposed to actually be living there."

Shakespeare nodded. "Anything else?"

"Beside the photo, which is obviously a plant, there's nothing. That apartment was wiped down clean from top to bottom. I swabbed all the usual places, plus our secret"—he signaled the significance with air quotes—"places, and still nothing. Even door jambs were wiped down. This guy knew all our tricks."

"A cop?"

Vinny's jaw dropped slightly. "God, I hope not. Not after—"

Shakespeare held up his hand. "Any chance at DNA?"

"I'm working on it, should have results tomorrow."

"Okay, keep me posted."

"Will do."

Shakespeare left the lab, never having fully entered, one foot the entire time in the hall. He took the elevator to see the kid. As he stepped out, he saw a vending machine beckoning him like a desert oasis. *Don't.* His stomach rumbled. *Are you kidding me? You just ate.* He stopped, hesitating. *Something small, but you have to take the stairs for the rest of the day.*

Rationalized, he headed to the machine, fishing out his wallet.

He punched B3 into the machine and frowned as his reward for a future effort yet to be completed dropped to the bottom, and the sense of guilt momentarily filled him.

You're pathetic.

He opened the Snickers bar and took a bite, finding momentary solace in the carbohydrate laden treat.

Completely pathetic.

Frank stared in stunned silence at the nearly perfect image before him. The descrambling process on the swirl hadn't taken long. Whoever had created the swirl had taken the generic settings of the program and used them with no variations. This was always used as the starting point when unswirling an image, but it never worked—most criminals disguising their faces like this were smart enough to randomize the settings, causing law enforcement to use brute force techniques to descramble the image, and that assumed they hadn't done something else to the image—one swirl could be undone. Two or more, with some other alternation, and there was no hope. Unfortunately many times law enforcement had to rely on the overconfidence of the offender, usually a pedophile. The cockier they were, the less effort they seemed to go to hide their identity.

But not today.

Today it was as if whoever had altered the photograph had wanted it to be unscrambled with ease, and alacrity. It had only taken a few hours, almost unheard of, but there it was. A woman's face. Beautiful, young, blonde.

And not Sarah.

Frank continued to stare, not sure what to make of it. If it wasn't Sarah, then who was with this unidentified woman in the photo? And if this wasn't Sarah, was the victim in the tub Sarah, or this woman? And if it wasn't Sarah, then why the hell was he in the apartment?

If only I could remember!

He smacked his palm against his forehead.

"Something wrong, kid?"

Frank nearly jumped out of his skin at the sound of the voice, his head twisting rapidly toward the entrance of his lab.

Shakespeare stood in the entrance, chomping on a chocolate bar, frowning.

"Ah, no, I mean—"

Get it together!

He took a deep breath and pointed at the screen. "Look."

Shakespeare walked over to his workstation and looked at the blown up image displayed there. "Is this the woman in the photograph?"

Frank nodded. "Yes. "

"I thought you said it would take a few days?"

Frank bobbed his head up and down, a little too quickly. He stopped. "Well, you see, it was too easy!"

"What do you mean?"

"I mean, whoever did this, didn't try very hard. They left everything at the defaults, like either they didn't know what they were doing, or—"

"Or they wanted it to be easy so you'd be guaranteed to identify her."

Frank nodded.

"What about the man?" asked Shakespeare.

"I've got him running now, but preliminaries look like he might be harder to identify, the default swirl pattern didn't work."

"Okay, print me off that photo, and run it through facial recognition, see if you can find a match. Make sure you hit missing persons."

Frank nodded and hit a few keys. A color laser printer nearby powered up, spitting out a perfect copy within seconds.

Shakespeare grabbed the photo and left the lab, leaving Frank trembling at his keyboard.

He had just lied to a cop, to one of his fellow co-workers who were supposed to uphold the law, just as he was. He had just lied for the first time in his career, and he was nearly sick over it.

He clicked a few keys, starting the analysis of the man for the first time, not, as he had told Shakespeare, for additional analysis. He had yet to try the "out of the box" reversal. Instead, he had told Shakespeare what he needed him to hear, just in case the photo did turn out to be him. He would know in a couple of hours if the analysis proved as easy as the first.

And if it was him, it would give him a day or two to decide what to do.

Shakespeare made a bold decision; he took the stairs. It was only six flights, down, not up, but it was the first time he had voluntarily taken the stairs in years.

Baby steps.

It still winded him slightly, and he stood in the stairwell catching his breath for a few moments. His racing heart calmed, he opened the door to the CSU labs and stepped into the hallway, nearly mowing Vinny down.

"Jesus!" exclaimed Vinny, his jaw dropping slightly when he realized who it was. "You took the stairs?"

Shakespeare frowned. "What's it to you?"

Vinny shrugged. "Nothin'." He made a show of looking down both ends of the hallway. "But if I see four horsemen, I'm outta here."

Shakespeare chuckled as Vinny walked toward his lab.

Me taking the stairs is one of the signs of the apocalypse. Now that's funny.

He pushed the double swinging doors open to the autopsy room and saw MJ sewing closed the chest of their victim.

"Shakes, you still here?"

Shakespeare had to admit he always felt good when dealing with MJ. He always seemed happy to see him, unlike most of the others. Shakespeare held up the photo, a smile on his face.

"Hey, MJ. Our young computer whiz has the first face from the photo. Thought I'd see if we have a match, now that you've got her cleaned up."

Jenkins reached up and focused the overhead light on the young woman's face, now cleaned of any blood, her hair neatly combed back from his search for trace evidence. "Let's have a look."

Shakespeare held the photo beside her face and raised his eyebrows.

"That's definitely not her," said Jenkins, echoing Shakespeare's thoughts.

"Well, if this isn't her"—Shakespeare shook the photo—"then who the hell is she, and why the hell was her photo left at this one's murder scene?"

Jenkins shook his head. "You're the detective, Detective. That's above my pay grade."

Shakespeare grunted. "If I had your money, I'd burn mine."

Jenkins stretched. "Hah! I think you have this poor public servant confused with a brain surgeon."

"Gotta have a brain to be—"

"Get your ass outta here before I open you up to see what's inside!"

Shakespeare laughed and headed to the door.

"Have you sent her to facial yet?"

Jenkins nodded.

"Yup, a few minutes ago. Hopefully they can find her in missing persons."

Shakespeare nodded.

"Once the kid figures out who the other person is in the photo, that might help."

"You never know." Jenkins held up a curved needle, examined it under the light, then leaned over, plunging it through the skin on one side of the chest cavity, then pulling it up and through the other side, yanking it tight, closing the wound a bit more.

Shakespeare grimaced.

I sure hope he gets paid more than me.

Trace stood in the center of the apartment, her trained eye going over every square inch, finding nothing. The body was gone, the CSU team had finished, the canvassing of the neighbors had proved fruitless, and Shakespeare had the lead. She couldn't believe it. Case after case over the past few weeks had gone to Eldridge, and now that he was gone, they were going to Shakespeare. *So much for getting my shot.* She knew it was a shitty way to get ahead, over the body of a fallen comrade, but sometimes that's the way things had to be. It wasn't like *she* killed him.

There was a knock on the door.

She spun on her heel and quickly walked toward the entrance, opening the door.

A young woman on the other side jumped back, her eyebrows shooting up in surprise.

"I-I'm sorry, I must have the wrong apartment."

Trace pulled her badge off her hip and showed it to the woman. "Detective Trace, Homicide." She noted the woman's face turn a shade paler. "And you are?"

"Jackie, Jackie St. Jean." Her eyes darted to the apartment number on the door. "Did you say Homicide?"

Trace nodded. *Uh oh, this won't be pretty.*

"Is, is Angela okay?"

Trace pulled out her pad and noted down the woman's name. "Did Angela live in this apartment?"

"Yes. Is she okay?"

"What was her last name?"

"Henwood. Would you please tell me what's going on?"

"Can you describe her for me please?"

"I don't know. Blonde, your height, I guess."

"White?"

"Yes."

"A little, shall we say, plump?"

Jackie frowned. "A little."

"Did she live here alone?"

She hesitated. "Yes."

"Who's Larissa Channing?"

"Who?"

Don't play dumb with me kid. "Larissa Channing."

"Oh, that was her Grandmother."

"Was?"

"She passed away about six months ago."

"And why was her name still on the lease?"

Jackie looked at the floor.

"Look, you're not going to get your friend in trouble."

Jackie looked up. "Well, you know, its rent controlled, so, when her Grandmother died, she just didn't tell the landlord."

Trace nodded, having heard it dozens of times before. If you could get a rent controlled apartment in New York City, it was something you held onto for dear life. She pulled out her cellphone and flipped to the picture of their victim, sent over by Jenkins earlier.

"Is this your friend?" She held the phone up so Jackie could see.

She gasped, her hand flying to her mouth, nodding. "Oh my God. What happened to her?"

"Is this your friend?"

Her head bobbed rapidly. "Yes!"

"And this is Angela Henwood?"

Again, her head bobbed. "Yes."

Trace waved Jackie into the apartment, motioning to a nearby chair. "Have a seat, I'll need to take a statement from you." She dialed

Shakespeare's number and waited. His gruff voice answered on the second ring.

"Shakespeare."

"Hey, Shakes, it's Amber. I've got an ID on our vic."

"Excellent! Who is it?"

"Angela Henwood. She lived here with her Grandmother, Larissa Channing, who passed away a few months ago."

"Let me guess, rent controlled?"

"Yup."

"Okay, I'll run her name through the system and see what we've got."

"Okay, I'm gonna get a formal statement from the vic's friend who just showed up here, and then I'll see you at the station."

"10-4."

She hung up and sat down beside a now visibly shaken Jackie. "Let's start at the beginning."

Jackie nodded. "Can I get a drink?"

Trace gave a by-your-leave wave.

Jackie rose from her chair and opened several cupboards before finding the glasses. Removing one, she filled it with tap water, then sat back down when Trace suddenly twigged on something.

"You didn't know where the glasses were."

"Huh?" Jackie shrugged her shoulders. "I guess Angela always got the drinks."

But Trace wasn't listening to the explanation, her mind fixated on one burning question.

How did Frank know where to get the glass from?

FOUR

Sarah woke, her head pounding, her mouth dry, but not dry enough for a hangover. She opened her eyes, and closed them again, not sure what she had just seen. She rubbed the corners of her eyes with her knuckles and opened them again. She was in a dimly lit—what? It looked like a featureless rectangle, about ten feet wide, maybe twenty feet long, with the ceiling also about ten feet high. The walls were featureless save for a door at the other end with no handle. The dim, reddish light came from above, but the actual source was hidden somehow. She stared at the ceiling and noticed the light seemed to pulse, with the occasional flicker of yellow and orange.

Then she heard the sounds.

And her heart stopped, then shoved against her chest in absolute terror.

Screams of horror.

Cries of pain.

Crackling of fire.

She sniffed.

It smelled like rotten eggs. *Sulfur?*

She noticed she was warm. She felt the floor with her hands. Warm to the touch. She felt the walls. The same. Then she noticed she was naked. She closed her legs and covered her breasts with her arms, trying to make herself as small as possible, embarrassment momentarily taking over from fear.

Where am I?

She began to sob, covering her ears, trying to block the sounds of horror on the other side of the walls, trying to remember what had happened. She remembered going for coffee with Frank, but nothing else. Something must have happened. Something sudden.

And there could be only one explanation.

She was dead.

And she knew where she was.

Hell.

What other explanation could there be? *But what did I do that was so bad to deserve this? I've led a good life. I've never hurt anyone, I've never stolen, or cheated, or killed.* She made a quick mental tally of the Ten Commandments, unable to remember them all, but certain she hadn't broken any of them, at least not in a way worthy of eternal damnation.

Why, God, why?

The sound changed.

She uncovered her ears.

A voice. Deep, growling, bestial, terrifying. Demonic.

"Sarah Paxman."

Her heart pounded harder, she felt the world start to spin.

"Sarah Paxman. Can you hear me?"

She said nothing.

"Answer me!" The room shook and she yelped.

"Yes! Yes! I can hear you!" she cried.

"Sarah Paxman, do you know where you are?"

"Yes."

"Sarah Paxman, do you know why you are here?"

"N-no."

"Liar!" Again the room shook. "Search your soul, you know the reasons, you know the sins you have committed."

She trembled as she pushed herself into the nearest corner, but there was no escaping the voice. It filled the room; it filled everything, as if it were actually in her mind. "I-I don't know!"

"I am the Lord your God, who brought you out of the land of Egypt, out of the house of bondage. You shall have no other gods before Me."

The first commandment? "I d-don't understand."

"Have you not prayed to other gods, practiced blasphemous superstitions? Have you not knocked on wood, tossed salt over your shoulder, shivered at the sight of a black cat, gambled and prayed for success?" The voice dripped with sarcasm, with scorn at each of the things it mentioned, and with a hint of delight as she nodded her head, knowing she had indeed done all of these things. "You shall not take the name of the Lord your God in vain, for the Lord will not hold him guiltless who takes His name in vain."

She cried out, "God forgive me!" She knew all were guilty of this commandment. *How can anyone escape?*

"There is no forgiveness here. Forgiveness is unknown. Here there is only pain. Here there is only suffering."

Her head throbbed, her rushing blood pounded in her ears.

"Remember the Sabbath day, to keep it holy. Six days you shall labor and do all your work, but the seventh day is the Sabbath of the Lord your God. In it you shall do no work."

Her heart sank. How many Sundays had she worked, trying to get ahead in her career? How many Sundays had she made excuses to not go to church, then, when out of her parents' house, had she even gone once?

"Honor your father and your mother, that your days may be long upon the land which the Lord your God is giving you."

How many times had she fought with her parents? How many times had she had ill thoughts toward them when she was younger?

"You shall not covet your neighbor's house."

How many times had she wished she had a bigger apartment, more money, a nicer car? How many times had she been jealous of others around her?

"These are your sins. Are you prepared to pay the price for your sacrilegious life?"

She wailed in terror, in heartbreak, in regret.

"Are you prepared?" the voice thundered.

She nodded. "Y-yes, y-yes I-I'm prepared."

"Then so it shall be. For eternity."

A deafening roar like nothing she had ever heard filled the space around her, so loud she felt the floor and walls vibrate. After a few moments it died away, leaving her with the comparably peaceful wails and screams of those who were sharing her experience.

She pushed herself harder into the corner and hugged her knees, burying her head between them, pressing them tightly against her ears.

And cried.

Trace wasn't sure what to think. Or do. *How did Frank know where the glasses were?* Of course, it could be completely innocent. Maybe everyone in that apartment complex kept their glasses in the same cupboard. Maybe there was something unique to the design that made putting the glasses in that particular cupboard an obvious choice. Or maybe he just made a lucky guess?

But she wasn't buying it.

The kid had fainted. *Who faints outside of women in old movies?* This kid saw the body, dropped like a sack of potatoes, and grabbed the only piece of solid evidence they had, damaging it in the process. But there was no way she could see him as a murderer. The kid was too meek, too quiet. *It's always the quiet ones.*

The elevator doors opened and she held out her hand, inviting her witness, Jackie St. Jean, to exit. She led her past the squad room and deposited her in an interrogation room. "I'll be with you shortly." She closed the door and walked back to the squad room. She spotted Shakespeare sitting at his desk, a frown on his face, almost looking a little green if she didn't know better.

"Hey, Shakes, you okay?"

He looked up and gave a half-hearted smile. "I'll live, at least for another day or two."

She wasn't sure if he was joking.

She thumbed over her shoulder at the interrogation room several walls away. "Witness in Interrogation Two, Jackie St. Jean, knew our vic."

"Why's she here?"

Trace hesitated. Should she tell him? *No. Not until you're sure.*

"Something came up I needed to check on stat, so I brought her here for a proper debrief." She started to walk toward the door. "I'll be back in a few." Shakespeare grunted and one last look over her shoulder found him frowning again, staring at his garbage can.

Fifteen minutes later she was in Queens, bounding up the stairs to Frank's lab. Taking a deep breath, her hand poised over the handle, she exhaled and dropped her hand, opening the door and pushing her way inside.

It was empty.

On a screen she saw an enlarged image of their victim, and on another screen, an enlarged image of a rapidly clearing picture of a man, his details still too obscured to recognize. She stared at it, fascinated, as tiny crosshairs appeared and disappeared, hundreds per second, imperceptibly changing the image.

Cool!

She sat down in a high-back chair in front of the monitors, and watched for a few minutes. She squinted slightly, in the hopes it might make the image clearer, to no avail. She leaned further back. No effect. She heard the door open as she noticed something that had become clear over the past few minutes.

The hair.

She felt her chair rock back and spin, then a yelp.

"Jesus Christ, Detective!"

She looked at Frank, one hand over his heart, the other gripping a Diet Pepsi. "Frank." She frowned. "A little jumpy today, aren't we?"

Frank shook his head. "No, just, well, I didn't see you there, and well, I wasn't exactly expecting anyone."

She pointed at a nearby chair. "Have a seat." She knew full well she was in his seat, but she wanted him uncomfortable. After all, this was his home, his territory, his lair. And she needed him unsettled. She could take him to an interrogation room, but that would make this formal, and if her hunch proved incorrect, she didn't want to ruin the kid's career.

Frank looked behind him, and sat down, clearly out of sorts.

"Now tell me how you're mixed up in this."

Frank's face went white.

If Frank hadn't been sitting, he probably would have collapsed again, but this time he kept a grip. *What kind of wimp am I?* He took a slow, deep breath, and focused on the Diet Pepsi bottle in his hand. Staring at it, rather than Trace, he gripped the top and slowly twisted, the satisfying hiss of greenhouse gasses escaping the pressurized container seemed loud in the silence that consumed the space between them, the hum and buzz of dozens of computers tuned out as the background noise it was.

He took a sip.

This is your lab. You've done nothing wrong. He knew that was bullshit, but he was sure he wasn't a murderer. At least he hoped he wasn't. He stole a glance at the screen. *Gray hair?* "Wh-what did you say?"

"I said"—Trace leaned forward—"tell me how you're mixed up in all this."

Frank's heart slammed against his chest as he tried to sound as calm as possible. "What do you mean?" He took another sip.

Trace's demeanor suddenly changed, her eyebrows narrowed, her eyes, cold and focused, glared at him. "How the hell did you know where the glasses were in that apartment!" she snapped at him.

He couldn't help it. He pushed back in the chair, the rollers sending him gliding several inches before slamming into a table behind him. His left hand squeezed the arm of the chair, his right squeezing the bottle, its cool refreshing cola spurting out the top like a grade six science experiment.

"Because it's where I keep *my* glasses!" he blurted out.

This seemed to catch her off guard. She paused in her attack for a moment, giving him time to recover. He leaned forward, dipping his head so he could hide his face, and switched the bottle to his dry hand. He shook the liquid off and wiped what remained on his pant leg.

"What do you mean, it's where you keep your glasses?"

She sounded unsure, as if the wind had been taken out of her sails. In fact, he knew he had her, his mind proving even more brilliant than he had thought possible under this kind of pressure. The truth was he didn't keep his glasses in the same place—their apartments were nothing alike. But somehow his brain had spit out a completely logical, reasonable response. Except it was a bald-faced lie, and if she were to check his apartment, she'd know this immediately.

But she'd need a warrant for that.

But he could never demand a warrant; they'd know for sure he was mixed up in this.

Now how do you get out of this?

"I mean, I put my glasses in the center cupboard, just like her. I guess it just seemed logical."

Good one!

Trace smiled and stood up. "I guess that explains that."

Frank breathed a sigh of relief, perhaps a little too loudly.

"How 'bout you show me."

Shakespeare sat at his desk, eyeing the empty one across from him. He closed his eyes and could picture the last time he sat here with his partner, going through stacks of threats. It was good old fashioned police work, something he hadn't done in a long time. And it had felt good.

His stomach growled.

He absentmindedly patted it. It wasn't a good growl. That chocolate bar with extra peanuts wasn't sitting well, probably his body's way of saying, "Huh? Are you serious with this shit?" He eyed the balled up wrapper at the bottom of the garbage can sitting beside his beat up press wood desk. *You're evil.* His stomach churned in agreement. He closed his eyes, a wave of self-pity rushing through him. *Why do you do it to yourself? You're so pathetic.*

"Shakes!"

Almost nothing startled him, not even the LT's yells across the squad room. He had always thought it was just his nerves of steel. Now however he wondered if it was just his body protecting itself from ever having to move quickly. He opened his eyes and turned his chair toward the voice.

"Yes, LT?"

"Is that your witness sitting in Interrogation Two?" Phillips stood in the doorway to the squad room, his three piece suit setting him apart from the rest of the slightly more casually dressed.

"Huh?" Shakespeare had to think for a moment. "No, Trace brought her in." He glanced at his watch. "Why? She not there?"

Phillips shook his head. "No."

Shakespeare threw his arms and legs forward, changing his center of gravity for the smooth, graceless motion required to exit his chair without a monumental struggle. "How 'bout I go do that interview, eh boss?"

"What a wonderful idea," said Phillips as he quickly crossed the squad room floor, his long strides chewing up the distance in moments, a slight smile on his face.

By now Shakespeare was standing. He stuffed his shirt tails back into his pants, grabbed his suit jacket from the back of his chair and, shoving one arm in, swung the rest around his back and shrugged his other arm in, taking a quick look at his armpit as he did so. *Damn!* A circle of moisture had appeared, the air conditioning in the squad room leaving something to be desired. He made a mental note to use his Drysol later that night, and headed down the hall to Interrogation Two. He rapped twice on the door then opened it to find a startled, teary eyed young woman sitting at the table.

"Wh-who are you?"

Shakespeare sat down across from her and pulled his notebook and pen from his coat pocket.

"I'm Detective Shakespeare. Detective Trace asked me to finish your interview as she had a more pressing matter to attend to." *What that could have been, who knows?* "Now, how about we start from the beginning, then we'll have you identify the victim."

She turned a special kind of pale. "Identify? Do you mean, see her? See her, you know, dead body?"

Shakespeare nodded.

Young Jackie St. Jean hurled across the table, covering his favorite shirt in her favorite lunch.

Trace eyeballed Brata for a reaction, but received the same scared, confused expression he'd sported all day. *What is this kid hiding?* How bad could it be that he had to lie to cops, to his friends? She simply couldn't picture him as a murderer; he just didn't fit the profile. And what happened to Angela Henwood did not appear to be some sort of accident he may have tried to cover up. *Then what the hell is it?* Her mind flashed to Eldridge. Could it be that? Could it be as simple as him still being shook up over the previous weeks' events? They were all shaken by it. The squad room was on eggshells, people continually eying his empty desk, that up until *the* night, you could expect to see him occupying when you came in early, or left late. He was dedicated to his job.

When the hell did he find the time—?

She cut off the thought. *Enough!* She, and the others, had to stop dwelling on this, had to move on. Her eyes focused on Brata again. *Maybe that* is *all that's going on.*

She slapped him on his shoulder as she rose from the chair. "Never mind, Frank, I'm sure you're telling the truth."

He seemed to blush at that.

Returning to the Bureau, she took the stairs two at a time to the squad room. Pushing open the door, she entered the hallway and saw Shakespeare closing the door to one of the interrogation rooms, his arms outstretched, holding his sport coat open, his upper back hunched over, and a look of disgust plastered on his face as he looked down at his shirt.

She looked.

Ugh!

"What the hell happened to you?"

Shakespeare looked up at her as she approached. And frowned.

"Your"—his tone did the jabbing his blazer filled fingers couldn't—"witness just blew chunks all over the Interrogation room and me."

Trace covered her mouth with her hand, not wanting Shakespeare to see the smile about to break out.

"Oh my"—she stifled a giggle—"I'm so sorry. Any"—another giggle, this time aloud—"anything I can do?"

Shakespeare tilted his head and raised his eyebrows. "Whaddaya think?"

She looked at his shirt. "How 'bout I call maintenance and have the room cleaned?"

"That'd be a good start." Shakespeare headed toward the men's room. "And have Little Miss Hurler formally ID her friend."

Trace watched Shakespeare push the bathroom door open with his back, and burst into laughter as his large frame disappeared.

"Glad someone's enjoying this!" she heard him yell as the door closed behind him.

"Ready?" Trace looked at Jackie St. Jean, who still appeared woozy from her earlier barf and bawl. *I wonder how Shakes is doing with those stains.* She smiled. Inwardly. After calling maintenance and collecting St. Jean, they had immediately gone to the morgue, something St. Jean was clearly not relishing. She squeezed Jackie's arm slightly, in an attempt to feed her some of her own strength. "It's okay, you can do this."

Jackie looked at her, apparently unconvinced, but nodded. MJ drew the sheet down, revealing their victim's face, and Trace, now gripping Jackie's arm, slowly lowered the now fainted witness to the floor.

"Well, that went well."

Trace frowned at MJ. "Love your gallows humor."

He shrugged. "Hey, you work down here all day, you kind of have to. Usually my audience collapses *before* my jokes."

Trace cringed. "Not funny."

"Whaddaya expect? I'm used to my audience not heckling me." He pointed at the rows of drawers containing dozens of the latest deaths from around their borough. "Actually, I'm used to dead silence."

Trace looked down at Jackie. "Please wake up soon, I don't know how much more of this I can take."

MJ looked over the table containing their vic, and at Jackie. "Take your time, the audience and I aren't going anywhere."

Trace looked at him. "You do realize you're not even funny?"

MJ nodded. "Like I said, whaddaya expect? I get no feedback from my audience, no critical reviews of my work."

Trace raised her hand to stop him as she saw movement from Jackie. She knelt down beside her. "You okay?"

Jackie's eyes fluttered, then opened. "Wh-what happened?"

"You fainted," the ever helpful MJ offered from out of Jackie's sight. Trace glanced over her shoulder and frowned, noticing the voice sounded as if it had come from the body occupying the slab.

Trace pulled Jackie to her feet, and dusted her off. "Let's get this over with so you can get out of here." She pointed at the body. "Is this Angela Henwood?"

Jackie took a quick glance and nodded, tears pouring from her eyes. "Yes."

"Good enough for me!" MJ pulled the sheet back over Angela's face as Trace turned Jackie away from the sight, leading her from the Morgue Comedy Club.

"Let's get you some coffee."

Sarah lazily opened her eyes, a restless sleep providing little in the way of comfort. She ached all over, her naked body still huddled in the corner. Her entire upper body was racked in pain from sobbing for hours before falling asleep. Now she was paying for both her self-pity, and her lack of bedding.

"Wh-where am I?"

Sarah nearly jumped up, instead her feet shoving her tighter into the corner as her head spun toward the voice. A man, perhaps in his late forties, was huddled in the corner opposite her, clearly terrified. She noted with a touch of bitterness he was fully clothed, a plaid tam-o-shanter hat covered his scalp, a patterned golf shirt, loud golf knickers, white socks and bright red shoes, the cleats knotted in freshly mowed grass, completed his ensemble.

"Where am I?" he repeated, staring at her.

She looked down at her naked body, and tried to cover herself by strategically placing hands, legs, and arms.

"Hell."

The one word, voiced by her, sent shivers through her body, the goose bumps raising the hairs on her arms, triggering an overwhelming sense of remorse, filling her from within, then spewing forth in an uncontrollable surge of emotion, tears pouring from her eyes, sobs shaking her body.

"We're in hell," she cried. "We're being punished for our sinful lives."

She couldn't hear what the man whispered, her own sobs too loud, the cries and moans on the other side of their prison walls seeming louder than before. The man curled up into a ball, mimicking her, and slowly slid to his side, the stunned expression on his face revealing the horror he now felt.

"What's your name?"

He looked up at her.

"Wh-what?"

"I'm Sarah. What's your name?"

"Patrick."

"What do you remember?"

Patrick sat back up, his eyes glazed over, as if searching back in time to when he had been alive, to a time before this infernal damnation they both faced.

"I was golfing," he said at last, his gaze still distant. "I missed a two foot putt. I was so angry. If that fuck Tony hadn't insisted on no gimmies—" Patrick took a deep breath and looked at Sarah, exhaling. "I threw my putter at the golf cart. It ricocheted off the back, and hit Tony in the head. The last thing I remember is a pain in my shoulder, then I collapsed."

"Heart attack?"

Patrick shrugged. "Probably." He looked around. "Doesn't explain why I'm here though."

"Maybe Tony died?"

Patrick nodded slowly. "Murder." He looked at Sarah. "And you?"

She tried to make herself even smaller, his gaze making her uncomfortable. He seemed to read her mind, and look away.

"I'm sorry, I didn't realize you were, well, naked."

Sarah didn't say anything.

Patrick looked at his own clothes. "If I'm wearing what I was when I died, why are you naked?"

Sarah blushed. All over it felt like. "I think I was with a man."

"Think?"

A new shade of red was discovered. "I don't really remember."

"Ahhhh, partying."

She shook her head. "No, that's just it. I remember going to a coffee shop with him, then nothing."

Patrick looked at her. "That's odd. Did he drug you?"

She shook her head. "No, not him. He works for the NYPD. So do I, actually. No, he wouldn't do it, but somebody must have. If I died, you'd think I'd have some memory of it, unless I was asleep, or drugged at the time."

"And you don't remember leaving the coffee shop?"

"No, not at all. I remember us ordering coffees, but only vaguely."

"I've heard those roofies or whatever they're called can cause retroactive short-term memory loss. Maybe that's why you don't remember being there."

She nodded. "Makes sense. But why? Why drug me? And if they drugged me, then they must have drugged him too."

"Maybe they drugged Frank too. Maybe you were both murdered."

Sarah looked at Patrick, momentarily forgetting she was naked, fear gripping her.

"H-how did you know his name was Frank?"

Patrick stood, a smile on his face that soon turned into a lip curling sneer. "Because here, I know everything!" He laughed then pushed against the door at the far end. It opened, the sounds of horror on the other side racing in like a plague of locusts. He turned to face her, his smile one of hate that sent shivers through her naked body despite the heat now pouring through the door.

"Goodbye, Sarah Paxman, see you soon."

The door slammed shut, and a demonic laugh echoed through her eternal chamber as she turned away, burying her head in her huddled corner.

FIVE

Richard woke, his head pounding as if from a hangover he had no recollection of deserving. The lights were out, the drapes were drawn, and it took a moment for him to remember where he was. He twisted himself to reach for the lamp he knew would be on the nightstand, and his elbow slipped in something wet, sending his chin into the pillow. He grunted and slid over some more, reaching for the lamp. Finding it, he fumbled for the switch and twisted the tiny knob, the click triggering a flood of light, momentarily blinding him. He blinked several times, then swung his legs over the edge of the bed, and stretched. He looked over his shoulder for Samantha, and gasped.

Blood was everywhere.

Everywhere.

He scrambled to his feet, his head spinning as he scanned the room for someone, anyone, who, he didn't know, his arms out behind him, searching for a corner to retreat into. Finding it, he pressed himself into the corner, the fear of getting jumped from behind slightly calmed, and listened. Nothing.

"Samantha?"

His call was tentative, barely a whisper.

Nothing.

"Samantha!"

This time louder.

And still nothing.

He ventured from his corner, slowly making his way around the bed, covered, no, soaked, in blood. *There's no way anyone survived losing that much blood.* He peered around the bed, at the floor, and found only a pile of sheets. And a bloody knife sitting on top. He reached for it and saw the blood on his hand. He looked at the bloody handle of the knife, and back at his hand. *Did I? Could I?*

He continued forward, into the large ensuite bathroom, and flicked on the light. He gasped. Lying in the tub was Samantha, covered in blood, her matted hair covering her face, slightly turned toward the wall, the tiny butterfly tattoo on the back of her neck unmistakable.

It was Samantha.

He looked at his hands and took a step back, toward the door.

What have I done?

He looked in the mirror. He was covered in blood, and there was something else. He tentatively touched his neck and winced. He looked closer in the mirror, bending his neck, exposing the left side, revealing three long scratches.

It was *me!*

He turned on the taps and immediately began to wash the blood off his hands, arms and face. He scrubbed and scrubbed, the hot water scalding him, rubbing his skin raw with the soap, the stubborn, sticky mess proving harder to come off than he had imagined. After several minutes he was clean. Exiting to the bedroom, he grabbed his clothes neatly piled on a nearby chair and hurriedly dressed. He retrieved his briefcase, looked about the apartment for anything he might have missed, and headed for the door. He looked out the peephole, saw no one, opened the door and hurried for the elevator.

What am I going to do?

Frank stared at the screen as the decryption program churned away, slowly revealing the face behind the swirl. It looked like it wasn't going to be as easy this time, it having run all night, and still not completed. The edges had revealed themselves; gray hair making an appearance he hoped wasn't just a calculation error. One thing he was certain of, he didn't have gray hair, although the past couple of days might certainly induce some premature graying. He glanced at his watch then at the screen, debating on whether or not to go home.

His phone vibrated with a text message.

TICK TOCK
LITTLE TIME ON THE CLOCK
I WILL MAKE YOU A BET
YOU HAVEN'T FOUND IT YET

Frank snapped his phone shut, and slammed his head against the desk. *Why me? What did I ever do to deserve this?* He sat back up, his tear filled eyes threatening to spill over the edges and down his cheeks. He pulled a handkerchief from his pocket and wiped them dry. Taking a deep breath, he slowly exhaled, then stared at the image on the screen, trying to decipher the message he had just received. What was it he hadn't found? If he was supposed to find it, then whoever was playing this game with him must think he'd be looking for it, but that didn't make sense—his job was not to search.

Could it be the photo?

He stared at the screen. That didn't make sense. How could this person, this killer, know how fast his computers were? No, it had to be something else. Something he was meant to find. He didn't expect it to be easy, but he expected it to at least be possible. After all, this person, this killer—he had to remember there was a killer, and it couldn't be him—this killer had warned him in the apartment to leave, seemed to be toying with him, more in a tormenting fashion, as opposed to a "trying to get him arrested" fashion. *God knows he could have had me arrested a dozen times by now.* His eyes, still staring at the screen, glazed over and drooped.

I need a coffee.

He opened the door to the hallway and looked out as nonchalantly as he could, keeping a wary eye out for Trace. The coast clear, he made for the stairwell, and took them two at a time to the ground floor. A brisk walk past the security checkpoints and he was outside, heading for his favorite coffee shop, and a reprieve, though momentary, from the pressures of lying to his fellow officers.

As he walked, he stared at his feet, only occasionally looking up to ensure he didn't barrel headlong into someone, lost in his own thoughts. He rounded the corner and saw his caffeine dealer's façade enticing him in, beckoning him for his thrice daily injection of one of the few legal substances that could get you high. Covering the final few paces to the door, he reached out to open it, and had a crystal clear vision of him opening that very door for Sarah just two days earlier.

He hesitated.

Would someone here remember him being with her last night?

He took his hand off the handle, leaving his arm still outstretched, his fingers hovering over the polished metal. *But maybe someone can give you some answers.*

He opened the door, and stepped inside.

Rachel Thompson's heart raced.

He's so hawt!

"Ouch!" she yelped, hot coffee overflowing the cup she was filling and burning her fingers.

"Si-ink!" sang Sandy, the manager and resident asshole. Okay, that was a little harsh. It was just that he seemed to notice everything she did wrong, whether it was here at work, or at drama class at NYU. And the last thing she needed was her mistakes pointed out to her in front of Frank.

He looks depressed.

Her burning fingers were momentarily forgotten.

Sandy tapped her on the shoulder and motioned with his eyes at her fingers. A sheepish smile broke free, and she quickly stepped over to the sink, running cold water over her fingers for several seconds. Not wanting to be taken out of the rotation of baristas, she quickly returned to her station and served up the offending cup after a quick wipe down.

Her heart leapt when Frank's order was taken, and it was her turn to make it. She smiled at him as she prepared his coffee, not even bothering to look at the ticket—he always ordered the same thing, a skim milk latte with a shot of espresso.

"How are you today?"

He looked at her, his eyes red, circles under them so dark it was as if someone had pitted them from his soul. But it was the sad look, the sagging outer edges of his mouth, the slack in his forehead, the paleness of his skin, that struck her. This was not the happy guy she was used to seeing.

Don't worry my darling, all things work themselves out eventually.

He seemed to realize she was talking to him after a few moments and shrugged his shoulders as his eyes focused. "Okay, I guess."

"You don't look so good."

This seemed to startle him slightly and she immediately regretted saying anything. *Keep it together; do you want him to know?*

"Ummm, well, rough night at work"—he glanced at his watch—"or I guess I should say day—" He stopped. "What day is it?"

"Sunday."

"Day, night and day I guess."

She took her time, not caring if the line got backed up.

"Is it that murder in your building?" *Shit!*

He bristled and his tone changed. "How'd you know about that?"

Think! The truth?

"I live across the street from you, I've seen you come in and out of that building for years, and when I saw all the cop cars there yesterday, I figured you may be involved."

This seemed to relax him again, and he nodded.

"Yeah, messy business." He looked at her as if he wanted to tell her something, his eyes yearning for a vessel to dump everything he was going through into.

Tell me what you're feeling! I'm here for you!

"Can't talk about it, of course." He motioned with his eyebrows at the coffee she held in her hand. "Is that ready?"

She was about to open her mouth when Sandy cut in, taking it from her hand and snapping a lid on it. "Of course it is. Here you go, Frank, hope your weekend improves."

Frank took the cup, gave a weak smile, and started to walk away.

Sandy turned to her. "Listen, Rachel, I need you to focus, we're shorthanded, and we're backed up." He pointed back and forth between her mouth and his. “Less chit chat, more”—he pointed at the tools of her barista trade—“this and that.”

She blushed, grabbed the next ticket, and when she looked up, was surprised to see Frank standing there.

“Sorry to bother you again.”

You can bother me any time.

“Problem with your order?”

He shook his head. “No, I was just wondering—” He stopped, as if nervous.

He's going to ask you out!

“Yes?”

He took a deep breath and rapid fired his question. “I was just wondering if you saw me here Friday night.”

How could she forget?

“Yes, I think so. Why?”

“Was I with someone?”

Yeah, that fat bitch.

“Yes, a girl.” She swallowed her bile. “You two seemed to be hitting it off.” He blushed. “Somebody from work?”

He nodded. “Yeah.” He paused. “Did you see us leave together?”

God, do I have to relive this?

She nodded. “Yeah, you two left about an hour after you got here.”

“Anything weird?”

Besides the fact you broke my fucking heart?

“Problem?”

The stern voice of Sandy startled both of them. Frank recovered first, shaking his head. “No, I was just leaving, thanks.” He turned and left without saying anything else as she turned to face Sandy, who was pointing behind him at the line.

“Take ticket, make ticket, hand over result of ticket, take next ticket. Got it?”

Her chin sunk into her chest. “Yes.”

I hate this life.

Richard sat in his car, staring straight ahead at nothing. He had pulled through the security gate and into the long drive ending in a cul-de-sac in front of the house, turned off the engine, and stared, his brain still not comprehending what he had seen. What he had done.

How could I have done such a thing? How could I not remember?

He shouldn't have left. He should have tried to help her.

He shook his head and slammed his palms into the steering wheel.

No, she was dead.

Or was she?

He hadn't actually checked. Maybe she was still alive.

I have to be sure.

He pushed the button to start the car and was startled when he heard his name called. He looked toward the front door of his sixteen bedroom abode, one he thought grossly oversized for their needs, but something his wife had insisted was necessary to match their "station in life", as she put it. *She would have fit well in Victorian England.* Her ideas on class made him cringe. Which was one of the reasons he enjoyed spending time with Samantha. She was down to earth, normal, not pretentious and fake like most of the people he was forced to associate with.

And none were worse than his wife, who now walked toward the car.

He hit the express-down button for the passenger side window.

"Yes?"

"I thought you had business to do?" The accusatory tone revealed none of the joy he felt a wife should feel at her husband unexpectedly coming home early from work.

"I finished early, but I just realized I forgot something at the office."

"Can't you get it Monday?"

He shook his head. "No, I need it today. I'll be back in a few hours."

She crossed her arms. "Don't think for a moment I don't know what's going on."

Richard gulped, a twinge of fear racing through him. *How the hell—* Then he realized it wasn't the murder she was talking about. "What do you mean?"

"You thought I was away this weekend, and now that you know I'm not, you're leaving again."

His mind reeled. He had forgotten she was supposed to be away at a friend's for some charity event. His eyebrows scrunched. "I forgot you were supposed to be away. Why aren't you?"

"How dare you turn this around on me?"

The screech made him cringe, another tweak of fear rushing through him, leaving a trail of goose bumps. *I hate her when she's like this.* "Can I go now?"

She nodded.

He slammed the car in gear. "I'll be back in a few hours."

He hit the gas, leaving her, and her bile, behind.

Frank sat on a bench, eyes closed, shoulders slouched, chin pressed into his chest. Somebody took the now lukewarm coffee cup from his hand. He tried to open his mouth to protest, but found he couldn't. Two hands were shoved under his armpits and he felt himself deadlifted to his feet, his own body unable to provide any assistance. It felt cool, almost like a ride at Disney, his body a puppet, his Good Samaritan the marionette. The puppet master swung his arm over their shoulder, and began to half drag, half carry him. He fought to wake up, but couldn't, his efforts using up the last of his energy as he felt himself drift away.

He woke, slightly, his only real indicator of anything beyond the fog filling his head was movement. The up and down sway as steps were taken. Steps not taken by him, but by the stranger who now controlled him. He struggled against their arms, but was too weak, and they were too strong, for him to break free. But then again, he could barely walk, so why was he struggling? This person was, after all, helping him. Weren't they? His head was porridge, the world a blur around him. His eyelids, heavy with fatigue, were impossible to lift to get a look at where he was. Sounds were distant echoes, as if he were at the bottom of a pool, listening to the delighted squeals of children playing on the surface and elevators chiming their arrival.

Elevators? In a pool? What am I doing in a pool? What am I doing in a pool with elevators?

He forced his eyes open for a moment as he felt himself dragged a few more steps. His back and side hit something hard, and a hand pressed on his chest, pushing him against whatever it was he had hit. And he saw a bright numeral 2 lit momentarily, then a 3. *I'm on an elevator!* His mind at ease, he began to drift again when he heard his benefactor mutter.

"Tick tock, elevator, tick tock. I'm on a schedule here."

Frank felt a momentary surge of panic, then blacked out.

Shakespeare nearly bowled Trace over as they both rounded the corner in opposite directions. He stopped with little difficulty, his pace never quick, but she appeared to have been almost running, and had to put a hand out, pushing against his chest. She took a step back and smiled.

"Sorry, Shakes."

Shakespeare shrugged his shoulders. "No worries. You woulda lost that one, though."

"Huh?"

"Physics."

"Uh huh."

Shakespeare had the distinct impression she didn't get his joke, and decided against explaining it.

"Were you able to save your shirt?"

Shakespeare shook his head. "Nope, lost cause. I don't know what that girl ate, but yoikes, it was nasty. I even tried spraying it with some Shout, but no go.

"Shakespeare the domestic?" Trace gave him an exaggerated, cockeyed look. "I can't picture it."

"I even pick out my own clothes in the morning." *Uh oh.*

She gave him the elevator from top to bottom. "I'd believe that."

Aaand there we go. The cop banter, back and forth insults, all in good fun; the only insults he'd experienced over the past few years hurtful, and one way. He had felt he deserved them, and rarely had fought back. But now it seemed his fellow cops were beginning to accept him again. And it felt good.

"How was our witness?"

"Oh, she's a drama queen that one. After spewing on you she fainted when identifying the body. Got her a coffee and sent her on her way before going home myself. I was just coming up to let you know I'm going to pull Angela Henwood's file, see if we can get a DMV photo, address, next of kin, some background before I start canvassing."

"Apartment building?"

Trace nodded. "And campus. According to St. Jean she was studying at NYU."

"Good. Let me know how that pans out. I'm going to see Frank and check on the status of that photo. He's not returning my phone calls."

Trace looked like she wanted to say something.

"What's on your mind?"

She looked at him then away. "Oh, nothing." She paused then shook her head. "Never mind, it's nothing. I'll call you if I find out anything." With that she swept toward the elevators. "Coming?"

Shakespeare was shocked to find himself shaking his head.

"No, I'm gonna take the stairs."

Trace and a few of the arriving morning shift stopped and stared, their jaws dropped.

"Oh piss off!"

Laughter erupted and everyone, including him, continued on.

And it felt good.

Richard pulled directly into the parking lot attached to the Waldorf Astoria, parked and hurried to the elevators. Using his express key, he swiped it for access to the suite floors, and the elevator quickly brought him to his destination, ignoring all other floors. He stepped off, careful to make certain no one else was in the hallway, and walked, as calmly as possible, to his room. Swiping his pass, he entered, closed the door, and pressed his back against it, closing his eyes and taking a deep breath as he tried to steady his racing heart. He opened his eyes and his calmed heart slammed against his ribcage, as if trying to escape what he saw.

A perfectly clean room.

He tentatively stepped into the main living area, where he distinctly remembered glasses being left the night before.

Nothing.

"Hello?"

His voice seemed to almost echo in the eerie stillness. But it wasn't eerie at all. This was how a hotel room should sound if no one was here. Completely still. Completely quiet. He stepped toward the bedroom, toward what should be a blood soaked crime scene. He tentatively took one step inside, leaning forward to look upon the bed.

It was made. As if no one had ever slept in it, the military precision inviting him to bounce a quarter off the center. He hurried to the bathroom, and again found nothing. Perfectly clean.

Had he dreamt it?

Impossible.

He knew it had definitely happened, he just didn't know how. But now someone had cleaned up after him.

Maybe the police had already come and gone?

No, he knew enough from television to know a couple of hours were not enough to process a crime scene, and it would definitely be taped off.

Someone had cleaned this up. Deliberately.

But why? Blackmail?

He was worth hundreds of millions or a couple of billion, depending on which accounting standard used, so that was definitely a possibility. In fact, he wouldn't be surprised to receive a phone call, or a brown envelope, before he made it back home.

Or to toy with him?

His thoughts turned to the most hateful bitch he could think of, but shook his head. He could see her doing it, and could think of a few good reasons why, but she had been at home. There was no way she could have done this.

Maybe she had help?

He held his breath, thinking, then in a burst, let it out. *It couldn't be.*

But there was only one question he truly cared to have answered. *Did I kill Samantha?*

He shook his head. No, not her, it wasn't in him. He peered around the bathroom, then returned to the bedroom, his eyes darting into every corner, trying to find any hint of what had transpired, and finding nothing.

What do I do now? He stood staring at the bed, trying to process what had happened, and what to do next. *You get the hell out of here!*

He walked quickly to the door when something nagged at him. He stopped, his hand on the doorknob. *What am I forgetting?* There was something. He turned, surveying the suite before him. He began a mental tally. *What did you bring with you last night?*

Jacket? He was wearing it.

Clothes? Ditto.

Briefcase? In the car downstairs.

Overnight bag?

That's it! He had arrived with an overnight bag, and he hadn't left with it, nor did he see it in the bedroom where he had put it when he arrived last night. He rushed back into the bedroom, searching every closet and drawer, under the bed, and behind the chairs and even curtains. Nothing. He moved to the living area, then the entrance. He opened the closet door, and breathed a sigh of relief. His Louis Vuitton overnight bag sat tucked in the corner. He reached in for it, when he noticed an envelope sitting on top.

He paused.

He knew this was it, this was the shoe dropping. He reached out, hesitantly, then grabbed the envelope. It was a hotel envelope, included on the writing table in every room, the hotel crest and address embossed in gold on the back flap. Nothing was written on the outside. He flipped it over, and shoved his finger under the folded top, the glue only stuck at the center, and slid his finger forward, ripping open the flap.

Inside was a folded sheet of paper. He pulled it out, and unfolded it. It too was Waldorf Astoria letterhead, and neatly written in the center, were words that shook him to his very core.

TICK TOCK
LITTLE TIME ON THE CLOCK
WHEN THEY FIND WHAT I HID
THEY WILL KNOW WHAT YOU DID

He clenched his hand holding the page into a fist, crumpling the paper, as his chest exploded in pain, radiating up and out. His free hand reached up, gripping his chest, squeezing it tightly, as if trying to rid it of the pain ripping it apart. He willed himself to the door as the pain racked his entire chest cavity, pulsing out to his back, his breathing becoming increasingly labored. Reaching out, he grabbed the knob and twisted. Pulling the door open with the last of his strength, he shoved his head, then shoulder through, and finally, completely spent of any remaining strength, collapsed, the upper half of his body in the exclusive hallway, the rest inside the luxury suite.

His mind screamed what his mouth couldn't.

Help me!

Frank's head pounded. Again. The sense of déjà vu sent his heart racing as he struggled to wake himself. His eyes heavy with sleep and whatever else had knocked him out, refused to open. He screamed in his head, and slowly, the adrenaline of panic started to course through his veins, and he willed his eyes open. But this time was different. This time, he knew exactly where he was.

He was in his own bed.

His heart started to settle, his panic eased, as he realized he was home, he was safe. *Maybe it was all a dream?* He looked about. Nothing out of place, nothing out of the ordinary. He looked down the bed at himself. He was fully dressed, still wearing the clothes he had worn to work. But how had he gotten here? He racked his brain, trying to remember. He left the station to get a coffee, he talked to that girl there, her name escaping him, then left, then…what? He had a vague recollection of someone carrying him, of the elevator, of them saying something.

Tick tock, elevator, tick tock!

He bolted upright in bed at the memory. The voice echoed through his head, repeating over and over. *Tick tock! Tick tock!* He jumped from the bed and grabbed for the wall, his head pounding, the room spinning around him. He leaned against the wall, steadying himself, concentrating on a spot on the floor, his wandering mind making a mental note to vacuum later. Settled, he rose, this time slowly, and as his first few tentative steps didn't send him tumbling into his furniture, he stepped from the bedroom and into the living area, cautiously peeking around the corner of his opened door.

Nothing.

He breathed a sigh of relief, and listened.

What is that?

He listened harder, cocking his ear. *Dripping?* He looked across the open concept living area and could see the kitchen sink and the tap, not dripping. He took several tentative steps toward the bathroom, when he spotted his cellphone sitting on the carpet in front of the door. He picked it up and saw there was a text message.

His heart started to race as he hit the key to view it.

TICK TOCK
LITTLE TIME ON THE CLOCK
COULD SOMETHING HAVE BEEN SLIPPED
WHEN THE POT WAS TIPPED?

The coffee shop? Could it be? Could someone have dosed his coffee today? And Friday? It made sense, it was the only thing in common he had with today and then, but why tip him off? And who? If he was carried here, it had to have been by a man. And Rachel made his coffee. There was no way she could have carried him. Could she be working with someone? He had always thought she liked him, but dosing him? That was no way to show it. Sarah! Could she have been jealous of Sarah? So jealous she dosed both of them, and killed Sarah?

But was Sarah dead? Right now she wasn't missing, she wasn't due at work until tomorrow, and he had kept his ears open for any new cases coming in, and had heard nothing about her, or any other Jane Doe's fitting her description, so right now his optimistic side was thinking she may still be alive.

But if Rachel had dosed them both on Friday because she was jealous, then she would have had to have known he would be coming there with a girl. And he never brought girls there. In fact, he almost never went out on dates. Scratch that. He never went out on dates. *You're a loser geek with no self-confidence and no idea how to approach a girl.* In fact, Friday's invite offer to Sarah had been so out of character for him, he was stunned when the words came out of his mouth, and equally stunned Sarah had said yes.

Getting shot gives you confidence?

It certainly had brought him attention from some of the women at work, but he hadn't followed through on anything. He had been given a few numbers and pecks on the cheek, but hadn't called any of them.

But Sarah. Sarah was different. She had always smiled at him, long before he had been shot, and she had always seemed like such a nice girl. He didn't care she had a few extra pounds on her; he thought they looked good on her. He had always pictured holding her against him, her softness a turn-on as opposed to a turn-off.

His phone vibrated again. He gulped, closed his eyes, and pressed the button to view the message. Taking a deep breath, he opened his eyes and swallowed his heart.

TICK TOCK
LITTLE TIME ON THE CLOCK
THE ONE ON THE CASE
BETTER NOT SEE YOUR FACE

His hand darted to his face, but felt nothing out of the ordinary. He rushed into the bathroom, flicking on the light and gasped.

His face was covered in blood.

Again.

Shakespeare stepped into the lab and was thankful to find it empty. He leaned against the wall and gasped for air, unable to do so moments before in the stairwell due to the lab's health-crowd traffic. After a minute of sucking in filtered, air conditioned air, he looked at his watch. *Too early for the kid to have gone home.* Then he remembered it was the weekend, and realized it wasn't early at all. *Maybe the kid did go home.* He was about to turn around when something caught his eye. A large screen at the far end was blinking a message, *Process Complete.* He approached the screen and stared at it, the swirl gone, a slightly imperfect image revealed of a man's face.

A man he recognized.

A man half of New York probably recognized, if they read a newspaper.

And a man the rest definitely knew the name of.

Richard Tate.

Shakespeare sat down and stared at the photo. It was a profile shot, so a little bit more difficult to recognize, and he was lip locked with a rather hot blonde who looked half his age, but he was sure it was him. His initial gut instinct was one of definite recognition, and that's what he usually went with. He tried never to let doubts creep in and make him second guess himself, but this was one situation where he had to be sure. You couldn't go around accusing one of the richest men in America of involvement in a gruesome murder.

And isn't he married?

Shakespeare leaned back in the chair and clasped his hands behind his head, tilting his head from side to side, trying to get different angles. It had to be him. And if it was, this case just got a lot more difficult. Billionaires had lawyers. Billionaires' lawyers had lawyers. Teams of lawyers. Teams of lawyers who would immediately advise their clients to not say a word, under any circumstances, then would start calling in favors.

The 1%.

Above the law, living a life the rest of us couldn't even fathom. It wasn't just the fancy cars and mansions, it was the complete disconnect from the real world. Anything you wanted at your beck and call, walk into the fanciest restaurants without a reservation, secretaries that were not only capable, but hot and willing to boot, trophy wives who didn't mind the philandering, butlers, maids, drivers, ass kissers and wipers, 'no' was a word never heard unless it was followed by 'problem'.

And they almost never saw the inside of a courtroom.

He stared at the screen. He needed to be sure. He knew he had seen in the movies tricks where they would take a profile picture, spin it and mirror it, creating a front-on shot of a full face. He had no idea what the technical term was, but his was 'fancy shit', and he needed Frank to work his magic on this photo, and he couldn't wait until Monday.

He dialed Frank's number, and after ringing several times, it went to voice mail.

"Frank, it's Shakespeare, call me ASAP, it's urgent."

He snapped his phone shut and clipped it to his belt, his love handles enveloping it like a protective layer.

Time to tell the LT.

Trace's phone rang and she hit the button on her steering wheel to answer as she waited, stuck in traffic.

"Trace."

"Hey, Trace, it's Shakespeare. You haven't seen Frank, have you?"

Trace's trouble radar went off. "No, why?"

"Can't find him at the station, not answering his phone. That photo looks like it's finished, but I need some more work done on it before I can confirm the ID of the John Doe."

"Who's it look like?"

"I'd rather not say, not over the phone. Let's just say if it's who I think it is, this case just got a whole lot tougher."

Trace didn't like the sound of that. But part of her was also titillated. *Who could be in that photo that Shakespeare of all people would be concerned about?* Then it dawned on her. *Frank!* It had to be. It made sense. Shakes wouldn't want to say anything to her, just in case it wasn't, but why would he be so horny to get a hold of him? There were other techs, why not ask one of them? *Because then they'd know.*

"Okay, I understand." She paused and looked at the street signs. "Listen, I'm only a couple of blocks from his building. How 'bout I go check and see if he's there?"

"Do that and get back to me. I've gotta talk to the LT."

The line went dead.

If he's talking to the LT about it, it has to be Frank.

She did a shoulder check then pulled a U-turn. She was nowhere near Frank's place, but was determined to be the one to bring him in.

Lieutenant Phillips looked up when Shakespeare tapped on the glass, and raised a finger for him to wait, the other hand jotting notes while his desk phone was cradled between his ear and shoulder. Shakespeare nodded and turned to survey the squad room. Walker passed by, staring at a file, and looked up.

"Hey, Shakes, what's shakin'?"

"Everything that shouldn't."

Walker laughed and sat at his desk, tossing the file over to his partner who sat across from him. Shakespeare looked at his own desk, and the now vacant one across from it.

I wonder who'll get assigned to me. And when.

The door opened behind him and he turned on his heel.

"Come on in," said Phillips.

Shakespeare followed and closed the door behind them. Phillips raised his eyebrows. "Problem?"

Shakespeare nodded. "I think so."

Phillips pointed at one of the chairs in front of his desk which Shakespeare gratefully accepted. Stairs were one thing; standing for too long a time would just have him sweating up a storm. He dropped into the uncomfortable wooden monstrosity and took a deep breath.

"I think we've got an ID on the John Doe in the photo."

"Really?" Phillips leaned forward, placing his elbows on his desk and clasping his hands. "Who?"

"Richard Tate."

Phillips let out a long whistle as he leaned back in his chair. "Are you sure?"

"No, not yet."

"Why?"

"Can't find the kid Brata to do some more wizardry on the photo to be sure."

"Can't another tech do it?"

"I'm sure they could, but how many people do you want knowing Richard Tate is involved in a murder investigation? It'd be all over the lab and then the press within hours."

Phillips nodded. "Good point. We better tread lightly here." He thought for a moment then leaned forward. "Crazy idea. Why not reach out to that reporter woman, Kai, and see if she'd do us a solid and let us know if there's a leak?"

Shakespeare thought for a moment. "Might be an idea. That photo has been sitting on a screen in the lab, unscrambled, for God knows how long. I recognized him right away, and I'm sure others will too."

"You didn't turn off the monitor?"

Shakespeare rose from his seat. "Have you seen that place, LT? You know me and computers, I'm liable to hit the wrong button and lose the whole damned thing."

Phillips shook his head and Shakespeare opened the door. "I think we need to schedule some computer training for you."

Shakespeare smiled at Phillips as he stepped from the office.

"I'm sick that day."

Frank scrubbed and scrubbed some more. The sticky, dried purplish blood flowed down his arms and neck, turning a bright crimson as he applied copious amounts of hot water and soap. He was making progress, but it was slow. And disgusting. He kept spitting as water mixed with blood entered his mouth. He tried holding his breath, but that made it worse, he tried breathing through just his nose, but he was in so much of a panic, he was beginning to hyperventilate.

There was a knock at the door.

Frank froze.

After a few seconds, another knock, this time a little more forcefully.

"Frank, it's me, Detective Trace."

Frank felt his chest tighten. He stared in the mirror. He was soaking wet, but at first glance he appeared to have rid himself of the blood. He grabbed a towel, dried his face, neck, chest and arms, then looked down at his shirt. Water splotches mixed with red stains covered it. He tore it off and threw it in the hamper behind the door. He wiped down the countertop with the towel, then tore open the shower curtain to throw the towel in the tub and screamed.

Like a little girl.

In the tub lay the body of another woman. And scrawled on the wall, in blood, was his name.

Now the knocking was more urgent. "Frank, are you okay?"

Frank stared at the body for a moment, then the towel still in his hand.

I'm not going to prison.

He closed the shower curtain, tossed the towel into the hamper, did a quick eyeball of the bathroom, then flushed the toilet. "Just a minute!"

The knocking at least stopped.

He took a deep breath and opened the door.

"Detective Trace, what are you doing here?"

Trace stared at Frank's naked chest. "Jesus, kid, don't you own any shirts?"

Frank blushed. "Yeah, well, you know, at home, comfortable."

She looked down at his pants. "In slacks?"

Frank shrugged.

"May I come in?"

He shrugged again and stepped back from the door. Trace entered, giving the apartment a quick once over with her trained eye, careful to keep Frank in sight the entire time. As far as she could see, nothing was amiss.

"We were worried about you."

Frank gulped. "Me, why?"

She stepped deeper into the apartment, keeping him in the corner of her eye. "Shakespeare was looking for you, something to do with the photo you were working on."

Frank closed the door and followed her. "Was there a problem with it?"

This time Trace shrugged her shoulders. "No idea, he just asked me to come get you, said it was urgent."

"No problem, let me get a shirt." He rushed to the bedroom and closed the door.

Seems a little too eager to get out of here. What are you hiding, kid?

She glanced over her shoulder and noticed the cupboards were not the same design as their vic's. *Lie number one.* The only other door besides the bedroom she assumed to be the bathroom. She covered the few feet swiftly, opening the bathroom door and looking in. Except for a slight fog on the mirror, everything seemed fine. She was about to leave when out of habit she pulled aside the shower curtain and gasped.

A noise behind her had her reaching for her weapon when she felt something hit her head, and the room turn to black.

Frank stared at his handiwork, and sobbed.

What have I done?

Trace was bound and gagged in his gaming chair with duct tape, still unconscious. The jade green sphinx statue he had hit her with lay broken, half still on the bathroom floor, the other half that had remained in his hand tossed on the living room carpet.

I hope I didn't hit her too hard.

His phone vibrated and he jumped. *Not again!*

TICK TOCK
LITTLE TIME ON THE CLOCK
TAKING OUT A COP
IS OVER THE TOP

He paused for a moment. *How does he know what I just did?* He spun around, searching the apartment for who, or what, he didn't know, but the hairs standing up on the back of his neck told him he was being watched. It made sense. In the other apartment he had received two text messages, too well timed, for someone to not have eyes on him. He looked at the large floor to ceiling window occupying one side of his apartment. The drapes were shut. There was no way for anyone to see in. He closed his eyes, and took a deep breath.

Think!

He hit Trace in the bathroom, tied her up in the living area. That eliminated the bedroom. Or did it? Had he opened the door? He searched back in time, through his jumbled, confused memories. Had he gone back into the bedroom?

No!

He opened his eyes. *Sometimes you gotta think like a criminal.* Shakespeare's words echoed in his head, something he had overheard him say to Eldridge. And it made sense. You can't think like a law abiding citizen when you're trying to catch one who's not. *If I were a criminal—and I'm not!—how would I keep eyes on my victim?* Curtains closed. No one else in the apartment besides him and Trace. Two different apartments, more than one floor separating them, but on the same side of the building. It couldn't be a hole in the floor or ceiling, otherwise they would have to have two apartments in the building, and he knew that was almost impossible. Almost. He shook his head. Not a peep hole.

He looked at the curtains again. They were closed, as they had been in the other apartment, and a peephole on the outer wall would be useless to anyone but a window cleaner. His heart leapt. He raced for the curtains, threw them open, but found no one. He looked up and down, but no window cleaning rig was in sight.

Okay, so not a peep hole.

Camera! He spun, his eyes quickly taking in the room, looking for anything new, anything out of the ordinary, but could see nothing. It would have to be something he wouldn't move, something hollow with a natural opening, something that gave a full view of his apartment, possibly including the bathroom. Possibly in the bathroom.

Trace groaned.

He whipped around to face her as her eyes fluttered open. It took a few moments for her to be fully aware of her situation, and she screamed against the gag, her eyes daggers. He stepped over to the chair she struggled against and knelt down. "I'm going to remove the gag, but you have to promise me you won't scream."

Tears rolled down his face as she nodded. He gently pulled at the corners, trying not to hurt her. He had a tight grip on one corner when she yanked her head to the side, ripping the tape from her mouth. She leaned toward him, her face only inches from his.

"What the hell do you think you're doing?"

Frank fell back on the floor, startled at the vehemence. *But would you be any different?* He thought about it. *I'd probably have pissed my pants then begged for my life.* Trace was looking around, probably for some means of escape, when Frank stood back up, resuming his search.

"Untie me now, Frank. You don't want to add a cop to your kill list."

Frank's heart thudded against his chest. "I'm n-not going to hurt you." His voice was a hoarse whisper, his throat having gone dry with the dismay his co-worker thought him a killer. *What did you expect? You attacked her and tied her up,* after *she found a body in your tub!*

"That's good, Frank, that's a start." She looked from side to side at the duct tape binding her arms to the chair. "Now how about you untie me and explain everything to me. We'll just talk, okay?"

He knew she was lying. She was trying to save herself from someone she thought was a killer. She'd say anything to get him to free her, then she'd use her cop training to kick the shit out of him. He shook his head. "I'm sorry, but I can't do that, not as long as you think I'm a killer."

Frank resumed his search, but could find nothing. The apartment was sparse. After all, he was just starting his life. His chest tightened. *I'm only twenty-six! My life can't be over already!* Another deep breath and a slow exhale. He looked up. And smiled. *If I were a criminal…*

He rushed to his desk, yanked open a drawer and pulled out a small black tool kit he used for working on his computers. He unzipped it as he rushed back to the kitchen then jumped up on the counter. Standing up, he was now eye to eye with the cold air return above his cupboards.

And he could see it.

He grabbed a Phillips head screw driver, and furiously removed one of the screws holding the grate in place. It fell to the floor and rattled on the tile as he pried at the grate with his finger tips and bent it away.

Inside sat a small camera, hooked to a cellphone, a piece of tape over the red light that would have revealed its presence had he thought to look. He ripped it from the duct, and in his excitement, forgot where he was, stepping back in triumph to show his prize to Trace, only to find nothing under his foot. He fell backward, his head hit the island countertop, and the world around him slowly went black. He heard a voice as if off in the distance, just before he passed out.

"Well that's just fuckin' lovely."

SIX

Sarah woke and rubbed her eyes. Her stomach rumbled slightly, but not as ferociously as she would have thought it should. It just felt—off. She wondered if she would ever get fed here. *Just another part of my eternal damnation.* She leaned against the wall, the feeling fading, but not completely, a dull reminder always there. Strangely she didn't feel weak. She had no idea how long she had been here, but it felt like at least a couple of days. And it already felt like an eternity. How she would last an actual eternity, she couldn't fathom. Already she felt herself slipping, her mind starting to feel crazed thoughts, thoughts of charging the door at the end of the chamber, and risking the horrors on the other side. Instead she prayed. She prayed for God to forgive her, to free her from her horror, to give her a second chance.

"Please, God, help me," she whispered.

"God can't help you here, my child."

She screamed and pushed herself away from the voice before she had a chance to look. Halfway down the wall to her right, she glanced back and saw an old lady, smiling at her. Smiling at her from under a habit. *What the hell is a nun doing in Hell?*

The old woman smiled at her, as if she could read her thoughts. *Maybe she can?*

"I suppose you are wondering how a nun ends up in Hell."

Sarah nodded.

The sister looked at the floor, her eyes sad, the corners of her lips turned down. "I was just a woman"—she looked up at Sarah—"like you in many ways, I suspect."

Sarah gave her a slight smile of encouragement to continue.

The sister took in a deep breath of the hot, dry air surrounding them, and continued. "I wasn't always in the Order, and during my youth I was, how shall we say, pretty wild?"

A chuckle almost burst from Sarah's mouth, but she stopped it after the first sound. "Sorry." But she wasn't. It was the first laugh she had had since being here. "Continue."

The sister smiled. "No need to apologize my child, I wouldn't believe it if I were you either." She arranged her robes as if to delay what she was about to say next. "My sin is I loved another man."

"Huh?" Sarah couldn't believe she had just said that to a nun. "I mean, pardon me? Another man? How is that even possible? I thought nuns weren't allowed to, you know, have relationships."

"Relationships. I like how you put that, my child." Again she straightened her perfectly black robes. "All of those in the Order are expected to love only one man. Do you know who that is?"

Sarah nodded. "God?"

"Our Lord and Savior, Jesus Christ. We love him with all our hearts, rejoice in his greatness, and his love for us and all mankind. But I loved another as well, and that is why I am here."

Sarah was intrigued, to the point where she almost forgot where she was. "Who? Who was it?"

The sister lowered her head. "Father Carmichael."

Sarah gulped. "You had sex with a priest?"

The sister's head darted up. "Heaven's no! How could you think such a thing?"

Sarah's mouth went dry. "Umm, well, you know, you said you loved him, and, well, you are *here*"—Sarah waved her arms indicating their prison—"so I just assumed—"

"That the only way to love a man is to have sex with him?"

Oh, God, I wish I had had sex with Frank. To have died with that memory…

Sarah shrugged.

The old lady chuckled. "Oh, you kids today. You know, I fear for the future of mankind with the attitudes I see displayed by the youth. Have you actually read the lyrics of some of these rap songs they play on the radio? Disgusting! When I was younger I used to listen to rock and roll.

Beatles, Stones, Kiss. But what they sang about was nothing compared to what the kids are listening to today." She jabbed her finger at Sarah. "Do you know that songs they play now talk about gangbangs, killing cops, raping women?" She sucked in a lungful of air. "And these are the hit songs. These are the songs playing on the radio."

Sarah wasn't sure what to say. She wanted to know how loving a priest would earn a nun a seat at Hell's table, but was also enjoying just listening to someone else's voice. "How do you know this?"

"Because I've been helping Father Carmichael do a study on the decay of our youth, and we have linked it to rap music."

Sarah frowned. "Sounds rather simplistic to me."

The sister nodded. "And it is. Think about this. Kids can't see a movie at a theatre if it's meant for adults because the movie theatre won't let them in. At home, parents can set a password to stop kids from seeing TV shows and movies they shouldn't see, and when watching shows or movies at home, they usually do so as a family. But music? Parents can't stand their kids' music, so they don't listen to it. The kids listen to radio or songs they download on their iPods, and the parents just assume the government is monitoring what is being sung about. People don't realize that the government only responds to complaints. If parents knew what their kids were listening to, they'd be horrified."

"So working on this, is that how you fell in love?"

She nodded. "Yes, we had decided we needed to start a campaign to inform parents of what was going on." Sarah sighed. There seemed to be no stopping the woman's tirade. "We were going to give parents a list of the top ten worst songs, all of which were in heavy rotation on the radio stations, give them the lyrics, and then ask them to check their children's iPods to see if they had these songs." She smiled and looked at the ceiling, as if remembering something. "It was his idea," she said, almost wistfully. "It was a brilliant plan to save our children. Fight back against the radio stations by getting legions of parents to phone in complaints, encourage parents to go on the Internet and type the word 'lyrics' followed by the name of the song, and read for themselves what their kids were listening to, and then stop them. If the songs stopped selling, then these so-called artists would stop making them." She sighed. "It was a brilliant plan. It would have been a long, hard fight, but in the end, I think we would have won. We might have saved the next generation of kids."

"But what happened?"

"I fell in love."

"I know that, but—"

"I fell in love, and told Father Carmichael how I felt."

"Oh." Sarah could read the pain on the woman's face. "What happened then?"

"He chastised me for breaking my vows, and told Mother Superior he no longer wanted to see me."

"What an asshole!"

The old lady lifted her head, shock written across her face. "No! No! Not at all! He was right; he reacted exactly as he should."

"Seems to me he didn't want you around because he'd be tempted."

This time the sister looked uncertain of what to say. Sarah pressed on.

"Think about it. He knew you loved him. You were like the forbidden fruit, dangling there, day in and day out, that he could taste at any time, and if he had let you stay with him, working on your project, he may have given into that temptation, and broken his own vows."

"Perhaps you're right, my child," the woman whispered.

"Damn right I'm right. I think he loved you too, but when you put it into words, he got scared, and like a little wimp he turned you in rather than face his own weakness."

The woman nodded. "I wish I had thought of that myself, before…"

Sarah waited, but nothing came. "Before?"

The woman raised both her arms, her robe sliding up to her elbows, revealing her bare skin. "Before I did this."

She slowly rotated her wrists, palms up, and Sarah gasped.

Both wrists were sliced open, their bloodless wounds revealing the sister's ultimate sin.

"Aynslee!"

Aynslee jumped in her chair and stared at the room around her, a dozen faces seated at the table turned toward her. She searched her mind, trying to remember what was just asked of her, but she drew a blank. She in fact didn't even know who had snapped her from her reverie, her reverie of horror, of pain, of sadness, of what could have been.

"What?" She looked at Jeffrey Merle, the news director for WACX News, the only one leaning forward with an expression indicating he might be waiting for an answer. She shook her head. "Sorry, Jeff, what was that?"

"I asked if you were sure you're ready to go back on tonight."

She nodded. "Definitely."

"Hmmmm." Merle didn't sound convinced.

She leaned forward, pleading her case not only to him, but to her unconvinced self. "I'm ready. I need this. I need to work again. I'm going crazy just editing copy, twiddling my thumbs. I need to get back in the game."

Merle grimaced then smiled. "Okay, you're on." He stood and began to clap. "Welcome back, Aynslee!"

The room erupted in applause as everyone stood to join him. Aynslee felt herself blush, and knew despite her slightly darker complexion there would be no hiding it. Tears filled her eyes and spilt down her cheeks at the outpouring from everyone in the room.

Except for that asshole Jonathan Shaw, who sat impassively staring at her with hate filled eyes. *Get over it, I'm the anchor, you're still the crime reporter. You got schooled by someone half your age. Live with it.* His daggers gave her strength and she smiled, standing up to join the others as they surrounded her. Hugs and back slaps abounded. Merle came around the table and gave her a big hug, his beer belly pushing against her toned stomach. He whispered in her ear, "Good luck, kiddo!" and planted a small peck on her cheek.

He stepped back and raised his hands in the air, quieting the room. "Okay, we still have a meeting to finish, and not a lot of time to do it in." Everyone returned to their seats.

"Okay, so what have we got?"

Shaw leaned forward and shoved a file folder down the table toward Merle. "Now that the sissy shit is over, here's what I've got." He turned to the room, making a point of curling his lip slightly as his eyes passed over Aynslee. She met his gaze with equal disdain. "Murder in Queens. Police found her body in a bathtub. No ID yet, but sounds like it might be interesting."

"Why?"

"My source says there's no suspect, the crime scene was scrubbed as if by a pro, and get this—"

Despite every effort, Aynslee found herself leaning in with the others after his dramatic pause.

"—they found a photo, sitting on the bathroom counter."

Shaw sat back and crossed his arms, his eyes making the rounds of the table as if in triumph. Aynslee quickly pushed herself back in her seat so she was out of his line of sight, obscured by the weatherman, Bryan.

She heard Merle grunt and she leaned forward again. "Okay, I'll bite. What do you know about the photo?"

"Nothing yet, except they went ape-shit over it. I'm still working my sources but—"

There was a knock at the door. Aynslee's head swiveled with the rest to see who would interrupt a story meeting when almost everyone was crammed into the room. When she saw who it was, she leapt out of her chair and rushed to the door, opening it with a smile.

"Detective Shakespeare! Are you here to see me?"

The large man blushed slightly at her attentions. He reminded her a little of her late father, and after he had saved her life, she had begun to think of him a bit in that way. *Father figure?*

"Sorry to interrupt, but I need to speak to you, if you have a moment?"

Aynslee didn't bother to ask. "I'll be back as soon as I can," she tossed over her shoulder as she led Shakespeare to her office. Safely secured behind the four floor-to-ceiling walls she had only recently earned, she sat in a comfortable high-back leather chair behind her desk and motioned for the detective to have a seat.

"How can I help you, Detective?"

Shakespeare looked about, as if to confirm they were alone.

"I guess I should have called—"

"I would have been disappointed if you had."

He blushed again. *How badly have you been hurt that any type of civility embarrasses you?*

"Well, ah, thanks. I-I guess I should have called, but I wanted to see how you were doing, and—"

He paused and looked around again.

She leaned forward. "And?"

He lowered his voice. "And I have a favor to ask."

She smiled. "Anything for you, Detective." Again a blush. She motioned at the walls. "And don't worry; no one can hear you through these walls. All the offices are soundproof. After all, we're reporters, dealing with confidential sources, et cetera, all the time."

He leaned back and sighed along with the chair he was squeezed in. She made a mental note to get a bigger chair for his next visit.

"I guess I'm being a bit silly, but this could be big, and I can't risk it getting out." He leaned in again. "Listen, what I'm about to tell you can't leave this room, okay?"

If it was anyone else, she would have just nodded with her fingers crossed behind her back, but with him, she nodded. And meant it.

"Have you heard of Richard Tate?"

"Unless you live on the moon, everyone's heard of him."

Shakespeare chuckled. "Yeah, stupid question, I guess. But I think you'd be wrong."

Her eyebrows furled. "Sorry?"

"I heard he bought the moon last month. Another casino."

She laughed and he joined in, the tension of her earlier meeting broken. "So, what about Richard Tate?"

"We're working on a homicide, and a photo was found at the crime scene."

Her reporter antennae shot full-up. "The scrubbed one from yesterday?"

Shakespeare's head jerked back. "How'd you know about that?"

She raised her hands, palms splayed out and shrugged her shoulders. "Hey, I'm a reporter. It's my job."

Shakespeare shook his head. "Somebody's head's going to roll."

"Well, let's just make sure it's not yours."

He huffed. "Mine rolled years ago." His eyes took on an unfocused, distant look. She wondered if he would ever open up to her about what had happened to him. She decided not to press it. He took a deep breath and continued. "Well, what your sources can't know, or at least I *hope* can't know, is that Richard Tate was in that photo, in bed with another as yet unidentified woman."

She let out a slow, long breath as she leaned back in her chair, elbows on the arms, her chin resting on steepled fingers. "You don't think—?" She stopped, not even wanting to say it.

This time Shakespeare shrugged. "I don't know what to think yet. But here's the thing. If he's involved, this is—"

"Huge."

He nodded. "Huge."

Her gaze, directed at the ceiling as she contemplated the implications, returned to Shakespeare. "What do you need from me?"

"I need you to tell me if you hear anything on the street, or your beat, or whatever the hell you news guys—sorry gals—people—hell, whatever you call yourselves and *it*"—she grinned—"about this photo, and who's in it. We can't risk this getting out there, but the department leaks like a sieve sometimes."

Aynslee smiled and nodded. "Don't worry, Detective, I'll keep my ears open and if I hear of anyone mentioning Richard Tate in any compromising photo I'll let you know right away." This seemed to satisfy him and he rose, extending his hand. She took it as she circled the desk. She pulled herself close to him and gave him a peck on the cheek, letting go of his hand. He patted her arm, his eyes conveying a fatherly concern that made her warm inside, and he stepped toward the door as something dawned on her.

"Hey, I wonder if that's why he collapsed."

Shakespeare stopped. "Huh?"

"Richard Tate. If he's involved in a murder, it might be why he collapsed earlier."

Shakespeare turned to face her.

"What are you saying?"

Aynslee looked at him, puzzled. "Don't you know? It's been all over the news. Richard Tate was taken to the hospital today. Possible heart attack."

Trace debated what to do. She could yell for help, but the fact she hadn't heard a damned thing since her captor had laid himself out, she suspected the walls were pretty soundproofed. *Break the chair like in the movies?* She shoved with her feet and back, trying to crack the chair in two, knowing full well it was a useless venture; the chair was a high-end office chair, not some cheap wooden glue-job from China. *Though it probably still is from China.* She could wait? Dispatch knew she was here. Eventually someone would come looking. But then he could wake up before then and kill her.

She leaned forward and with all of her strength pulled her arms up at the elbows, trying to tear the tape. Pushing as hard as she could, her hands gripping the ends of the chair arms, her entire being strained as she felt the elbow of her left arm rise slightly. Filled with a rush of expectation, she pushed even harder, but the elbow remained stubbornly still, until she at last gave up, relaxing her taught body, and to her dismay, noticing her left elbow did not lower any further than her right, the perceived gain only in her imagination.

A deep, guttural growl slowly built in her throat, erupting in a roar of frustration as she slammed her head into the high cushioned back of the chair. Her outburst over, she closed her eyes and steadied her breathing. *If you're going to die, you're going to die.*

But none of this made sense.

If the kid was a killer, why wouldn't he have just killed her? Hell, he had one body in the tub already, what's two? And what was that he had found behind the grate? She could have sworn it was a webcam. And if it was, it wasn't his secret date-rape cam to tape unsuspecting women—he had searched for this thing, had found it.

Or it could have been a show for her.

She thought about that. Was he that good an actor? She shook head and whispered, "No way." No, this kid wasn't acting. He found that webcam. And it wasn't his. And his reaction. He had been so pleased, as if he had just proven he wasn't crazy, that the camera must be the key.

The key to what?

The key to the murder? No, something more. *Pull the kid out from the equation.* Okay, dead body in the tub. Webcam hidden in the grill to monitor the apartment. Connected? Obviously. The only way they wouldn't be was if the owner of the apartment had placed the camera there, and since he didn't, and she didn't believe in coincidences, they were clearly connected. She visualized the problem, pictured the body in the tub, the camera broadcasting the apartment. Broadcasting what? To whom? The whom was easy. The killer. That's the only explanation for the camera. If the body and the camera are linked, then obviously the killer planted the camera. But why? Perhaps to watch the kid's reaction to the discovery? The investigation. In fact—

A chill ran down her spine as a horrid realization dawned on her.

In fact, the killer could be watching right now.

Or rather, would have been, but since Frank was passed out behind the counter with the camera somewhere on the floor, he would have nothing to see.

And if I was a homicidal maniac, wanting to get my kicks, I might just come back and—

There was a noise at the door.

Her heart leapt as her head spun toward the sound. It wasn't a key. There was no knock. Nothing indicating a visitor, or someone who was supposed to be there. But there was a noise, a scraping sound, something odd she couldn't place. *Is someone picking the lock?* Her heart thudded in her chest as she focused on the door. What would the killer do if he found a cop, tied to a chair?

He'd kill you, obviously.

But maybe not if he thought she was passed out. She closed her eyes and turned her head away from the door, trying to steady her rapid breathing. The sound continued, each little scratch like a roar of thunder echoing between the Manhattan towers. She could hear her pulse drum through her ears, every sound in the apartment, on the street below, and at the door ten feet away, amplified like a speaker cranked to ten.

Then a quick, final scrape, as if something were sliding, then…nothing.

She waited. Could he have opened the door? Could it have been that silent? He would want to sneak in, just in case someone was inside. He would want to open and close the door as gently as possible. She strained to hear. A moment ago everything was so loud. But now she could hear nothing.

She opened her eyes a crack, her head still facing away from the door.

Nothing.

Straining, she held her breath, but all she could hear was her own heart thudding in her chest. No footsteps, no breathing, no nothing. She had to risk it. By now whoever it was would have seen Frank out cold in the kitchen, and she was in plain sight from the door. He would know no one would be in the bathroom other than the victim, and would most likely know Frank lived alone.

She turned her head slightly, pushing her eyeballs in their sockets as far to the right as she could, trying to maximize her peripheral vision.

Nothing.

She turned her head some more, then all at once opened her eyes and spun.

And breathed a sigh of relief.

Tucked in the door of the apartment was a flyer, probably for some pizza joint she could ask Shakespeare for an opinion on. She heard a clicking in the hallway, the distinctive sound of a stairwell door closing.

And an opportunity for help, lost.

The old lady was gone.

Sarah sighed, eyeing the door outlined at the end of her prison, wishing she too could just walk out like her guest had while she slept. But she couldn't. This was *her* prison, not theirs. Were they even real? Or merely demons sent to torment her. To remind her of the world she had lost, and the isolation she would now experience. If she was isolated permanently, there was a risk she might forget about companionship over time, and learn to accept her isolation. But if occasionally she were reminded of what she had lost, she may never become accustomed to the loneliness. It was clever. It was cruel.

It was evil.

"I wonder what happened to Frank," she said aloud.

"He will be joining us soon."

The voice startled her, deep, rumbling, the entire room vibrating from the deep bass in the voice. She pushed herself further into her corner, burying her head. *Face your fear! How can it get any worse?* She raised her chin slightly, exposing her mouth.

"Why? Why do you have to punish him too?" Her voice trembled, her heart screamed in her chest as terror gripped her.

"You dare question me?" The room shook as if an earthquake had hit. Sarah's arms darted out to the two walls and she braced herself.

"I'm sorry," she whimpered.

"The list of your friend's sins is long." There was a pause. "Perhaps you would like to hear them?"

She shook her head. "No, no I wouldn't."

The voice chuckled. "Then let us begin."

Half a dozen commandments were read, but when she heard the last one, she gasped.

"Thou shalt not kill."

Kill? It made no sense. Frank didn't even carry a weapon. And besides, she had always been taught that by "kill", God had meant "murder". Killing without cause. There was no way Frank could be guilty of breaking that commandment.

"There's no way Frank is a murderer."

A soft chuckle echoed off the walls.

"Oh really?"

The chuckle built, becoming deeper, turning into a growl, almost a barking laugh.

"Then why are you here, Sarah?"

Frank moaned. His head throbbed with a splitting headache he couldn't explain. For a moment panic surged through him at the thought of being drugged again, but when he opened his eyes and found himself staring up at his kitchen ceiling, he remembered what had happened.

The camera!

He bolted up, immediately regretting it, grabbing the island countertop until the room stopped spinning. He opened his eyes again and surveyed the floor. He bent over, slowly, picking up the webcam and transmitter lying on the floor.

"It's about goddamned time."

He spun toward the voice and moaned in pain. *Trace!* He had almost forgotten about her in his excitement and pain. "See this?" He held up the camera triumphantly as he disconnected the transmitter. "This"—he shook the camera—"is the proof that I'm innocent."

Trace was looking at him, but he couldn't read her expression. At last she spoke. "Okay, boy wizard, what the hell are you talking about? Explain it to me, pretend I'm dense, I don't have all the facts. Give them to me!"

He grabbed another chair and pulled it up in front of her, showing her the camera and transmitter. "This"—he held up the camera—"is a web camera. This"—he held up the transmitter—"is a transmitter. It's been transmitting the signal from this camera, to the Internet." He leaned back triumphantly.

"So?"

So? How could she not see it? "Don't you get it? This is the killer's. He planted this in my apartment so he could watch me."

"How do I know you didn't put it there yourself?"

Frank opened his mouth to respond but stopped. She was right. How could he prove it? Then it dawned on him. He reached into his pants pocket and pulled out his cellphone, scrolling to the latest message he had received and showed it to her.

"See? I've been getting these all weekend. I'm being set up!" He scrolled through each of them so she could read them.

"How do I know you didn't just send those to yourself?"

"But why would I?" Frank was getting frustrated. Why couldn't she get it? Was she really that stupid?

"So that if you ever got caught, you could claim it was someone else."

His shoulders slumped. He had to admit she was right. All of it was circumstantial. All of it could be explained away. All of it—

The phone vibrated.

They both jumped. He pressed the button to view the message and smiled, turning the phone to her so she could read the newly arrived message.

TICK TOCK
LITTLE TIME ON THE CLOCK
MY CAMERA MAY HAVE BEEN FOUND
BUT I'LL BE SEEING YOU AROUND

Frank whispered, "Do you believe me now?"

Trace nodded and visibly relaxed, her hands releasing their grip on the chair, her shoulders easing back into the leather. "Yes."

"Thank God." His voice cracked and tears rolled down his face as he leaned forward and began to yank at the tape. Relief swept over him as the realization the terror of the past two days was over, and he could finally tell his colleagues, his friends, what had been happening to him, and to find out what, if anything, had happened to Sarah.

"I think you better get a knife."

He leaned back and looked at her, a little chagrined. "I didn't know how much to use, so I used it all."

She chuckled and he grabbed her in a hug, his head over her shoulder, his chest heaving. "Thank you for believing me."

"Don't worry about it, kid, but how about we do the hugging after I'm free and clear of this chair?"

He let go and stood up, wiping his eyes, his cheeks flushed with emotion and embarrassment. "I'm sorry, you just have no idea what I've been through." He stepped into the kitchen and grabbed a steak knife from a butcher's block and walked back toward her.

A loud pounding on the door startled them both. Frank turned pale as the pounding repeated, and his phone, sitting on the floor beside Trace, vibrated. He looked at Trace whose eyes were wider than just seconds ago. He reached for the door when she whispered loudly, "No! Cut me loose first!"

Frank turned and rushed over, kneeling down in front of her when the door burst open.

Shakespeare wasn't sure what he was looking at, but he didn't like it. Trace was tied to a chair, jaw dropped, a look of shock on her face. The kid was in front of her, no shirt on, looking panicked, and gripping a knife. Shakespeare raised his weapon and pointed it at Frank. "Drop it!"

Frank just stood there, shaking.

"I said drop it!"

Frank's head bobbed rapidly and he opened his hand, the knife dropping to the carpeted floor with a dull thud. Shakespeare flicked his gun, indicating Frank should move away from Trace. "Over there, keep your hands where I can see them." He looked at Trace who now had a smile on her face, one side more pronounced than the other, as if she were enjoying the situation. "Are you okay?"

She nodded. "Yeah, I'm fine," she said, slightly exasperated. "The kid was just about to cut me loose."

"Huh?"

"This isn't what it looks like." Shakespeare looked at Frank. *Yeah, right.* "Just let him cut me loose and I'll explain everything."

"You sure?"

She nodded. "Yes, let the kid cut me loose, I wouldn't want you to hurt anything."

"You're such a sweetheart." Shakespeare motioned for Frank to come over and stepped back a few paces so he could cover him.

"What are you doing here, anyway?" asked Trace as her left hand was freed. She immediately scratched her nose, sighing.

"When I never heard from you I called your phone and you didn't pick up. I called dispatch and they said you were still here, so I figured something must be wrong." He waved at the scene with his gun. "Never expected this."

"Yeah, well go check the bathroom if you want a real surprise." Both hands were now free and Frank was bent over between her legs, working on the tape binding her feet together. She leaned forward and tapped him on the shoulder. He looked up. "Howsabout I take care of the rest since you haven't even bought me dinner." He looked puzzled and Shakespeare grunted a laugh.

Kids.

He stepped into the bathroom and saw a body floating in the bathtub. "Holy shit!" He looked about for a photo, but found none. He stepped back into the living area and looked at Frank. "You better have a damned good explanation for this."

Trace stood up. "He does. And he was just about to start explaining everything, from the beginning." Frank nodded furiously. "My gun?" Frank pointed to the kitchen counter. Trace retrieved her weapon, holstering it, as Shakespeare retrieved the key building management had given him from the door lock.

"Okay, let's everybody take a seat, and work this thing out," he said, sitting in what looked to him to be the most comfortable chair there—the high-back office chair Trace had just been freed from. Trace gave him a look. "Hey, figured you wouldn't want to sit here again." She gave him another look as if she thought he might just be right, then sat on the couch lining the window, and sighed. Shakespeare had the distinct impression she was trying to make him second guess his choice.

Frank paced back and forth between them, before at last sitting down in the couch's matching chair. All three leaned forward in their little triangle, both Shakespeare and Trace pulling out their note pads. "Why don't you start at the beginning?"

Frank nodded and took a deep breath.

"Okay, it all started I guess Friday after work. I met Sarah in the elevators—"

"Sarah who?" interrupted Trace.

"Sarah Paxman. I think she works in HR."

"Pretty, chubby?"

Shakespeare was about to leap to the poor girl's defense when an angry Frank beat him to it.

"Hey! She's a really nice girl. Don't judge her because she has some weight issues."

Way to go, kid.

Trace threw up her hands, conceding his point. "Okay, okay, I'm sorry." Then she stared straight at him. "Is that who's in the tub?"

Frank paled. "God, I hope not!" He jumped up and rushed to the bathroom before either of them could stop him and returned a moment later, shaking his head. "No, this one's skinny like you," he said, jerking his chin at Trace who Shakespeare noted was about to smile at what clearly was not meant to be a compliment but caught herself. Her eyes darted at Shakespeare and he gave her a knowing smile.

Vanity, thy name is Trace? No, he didn't think that. She dressed well enough and appeared to take care of herself—light makeup, simple but neat hairstyle, a rockin' body as the kids might say, but she was one of the boys. Nothing girly about her. *She's only human. Everybody loves a compliment, even if they won't admit it.* He tried to remember the last time somebody had complimented his looks and gave up.

"So, you like this girl?"

Frank looked at Trace and shrugged his shoulders. "I guess. I don't really know. I've seen her around work here and there, you know. Talk to her in the elevator, whatever."

"So what was different about Friday?" asked Shakespeare.

"I asked her out for a coffee."

"Frank, the ladies' man, I never would have thought it." Shakespeare watched as Trace gave Frank the twice over, her eyes momentarily drawn to his abs.

"Frank, why don't you put a shirt on? It's like looking in a mirror here."

Frank missed the humor and left to get a shirt, while Trace watched him leave then turned to Shakespeare.

"Youth is wasted on the young."

He nodded. "You're telling me. That kid doesn't even know what he's got." He leaned forward. "Are you okay?"

"Yeah, my pride is wounded more than anything else. Taken down by a computer nerd." She jabbed a finger at him. "If you tell anyone about this at the squad, I'll punch you in the throat."

They both sat upright when Frank returned sporting a Steve Jobs style turtleneck. *These kids still worship that guy.*

"Okay, so where were we?" asked Trace as she looked at her notes. "Oh yeah, you asked her out for coffee. What happened then?"

"She said yes." He sounded surprised.

"Rare event for you, girls accepting your invitations?"

He shook his head. "No, me asking is what's rare."

Shakespeare felt a twinge of sympathy. He had always had an extra few on him, and it had always shaken his self-confidence. Rarely did he ask someone out, in fact, over the years he could count on one hand how many he'd asked, and unfortunately he needed even fewer fingers to count how many had said "yes". "So you're on the elevator, you ask her out, she says yes. What now?"

"We go to this coffee place I go to, La Barista, just a couple of blocks from here—"

"I know it." *Great cinnamon rolls.* Trace shot him a look as if she had read his thoughts.

"—and that's all I remember until the next day."

Trace looked up from her notes. "What do you mean?"

"I mean, we went in the shop, I have some fuzzy memories of sitting down with our coffees, talking, laughing—" He paused and blushed.

"Yeeeessss?" prompted Trace.

"Kissing."

Trace almost looked jealous.

"Then nothing. I woke up in that apartment downstairs yesterday morning. That's my first memory."

"You woke up where?"

"Downstairs."

Shakespeare and Trace both leaned back, looking at each other wide-eyed, each reevaluating the entire case. Trace spoke first.

"Sounds like you were dosed." Trace looked at Shakespeare. "How long does that stuff stay in your system?"

"Not sure. We might—"

"I took a sample."

"Huh?" Trace and Shakespeare echoed.

"I took a sample, you know, pissed in a cup, just in case."

Smart kid. "Where is it?"

"In my fridge at the lab."

"Remind me never to go into your fridge." Shakespeare racked his brain, trying to remember if he had ever taken anything out of the fridge over the years he had known Frank and drew a blank. *Thank God.*

"We'll test you again, just to be sure."

"Well, it wouldn't matter, because I got dosed again today."

"What?" Trace seemed to be echoing each of Shakespeare's outbursts.

"Yeah, I was just waking up when you arrived."

"Okay, we're getting ahead of ourselves here," said Shakespeare. "Back it up to yesterday; you woke up the next morning in the apartment downstairs. Then what?"

"I discovered the body in the bathroom and panicked."

"Meaning you did…" Trace's hand made a circle in the air, indicating he should move the truck that was his brain forward.

"Meaning just that. I panicked! I didn't know what to do! I knew that I'd go to prison because I was covered in blood, there was a dead body in the tub, and my name was written on the wall."

Shakespeare's eyebrows narrowed. "There was nothing written on the wall."

Frank looked at the floor. "I washed it off."

"You did what?" roared Shakespeare.

The kid turned pale, even Trace jumped. "I-I didn't know what to do, I just didn't want to go to prison, so I cleaned the entire apartment, top to bottom."

"Why didn't you take the photo?" asked Trace, giving Shakespeare the "take it easy" eye.

Frank looked up at her. "It wasn't there when I left!"

Trace and Shakespeare looked at each other. "Seems to corroborate your claim someone else is doing this." Shakespeare leaned back in the chair. "There's no way you'd leave the photo if you had done this, unless you're a psycho trying to lead us on a wild goose chase and just got caught sooner than you had expected." Shakespeare didn't believe that for a second, but he didn't want the kid getting too comfortable. If he thought there was still a chance they thought he was guilty, he'd volunteer much more information, trying to prove his innocence.

Frank frantically shook his head. "No, no, I'm not crazy! I thought I was, going crazy I mean, I just didn't know what was going on, and then I started to receive these text messages—"

"Text messages?"

"Yeah." He handed his phone to Shakespeare who scrolled through the messages, his eyebrows climbing his forehead with each one. "When did you get the first one?"

"In the apartment, the first two in fact. It was like I was being watched. And like he was trying to help me."

"He?"

Frank shrugged his shoulders. "I'm guessing it was a he, because whoever carried me here was definitely a guy."

"Huh?" Trace beat Shakespeare to it. "Carried you here? When?"

"Earlier today. I'll get to that." Frank seemed to be enjoying himself a bit, his voice stronger, his hand motions more controlled. "So I snuck out of the apartment, tossed some stuff down the garbage chute, ran up here—"

"So it was you I chased!"

Frank nodded. "Yeah, sorry about that."

Trace made a note. "That's fine, it's just one loose end tied up."

"I flushed the rest of the stuff down the toilet, and then got the call to come to the scene to pick up the photo."

"Which wasn't there when you left, which is why you fainted when you saw it."

Frank blushed, his eyes roaming the room. "Yeah, I couldn't believe it when I saw it."

"Is that why you grabbed it?" asked Shakespeare.

"No, I didn't do that on purpose, that was an accident, I swear!"

"Okay, so you wake up, scrub the place down, get some text messages, outrun Trace"—Trace shot him some daggers—"then get the call to come back to the crime scene, see the photo, pass out, wake up, leave with the photo, then what?"

"Well, that's when I found out it wasn't Sarah who was dead, which really freaked me out." He looked back and forth at both of them, his eyes pleading, filled with tears. "We need to find out what happened to Sarah!"

"Did you try calling her?"

Frank shook his head. "No, I was too scared to, I was afraid that if something had happened to her, then I'd be questioned as to why I called her."

"You must have known we'd see the two of you leaving together on the surveillance tape at the crime lab?"

Frank nodded. "Yeah, but like I said, I wasn't exactly thinking straight."

Shakespeare nodded. "Go on."

"Well, I did the analysis on the photo, unscrambled the woman who wasn't the victim apparently, then set it up for the guy in the photo. That's when Trace came in and scared the shit out of me."

Shakespeare turned to Trace. "Explain."

"He slipped up. When he fainted he went to get a glass of water and knew where the cups were."

Shakespeare snapped his fingers, nodding. "That's what it was. I knew something was bothering me about that entire scene." He looked at Trace. "Good catch!"

She grinned. "I didn't get a chance to follow up because of the witness showing up, but I had planned on it. I just didn't want to voice anything, just in case the kid turned out to be innocent. Especially with what just happened with Eldridge. One whiff and the kid's career is over."

Shakespeare turned back to Frank. "So Trace fills your drawers, now what?"

"Next morning I come in, do some more work on the photo, leave to get a coffee, then wake up here."

"Same coffee place?"

Frank nodded.

"You got your coffee, and don't remember anything else?"

"I have a vague memory of being on the elevator with somebody holding me up, and they said the words 'Tick tock'."

"Just like the text messages."

"Yeah."

Shakespeare looked at the messages again, finishing with the last one. He decided to wait before asking about it.

"Next."

"So I wake up, discover the body in the tub, and Trace arrives. I panicked and knocked her out."

"What did you hit me with?" asked Trace, rubbing the back of her head.

Frank pointed at the piece of broken statue on the floor. "With that."

Trace looked at her hand.

"Any blood?"

She shook her head. "No, just a nasty bump."

"You should get that checked out."

She waved her hand at him. "Nah, I'll live."

"Okay, so you take out a highly trained detective"—daggers—"with a single blow to the head"—more daggers—"and now what?"

"Well, I get a text message about her, about what I had just done, which makes me realize I'm being watched. So I search the apartment and I find this"—he got up and picked up something from the floor, handing it to him—"behind the grate in the kitchen." He pointed, indicating the grate, now hanging by a single screw.

"What is it?" asked Shakespeare, turning the device around in his hands.

"It's a wireless camera that streams its feed to the Internet."

"What does that mean?"

"It means that anybody, anywhere, who knows the right website, shall we say, can watch the feed."

Shakespeare eyed the lens. "Is it on?"

"No, I disconnected the transmitter."

Shakespeare put the camera on the table in front of him and leaned back in his chair. "And then you received this text message."

Trace pointed at the phone. "That's when I realized the kid was being set up."

"Yeah, I was cutting her loose when you arrived."

"Just *after* the nick of time, I might add."

Shakespeare let her have that one. "You just be thankful it was me who discovered you. If a couple of uni's had come in here, you two'd be in deep shit." He leaned back. "I guess that just leaves one thing." He looked at Frank then at Trace. "Do you want to press charges?"

Frank gasped.

"Absolutely," said Trace. "Nobody assaults a police officer and gets away with it. I don't care what the excuse is."

"But I was being framed! I thought you believed me!" Frank started to panic again and Shakespeare held up his hand, deciding he had had enough.

"Relax kid, we're joking." He shifted his eyes to Trace. "We *are* joking, right?"

She laughed and leaned over, slapping Frank on the knee. "Take it easy, kid, you need to learn to have a sense of humor about these things otherwise this job will eat you alive."

"Easy for you to say. You haven't had to lie to your friends, break every rule you've sworn to uphold, and been stalked by a killer for forty-eight hours."

Shakespeare suddenly regretted his joke. "Sorry, kid, I guess I wasn't thinking about what you've been through." He leaned in. "But it's over now."

Frank gave a weak smile. "Yeah, I guess so. Now what?"

Shakespeare stood up. "Well, that should be obvious, shouldn't it?"

"What?"

"We check out the other apartment for a camera." He pointed at Trace. "You stay here and call this scene in. And put an APB out on Sarah. We'll go check out the apartment." Shakespeare held open the door for the kid as he grabbed his small tool kit off the kitchen counter. A quiet elevator ride to the fourth floor and they were soon inside the apartment by way of the master key Shakespeare still had.

Frank pointed at the grate above the kitchen cupboards. "I'm guessing it's in the same place."

Shakespeare nodded and waved for him to proceed. Frank grabbed a chair, climbed up and quickly removed the screws holding the grate in place, letting it clang to the top of the cupboard. He reached in, pulling out a camera in triumph.

Frank's phone vibrated. Shakespeare, still holding it from earlier, raised it and pressed the button to view the message that had just arrived.

TICK TOCK
LITTLE TIME ON THE CLOCK
TO THE DETECTIVES ON THE CASE
I WELCOME YOU ALL TO THE RACE

Shakespeare frowned.
This isn't good.

SEVEN

Vinny glanced up from his customary walkthrough to see Shakespeare and the kid enter the apartment. He noticed Shakespeare had a hand on Frank's shoulder, apparently trying to comfort him. *I know I wouldn't want to see this coming home.* There were half a dozen techs working the scene along with several uniforms outside providing security. And Trace, sitting on a couch near the window. All she had said since he arrived were "body's in the bathroom" and "ignore the chair". He eyed the office chair with bits of duct tape still stuck to it. *Why the hell am I ignoring a key piece of evidence?*

Shakespeare walked toward the bedroom with Frank in tow, and motioned to Trace and Vinny to join him. Vinny was about to tell him he was busy when he decided against it. Something was going on here, and he wanted to know what. For example, why wasn't the kid in handcuffs? This was his apartment, so he'd be the most likely suspect. And he'd been acting a little strange lately, so he was at least a person of interest.

"Close the door."

Vinny closed the bedroom door and walked over to the dresser, half sitting on it. "Okay, is someone going to tell me what the hell is going on?"

Shakespeare looked around, frowned, and sat on the bed. Trace leaned against an armoire occupying one corner, and Frank merely sank down on his haunches, leaning against the wall, the lone window above his head.

"Okay, what we're about to tell you doesn't leave this room until I say so, got it?"

Vinny frowned at Shakespeare. "What is this, national security? Let's get serious; what the hell are you talking about?"

"Promise it." This time it was Trace asking. Her arms were crossed; there was no humor in her eyes. She was serious.

"Jesus," muttered Vinny. Then, raising his hands in defeat, "Okay, I swear, not a word."

The room seemed to let out a collective sigh, and Shakespeare began. "Our friend over here has gotten himself into some trouble."

"Don't tell me—"

"I'm not a murderer!" yelped Frank.

"Shhh!" admonished Trace. "Do you want everyone out there to hear you?"

Frank's head dropped between his knees.

"Here's the skinny. Friday night he meets Sarah Paxman from HR in the elevator. He asks her out for coffee and they go to his regular haunt, La Barista, two blocks from here. He wakes up the next day, remembering almost nothing, evidently dosed the night before."

Vinny let out a slow whistle. "Where's Sarah?"

Shakespeare ignored the question. "He woke up in the apartment downstairs, our crime scene from yesterday"—Vinny's eyes shot open—"with the body in the tub, no photo in sight. He then proceeded to scrub the scene clean—"

"You did what?"

"—then was about to leave when he received two text messages." Shakespeare handed a cellphone to Vinny. He read the first message, then the second, his eyes now even wider. He glanced at the kid, starting to understand why he wasn't handcuffed. "He then made it back to his apartment, flushed the evidence of his cleanup, and cleaned himself up when he was called to come and look at the photo."

"So that's why you missed the funeral."

Frank's head popped up from between his knees, his eyes red with tears. "I really wanted to go, I swear it, but—" He shrugged and splayed his hands.

"I understand, kid, don't worry about it."

Shakespeare continued. "He then went about doing what we asked him to do, analyzing the photo, and during this time, received additional text messages. Earlier today he went to the same coffee shop, and woke up here, with no memory of how he got here. He remembers a man's voice saying the same first line from the text messages, but nothing else.

That's when he found the body in the tub, and Trace arrived. He knocked her out"—Vinny shot a glance, mouthing 'are you okay?' to which she replied with a nod—"and taped her to the chair. He then received another text message suggesting whoever was behind this knew what he had just done"—Vinny scrolled through the messages finding the one in question—"and proceeded to search his apartment, finding a camera hidden in the duct work in the kitchen. He was then about to free Trace when I arrived. He gave us a full statement, and we then proceeded to check out the original crime scene, and found another camera. That's when we received the last text message."

Vinny read it and let out a slow breath. "Man, this is heavy. How're we going to handle this? The kid tampered with a crime scene, withheld evidence, attacked a cop, hell, he broke nearly every damned rule in the book."

"He was being framed. Would you have done any different?" asked Trace, pushing herself off the armoire with her hips.

Vinny shrugged. "I have no idea." It was an honest answer. He really did have no idea. He looked at Frank. *The poor kid must have been going crazy.* "Looks to me like we need to think about this logically."

"We're open to suggestions," said Shakespeare. "Shoot."

"First, where is Sarah?"

"APB out on her now."

Vinny nodded. "Second, there's no evidence of Frank being at the first crime scene. Does anybody need to know he was there?"

Shakespeare nodded. "I see where you're going with this. No, there's no need, since there's no evidence, however, if evidence is discovered placing him there, and he hasn't come clean, then he's up shit creek."

"Agreed." Vinny looked at Frank. "That camera you found, do you think you'll be able to trace where the signal was going?"

Frank nodded. "Sure, I just need to get it and my equipment together, and I'll be able to pull the IP address—"

Vinny help up his hand. "No details needed, the 'Yes' is good enough for me."

"So we're agreed he has to come clean on everything about the first crime scene?" asked Shakespeare.

Everyone in the room nodded, including Frank who pushed himself up the wall and now stood in front of the window.

"Okay, so then now the only question that remains is the second crime scene. Nothing to really hide here, except what he did to Trace."

"I don't see why anyone needs to know about that," said Trace.

"Agreed. Is there any way to hide that the chair exists? Not to mention the knife on the floor and the wads of duct tape?" asked Shakespeare.

"Most of that isn't a problem," said Trace, patting her jacket. "I've got the knife in here, and pulled all the duct tape I could off the chair. "Unless someone else thinks to check the chair, we should be okay."

Vinny shook his head. "The residue from the tape's already been noticed by me so someone else most likely noticed it as well."

"Yeah, but with no other evidence surrounding the chair, it could be explained away somehow." Trace paused, tapping her chin. "But how?"

Shakespeare snapped his fingers. "We don't know what happened to Frank while he was out. He could have been taped to the chair by the killer, then freed, and the killer cleaned up the evidence. We have no way of knowing. Let's just leave it as an unexplained."

"That works," said Vinny as Trace nodded her consent.

"Guys, you're forgetting one thing."

The room turned to Frank.

"What's that?" asked Shakespeare.

"The camera. Anything I did was caught by that camera. If that video gets out, then we're all in deep shit and I don't want anyone getting in trouble for what I did."

"Dammit, forgot about that!" muttered Shakespeare. He took a deep breath. "Okay, so basically, what we're saying here, is that he has to come clean about everything, including Trace."

"Yes, but I won't be pressing charges, so hopefully he won't get in trouble for that, we should be able to keep that fairly quiet. And if we can convince the LT and the DA that he's been manipulated by the killer through those text messages, he might be okay."

"It's a stretch, but I don't see that we have any other choice," said Vinny.

"Agreed." Shakespeare struggled up from the bed. Vinny was about to extend him a hand when Shakespeare at last stood up. "Okay, kid, whaddaya think? How about you and me go down to the Bureau and talk to the LT, get this all out in the open?"

Frank nodded. Vinny's heart went out to the kid. He was clearly trembling. He walked over and gave the kid's shoulder a squeeze. "Don't worry, Frank, we'll get you through this. Everyone knows you're a good guy, and there's no way any jury would convict you of anything, so now let's just save your career."

Frank took a deep breath and looked at Vinny with a weak smile, nodding. "Yeah, thanks, I guess you're right." He looked at Trace and Shakespeare. "You're all right. I've got to come completely clean, and see where the chips fall."

The cellphone vibrated in Vinny's hand. The whole room turned, staring at the phone. Vinny pressed the button and read aloud the text:

TICK TOCK
LITTLE TIME ON THE CLOCK
IF YOU TURN YOUR FRIEND IN
SARAH DIE'S FOR HER SINS

Vinny looked up at the room. "It looks like your friend just solved our problem."

Shakespeare nodded. "Agreed. Now we can't tell anyone."

"LT, got a few minutes?"

Phillips looked up from his laptop and nodded, his eyes shooting up a little when he saw Frank follow Shakespeare into the office. Shakespeare closed the door and drew the shades, blocking anyone outside from seeing their conversation. "Okay, what have you got yourself into this time?" He pointed at Frank. "And how did you involve him in it?"

Shakespeare pointed at one of the two chairs in front of the LT's desk and Frank sat in it, saying nothing. Shakespeare sat in the other chair and looked around to make sure they were alone. "We've got a problem."

"Obviously."

"No, I'm serious. We've got a big problem."

"Okay, what is it?"

Shakespeare shifted in his seat, suddenly uncomfortable. "I can't tell you."

"What the hell do you mean, you can't tell me?"

Shakespeare sighed. *I knew this was a bad idea.* They had agreed they couldn't turn Frank in, but there was no hiding that a body had been found in his apartment. He needed to convince the LT to let Frank continue to work on the case, otherwise the other techs might trace the Internet video first, and Frank, and the rest of them, would be in it up to their eyeballs.

"Do you trust me?" He cringed inside as he asked the question.

Phillips leaned back, steepling his fingers in front of him, elbows resting on the arms of his chair. His head tilted to the right, his eyebrows scrunched inward. "What's going on?"

"Do you trust me?" repeated Shakespeare. "You've known me for over twenty years, worked with me most of that time, and been my boss for the past five years. Do you trust me?"

Phillips sighed. "Shakes, do I trust you? Ask me that five years ago, and I'd have answered 'yes' in a heartbeat. But you haven't exactly been a spectacular example of the hard working detective for the past few years."

Shakespeare felt his chest tighten. It hurt hearing that from a man he considered his friend. But he was right. And now this poor kid sitting next to him might be screwed because of him. He was about to open his mouth when Phillips raised one finger to stop him.

"But, no matter how much of a slacker you've been the past few years, I've always trusted you to do the right thing, and that hasn't changed."

Shakespeare could have sworn he heard Frank expel a lungful of air. Shakespeare smiled at Phillips. "Not exactly a ringing endorsement, but I'll take it." He leaned forward. "You know we found a body in Frank's apartment today."

Phillips nodded.

"Well, there's more to this story, much more, but I can't tell you anything yet. When I can, you'll understand why. The key here is I need you to let Frank continue to work on this case."

"Out of the question. He's involved!"

Shakespeare nodded. "I know, I know. It goes against protocol. But we need him to be the tech on this. Again, you'll understand why when we solve this thing. For now, believe me when I say, lives depend on it."

Phillips frowned, his fingers now interlaced, his thumbs beating against each other as he processed what he was being told. He looked at the kid sitting quietly then back at Shakespeare. "If this blows up, how much shit am I in?"

"Ankles. As for us, necks. But I can live with that. There's too much at stake here not to continue forward."

Phillips frowned even more. "How are you going to keep this from Trace and Vinny? Weren't they there?"

"They know what's going on, and are in complete agreement with what I'm doing."

"So essentially what you're telling me is that I'm the only goddamned person in my squad who has no clue what's going on."

Shakespeare chuckled. "As it should be?"

Phillips shook his head. "Get out. Just try to keep it below my knees."

"Thanks, boss," said Shakespeare as he rose, motioning to the kid to follow.

"Thanks," whispered Frank.

Phillips said nothing, staring only at his computer screen as Shakespeare spun the rod, opening the blinds.

Trace looked up from her desk when the LT's office door open. When Shakes and the kid came out, she stood up and walked out the door of the squad to the elevators. All three boarded an elevator, along with several others, and rode in silence. Out of the building, they all piled into Shakespeare's Caddy, her in the back, Frank in the passenger seat.

"What happened?" she asked, dying in anticipation.

"It worked," said Shakespeare. "He's agreed to let Frank stay on the case. He knows something's going on, but he's agreed to let me run with it for now."

"Thank God." She thought Shakespeare crazy for suggesting he go to the LT, especially after they had all just agreed to saying nothing to no one, but when he pointed out they needed Frank working the tech end, and protocol would dictate he be taken off the case, they all realized they had no choice. They needed to bring the LT in, albeit only slightly. How had Shakes put it? "We only need him to dip a toe into the pool of shit we're swimming in." *The man has a way with words.* "Now what?"

Shakespeare looked at Frank. "I'll drop you off at your lab. You confirm the photo is Richard Tate and then turn off that damned screen, or whatever it is so it's not there for the world to see, then try and track down where those cameras were sending their signals."

Frank nodded. "Will do."

Shakespeare turned to Trace. "You and I are going to the coffee shop. That's clearly the center of this thing. Take your car, because after that I want to go to the hospital and interview Tate, and I want you to go to NYU to follow up on our first vic, Angela Henwood."

"What should I do while I'm waiting for you?"

Shakespeare smiled. "Have a coffee." Frank climbed out of the car to let Trace out, and as she stepped onto the pavement, Shakespeare added, "And try not to get dosed."

"You're all heart, Shakes; don't let anyone tell you different."

The door slammed shut and she heard Shakespeare laugh as he started the car. She watched the car pull away, Frank giving a shy wave. She gave him a million dollar smile to make him feel good, and noticed his spread a little further across his face. *You've still got it.*

If someone had told her a few weeks ago she'd start to like Shakespeare she'd have told them to call their village, because she had found their missing idiot, but she had to admit, working this case with him was unlike anything she had expected. First off, he was actually working. That was almost unheard of, with Eldridge having carried him for most of the past three years, and the LT having protected him out of some sense of loyalty and homage to a phenomenal career prior to "the fuck up" as it was referred to in whispers around the precinct. *I wonder what really happened.* Whatever it was wasn't anywhere near the rumor mill version, she was sure. There's no way a cop with that kind of experience leaves critical evidence in a murder investigation, a gun no less, on the front seat of his car just because he's hungry. She knew enough about Shakespeare's previous reputation, and just in the way he was handling himself on this case, to know he would have at least locked it in his trunk. She could believe him stopping to eat, there was no doubt about that, but not the part about the evidence.

But if it wasn't true, why didn't he come clean about it? *There's no effin' way I'd let anybody say the shit that's been said about him, about me. Not if I were innocent.* She unlocked her Mustang and climbed in, pressing the button on the dash to start it. She gave the gas a gentle push, the roar from the tailpipes sending vibrations through her body, leaving a tingling sensation in her core. She sighed. *I love this car.* She put it in gear, and soon found herself searching for a spot near the coffee shop in question, her *Guilty Pleasures* playlist on her iPod having pumped up her adrenaline to the point where a coffee wasn't needed except to keep the high going.

Minutes later she walked into the shop, her trained eye taking everything in. There were a couple of dozen seats of varying types, from straight back to couches, mostly lining the windows surrounding small, circular tables. About half were filled with patrons either chatting with each other, or solos reading papers or their Kindles. There was one staff member making the rounds, cleaning tables, straightening chairs, tidying up. She seemed to avoid tables with patrons at them, and Trace put her near the bottom of the dosing 'possibles' list. Behind the counter were half a dozen workers, two working the cash, alternating with each order, two in the back making sandwiches from what she could see, and two baristas who were making the specialty coffees. If this were the typical setup, there were no less than four, and possibly five stations, that could dose a coffee.

She texted Frank. *What type of coffee do you order?*

A moment later he replied. *Large skim milk latte with an extra shot of espresso every time.*

"Next!"

She stepped up to the cash. "One large skim milk latte with an extra shot of espresso, please."

She choked at the price that popped up on the screen and handed over a few more bills than she had expected, normally a straight black coffee drinker herself. He handed her a ticket, and she moved down the line. One of the baristas looked at her computer and went to work, making her artsy coffee. Trace noted the two baristas chatting, handing each other things, and passing within inches of each other's coffees. As well, the other two at the cash were within feet of them. She quickly realized any of them could dose a coffee without the other knowing. The girl who was clearing tables entered the coffee prep area and began wiping things down with a damp rag. *Make that five.*

A petite girl handed her the coffee with a smile, and she went to one of the more comfortable chairs in the corner and sat down with a full view of the shop, as well as the coffee prep area. She took a sip. *Woah, sweeeet!* She took another sip. *But tasty.* She could picture herself developing a taste for these, and a waistline to match. She put the coffee down, and pretended to do some texting.

Shakespeare took one look at the photo and was convinced. It had to be Richard Tate. He looked at Frank. "Well?"

"Well what?"

"Is it him?"

"Who, Richard Tate?" He shrugged his shoulders. "Looks like him to me, but it's not a great angle."

"Isn't there anything you can do to get an ID?"

"Nothing positive, there's not enough to work from."

"Can't you do like in the movies, flip the face, map one side to the other, and do facial recognition."

Frank chuckled. "You've seen too many movies. I can do the 'flip' as you call it and give you a face, but it's useless for facial recognition, because the points on the other side of the face are just guess work."

Shakespeare growled in frustration, about to push himself from the chair he had commandeered.

"But—"

"But what?" Shakespeare felt a touch of hope creep back into the room.

"—I can tell you if it's definitely not him."

"How?"

"Well, I do have a few points to work from, and can map them against a known photo of him, and if they don't match, then we know it isn't him. If they do match, then we know it *could* be him."

I'll take what I can get. "Okay, do that. How long?"

"Not long, I'll phone you with the results."

Shakespeare pushed himself up and stretched. "Okay, can you send me that photo to my phone?" As he tucked his shirt back into his pants, Frank hit a few keys and Shakespeare's phone vibrated.

"Done."

Technology. Gotta love it.

"Thanks. I'm heading over to the coffee shop. Let me know what you find."

"Will do."

"And make sure nobody sees that damned photo."

"Will do."

"And if you get any more of those texts, you let me know right away."

"Will do."

"And stay put. I don't want you getting dosed again."

"Will do."

"Vinny should be back soon to check on you, so if you need to go anywhere, do it with him."

"Will do."

He felt like a mother hen. *Was the kid even listening?*

"And when Trace comes by, try to have a shirt on, you're distracting her."

"Will d—" Frank blushed. "Are-are you serious?"

I guess he was listening.

He left his last statement hanging as he walked from the lab, a grin on his face.

MJ flipped the girl over in the tub, revealing her badly beaten face. He pulled out his phone and took a photo, then swept his finger over the display, finding the photo Frank had decrypted earlier. "Definitely looks like a match," he said to no one in particular.

"To who?"

MJ looked over his shoulder and saw Vinny in the doorway. He handed him his phone. "Look, that's the girl from the picture; the next one is our vic here."

Vinny's eyebrows furled as he flipped back and forth between the two. "Looks like it could be the same girl." Vinny suddenly brought the phone closer. "Look at this." He handed the phone back to MJ. "Is that a tattoo on the back of her neck?"

MJ took the phone, then shoved it in his pocket. He rolled the body back and moved her hair from her neck. "Butterfly."

"Same as the photo."

MJ gently let go of the body. "Looks like it's the same girl."

Vinny leaned over to take another look. "This obviously ties the two crime scenes together, not that there was any doubt of that."

"Nope. I'll know more when I get her back, but I'd say she was probably killed last night, between six p.m. and midnight."

"Cause?"

"Not sure. Our other vic had her throat slit, ear to ear, just like this one, but I also found traces of Rohypnol in her system. I'm suspecting whoever did this dosed his victim, then killed them later."

"Any evidence of sexual interference?"

"Nothing obvious. I'll know more later." MJ rose to his feet and stretched out his aching back. "At least this one isn't covered in bleach. There might actually be a chance at retrieving some DNA." He noticed Vinny divert his eyes at his last statement, looking at the toilet, the sink, anywhere but him. "Something I should know about?"

Vinny shook his head. "Nope, why?"

MJ looked at him thoughtfully for a moment. "Never mind." *But I know when I'm being lied to.* He pulled off the latex gloves he was wearing, packed up his kit, and followed Vinny from the tiny bathroom. He looked at his body baggers and nodded. "I'm done in there. Bag her and tag her, then bring her straight to the autopsy room, she's my new number one."

Both men nodded and disappeared into the bathroom. "And make sure you don't drain the tub," yelled Vinny after them. "We need to strain that in case there's any trace."

"No problem!" he heard a voice call from inside.

MJ looked at Vinny. "They do know their job."

Vinny nodded. "Yeah, but it wouldn't be the first time somebody forgot, would it?"

MJ couldn't argue with him, he was right. He just didn't like to see his people treated like rookies. But then, how many times had he said the obvious to Vinny over the years about his investigators? "Okay, I'll head back to the cooler and I'll let you and Shakes know when I find something." He looked at the office chair he had noticed when he arrived, looking rather out of place near the couch and matching chair. He pointed at it. "What's up with the chair?"

Vinny's head darted a little too quickly in the direction he was pointing. "Oh, nothing, must have got moved there by one of my guys."

MJ now knew he was being lied to for sure. There was no way one of Vinny's techs would have moved that chair, and for Vinny to suggest it, rather than yell at his people about moving something without first labeling and photographing its original position, confirmed something was wrong.

But what the hell could it be?

Shakespeare's phone vibrated as he pulled into a parking spot a block away from the coffee shop. He flipped it open without checking the call display. "Shakespeare."

"Hi, Detective, it's Vinny."

Shakespeare paused for a moment, trying to remember the last time he had received a call from him, and couldn't.

"What's up?"

"First, it looks like the vic at Frank's place is the girl from the photo."

"Okay, I guess that's not much of a surprise."

"And I think we may have a problem."

He didn't like the sound of that, their little secret only in play for a couple of hours. *How can there be a problem already?* "What?"

"I think MJ knows something's up. He asked me if something was wrong, kind of looked at me funny, you know, as if he suspected something."

Shakespeare felt relieved. "Is that it?"

"And he pointed out that the chair was over in the living room area, sort of out of place."

Shakespeare's heart skipped a beat. "Shit! Forgot about that." He thought for a moment. "I wonder if we should bring him in on this."

There was a pause, then a deep breath. "I don't think we should. After all, he knows nothing, the body shouldn't show anything involving Frank, and who's he going to go to? Most likely the LT, and he'll keep him straight for now. I say we keep this as tight a circle as we can."

Shakespeare nodded. "Agreed. I'll drop by and see him later, just to see what kind of vibe I get off him."

"Okay, talk to you later."

Shakespeare ended the call and stuffed the phone back in his pocket as he climbed from the Caddy. A quick huff to the shop left him slightly winded. He stepped inside, gulping air for a few seconds, and nodded to Trace who stood up and quickly joined him.

"Hey, Shakes," she said as she stepped up beside him, then gave him a look. "You okay?"

He took another deep breath, nodding. "Just payin' for years of neglect."

"You need some cardio."

That's what he liked about Trace. She was no nonsense, just said it like it was, without the insults. "You're tellin' me. I'm afraid my old heart might explode just at the sight of a treadmill."

Trace chuckled. "Well, if you don't do something, it'll explode anyway."

He looked away so she couldn't see the pained expression on his face at the thought of a heart attack he knew was probably just around the corner. "What've we got?"

"Looks like seven employees, five with dosing access. Two in the kitchen making sandwiches are probably in the clear, the rest would have access. We find out who was working behind the counter, and who was bussing these tables when Frank was in here those two times, we'll have our guy, or at least a very short list."

Shakespeare flashed his badge at the oldest looking person he could find behind the register, the rest all looking like they were barely out of high school. At least this one looked like he may be in his mid-twenties. "Detective Shakespeare, Homicide. Who's in charge around here?"

"That would be me, I'm the evening manager."

"Can we ask you a few questions?"

He nodded and tapped the other cashier prepping a coffee on the shoulder. "Take over, I'll be a few." The man walked out from behind the counter. "What's the problem? Did you say 'homicide'?"

Shakespeare nodded and Trace responded, her voice slightly elevated. "Yes, we've had two murders recently and this coffee shop seems to be involved."

A few of the patrons stopped their conversations and looked. The young man blanched, and ushered them into the back where they found a tiny office. He sat behind the desk, leaving Shakespeare to take the one lone chair for guests.

"Chivalry is indeed dead," said Trace, looking at him.

"Hey, respect your elders." Shakespeare turned his attention to the evening manager. "Your name?"

"Calvin Tickle."

"Okay, Calvin, here's the skinny. We think one of your staff is dosing coffees here."

"Dosing? You mean, putting something in their drinks?"

"Yes, something like Rohypnol," said Trace, her notepad out.

"You mean the date rape drug?"

"Yes."

"Who?"

"That's what you're going to tell us," replied Trace.

Shakespeare was content to let her be the bad cop.

"How?"

"By providing us with a list of everyone who was working here from three p.m. Friday until midnight, including when they started."

"Do you have timecards here?" asked Shakespeare.

Tickle nodded. "Yeah, it's all computerized." He started hitting keys on the computer and a report soon spit out of a printer behind him. "Here's the ins and outs from Friday."

"And we'll need today as well."

"Today?" Tickle hit some more keys. "You mean this happened today as well?"

Trace and Shakespeare kept silent as they looked down the list, none of the names jumping out at Shakespeare, but he hadn't expected any to. Another sheet spit out of the printer and Tickle handed it to Trace. "Christ, there's half a dozen matches on both lists." Trace put X's beside the names unique to one list, eliminating them from their pool.

"These lists are accurate?" asked Shakespeare.

"Oh yeah, otherwise they don't get paid."

"And what if they were to leave during their shift, and come back?"

"Well, we would trust that they punch out and back in, but to be honest, no one ever does." Tickle leaned back in his chair, scratching his goatee. "Let's face it, this is minimum wage work. Someone abuses the system, their co-workers complain to me or one of the other managers, we fire them, and get another. In fact, I fired somebody just today."

Shakespeare looked up from the two lists he was examining.

"Who?"

"Sandy Thorton."

"Why?"

"I found out he took off during his shift for over an hour. When I got in today, one of the staff from his shift had stuck around after he left and complained to me. I left a message on his voice mail firing him. It wasn't the first time he'd done something like that, and he hadn't even been here two weeks."

Shakespeare looked at the lists and confirmed Sandy Thorton was on both. "What time did he disappear today?"

"Roughly ten to eleven."

Bingo! Shakespeare gave Trace a quick look and could tell she was as excited as him.

"We'll need personnel records for the employees on these lists. Names, address, phone numbers."

Tickle hit some more keys, and within minutes employee tombstone information was spitting out of the printer. He handed them to Trace as Shakespeare pushed himself from the chair.

"Thanks for your help," said Shakespeare as they were leaving.

"And don't leave town," added Trace.

"Why?"

"Because you're on both these lists as well."

Tickle looked aghast at the idea, his jaw dropped so far you could park a fist in his mouth without hitting teeth. "But—"

Shakespeare chuckled at Trace's bad cop routine. "It's just routine. Everybody's a suspect until we eliminate them." He paused and raised a finger in warning. "But listen to me carefully. If I find out you called this Sandy character and warned him, I'll have you up on charges so fast, you'll forget what good coffee tastes like by the time you're out of Rikers."

Tickle was too terrified to say anything, he simply nodded and sat in one of the leather chairs in the front as Trace and Shakespeare left. Outside, Shakespeare looked at the personnel sheet for Sandy Thorton. Trace was smiling.

"Looks like we've got our man."

Shakespeare grunted. It just didn't feel right. His phone vibrated in his pocket. He fished it out and flipped it open. "Shakespeare."

"Hi, Detective, it's Frank. I've finished analyzing the photo. The few facial recognition points I could pull are a match for Richard Tate. It's not a positive ID, but I haven't been able to rule him out scientifically, and just looking at the photo, flipped and mirrored like you asked, it sure looks like him to me. I'm sending it to your phone right now."

"Okay, good work kid, any luck on tracing those cameras?"

"Just starting on them now. I figured you wanted this photo analysis done first."

"Okay, get to work and let me know as soon as you find something."

Shakespeare ended the call just as the phone vibrated with a message. He opened the photo attached and grimaced. *Definitely looks like him to me.* "What do you think?" He held the photo up for Trace to look at.

"Richard Tate? Definitely. There's no mistaking that guy."

"Okay, I'm going to go to the hospital to interview Tate. You phone this in, then sit on Thorton's place until the warrant arrives. I don't want him making any sudden departures."

Trace got on the phone and Shakespeare headed for his car, the feeling in his stomach he usually got when he was about to bust a case wide open not there. But the timing fit. Sandy had worked Friday night and today. He was there both times Frank was, and more importantly, he had left during the exact same time frame Frank was drugged. He felt a slight tingle. *Okay, maybe it is the guy.*

Or he could just be hungry.

"What the hell does it mean, Richard?"

Aynslee stood just out of sight, but not earshot, of the rip roaring argument that had ensued when a large bouquet of flowers had arrived moments before. After Justin's visit earlier, she had asked Merle for the Tate story, knowing it would eventually become a bigger one. She had argued that he and his wife knew her from the entertainment beat coverage she had been doing only weeks before, with them quite often being the story. They might open up to a familiar face. Merle had agreed, and she was here with her camera crew, Mike and Steve.

"What the hell was in that note?" asked Steve.

"Must be from a girlfriend," said Mike.

"Shhh!" She leaned in, trying to hear what was now being said, the door still open from when the flower deliveryman had left moments before, the twenty she had slipped him to leave it open money well spent.

"Tick tock, little time on the clock, have you told your dear wife, about your second life?" The glass vase the flowers had arrived in shattered on the floor. "What second life, Richard? What the hell does it mean?"

Aynslee couldn't hear Tate's response, his voice apparently too weak.

"Anything interesting?"

Aynslee jumped at the voice right next to her ear. She spun around as if caught with her hand in the cookie jar, and smiled, seeing

Shakespeare standing there, a slight look of what might be disapproval on his face. And she knew why.

"Detective, three times in one weekend?" She gave him a quick hug and pointed to Mike and Steve. "Not sure if you've met my crew, Mike Parker and Steve Davis." Shakespeare shook their hands and turned back to her.

"What are you doing here?"

She raised her hands. "Don't worry, it's not what you think. I'm here on the heart attack story, not the other thing," she said in a whisper. "I've been keeping my ears open and nothing has come in on that yet. But—" She stopped and looked around.

"What?"

"There's something going on in there. Some flowers were just delivered, and the wife flipped out. I think there was something written on the card, some poem."

Shakespeare's eyebrows shot up. "Poem?"

"Yeah, it was kind of weird. Something about a clock, then asking if he'd told his wife about his second life." This clearly excited Shakespeare. He stood up straight, his cheeks slightly flushed, his eyes bright with energy. It was a good look for him. A look she couldn't remember having ever seen. "What, does it mean something?"

He looked down at her. "It could mean everything." With that he stepped into the room, and closed the door, smiling slightly she was sure at her look of dismay.

"Who the hell are you?"

Shakespeare held up his badge to the clearly irate Mrs. Tate, her fake tanned cheeks flushed, her eyes red from crying. "Detective Shakespeare, Homicide." He looked at Richard Tate, lying in the bed, his face pale but cheeks slightly flushed, perhaps from the tongue lashing his wife had given him.

"H-homicide?" Tate looked nervous. Too nervous. "What do you want?"

"I need to ask you a few questions, in private."

"Like hell you are, anything you want to ask him you can ask in front of me!"

"Don't I have the right to have my lawyer present?"

Normally Shakespeare's guilt-dar would have gone off, but when dealing with the rich, you usually expected an emergency lawyer to step out of the closet within moments of arriving. "You're not under arrest, sir, I just have a few questions for you."

He slumped into his pillows. "Okay, go ahead."

"What did you say your name was again?" asked Mrs. Tate. "Shakespeare? What the hell kind of name is that?"

Shakespeare shrugged his shoulders. "My dad's?"

She went several shades of red darker. "Don't get smart with me, boyo!" She snapped her fingers. "Do you have a card? I'm going to talk to your supervisor."

Shakespeare pulled a card from his wallet and handed it to her. "Feel free. He always enjoys hearing from concerned citizens." He turned back to Richard Tate. "Are you sure?"

Tate glanced at his wife who glared back. "Of course."

There's no way he knows about the photo. Shakespeare took out his cellphone and flipped to the unscrambled photo, holding it out for Tate to look at. "Can you confirm this is you?"

Tate went as white as his sheets, his eyes darting to his wife who stepped over and grabbed Shakespeare's wrist, twisting the phone so she could see it. "Woah ho, I'll see you in divorce court." She shoved Shakespeare's wrist away from her and stormed from the room, the tension level, at least for Shakespeare, easing quite remarkably. He looked at his witness. *I guess I'm alone.*

"You just cost me half a billion dollars."

Right, like I'm the one who was slipping it to another woman.

"So you confirm this is you in the photo?"

The man nodded, defeated. "Yes."

"And who is the woman?"

"Samantha Alders."

We have a name! Shakespeare decided to play a game. "And where can we find her?"

The man looked nervous, his head turning slightly away, his eyes wandering the room then settling on the heart monitor which was now beeping slightly faster.

"I d-don't know," he whispered, his voice cracking.

Okay, that's a little different than I was expecting. "Would you be surprised to hear that we found her body today?"

"Oh, God no!" Tate's head swung toward Shakespeare and he pushed himself up onto his elbows. "You've got to believe me. I didn't kill her! I don't remember a thing! I just woke up and there was blood everywhere, and her body was in the tub. I left her there, then when I came back, she was gone; there was no blood, there was nothing. Nothing except—" He stopped, looking about the room. His eyes settled on a chair in the corner. "There, get me my jacket."

Shakespeare walked over and picked up the suit jacket lying over the back of the chair. "Just tell me where?"

"Inside pocket."

Shakespeare carefully reached in, not expecting anything sharp with this type of witness—suspect—but still wary nonetheless. He felt a piece of paper and pulled it out. It was a crumpled envelope, the Waldorf Astoria seal emblazoned on the back, the seal torn open. He reached inside and fished out the lone piece of paper, opened it, and read the four lines, his heart racing.

TICK TOCK
LITTLE TIME ON THE CLOCK
WHEN THEY FIND WHAT I HID
THEY WILL KNOW WHAT YOU DID

Shakespeare pulled an evidence bag from his inside pocket and placed the envelope and paper inside, sealing it. "The Waldorf, is that where it happened?"

Tate nodded.

"Give me the full story."

"I left the office Saturday, went straight to the Waldorf, about six p.m., went up to the room, and Samantha arrived shortly after, maybe ten minutes later. We, you know, made love, then she poured us drinks, then the next thing I know it's the next morning, I'm lying naked in bed, blood all over me and the sheets, and she's floating in the tub, dead."

"Then?"

"Then I got the hell out of there, went home, got in a fight with my wife in the driveway, left without even leaving my car, and decided I had to go back to the hotel."

"To do what?"

"I don't know! I wasn't really thinking straight. I guess part of me was thinking I needed to get rid of any evidence I was there, but that would be impossible since the room was in my company's name, and part of me thought she might still be alive and need help. I don't know what I was thinking, I was panicking."

"So you went back, then what?"

"Nothing. It was completely cleaned up. The body was gone, there was no blood anywhere, the bed was made, just as if housekeeping had come through."

"And how long had you been gone?"

"About four hours I guess. I drove out to The Hamptons and back, so however long that takes."

"Sounds about right. And the note?"

"It was sitting on my overnight bag. I had forgotten it when I left, and found it in a closet. I opened the note, then had this damned panic attack or whatever they're calling it."

"Not a heart attack?"

"No, panic, anxiety, whatever. Pretty clear what caused it though."

Shakespeare grunted in agreement, furiously scribbling notes.

"Have you ever been to a coffee shop called La Barista?"

Tate shook his head. "No, never heard of it."

"Does the name Sandy Thorton ring a bell?"

Tate shook his head. "Should it?"

"What can you tell me about Samantha? Where did you meet her?"

Tate looked away, his cheeks flushing. "I met her on a sugar daddy website. I needed a release, my wife and I haven't been getting along for years now, and rather than divorce her, I decided to take action, and solve my problem."

"With a hooker."

"Not a hooker!" Tate clearly was upset at the suggestion, his glare aimed directly at Shakespeare. "She's a college student, trying to pay off her student loans."

"How does this sugar daddy arrangement work?"

"Basically you meet, if you hit it off, you work out a, shall we say, arrangement. Give them an allowance, and they come by whenever you want them to."

"And how much were you paying her?"

"About two grand a week."

Shakespeare whistled. "I'm in the wrong business."

"You'd be lucky to get fifty bucks."

Shakespeare chuckled. "And what college was she going to?"

"NYU."

Bingo! Yet another link to NYU. *Maybe the coffee shop is a red herring?* "Have you received any text messages, or any other type of message, that seemed odd?"

Tate pointed at the flowers scattered across the floor. "Yeah, those fucking things came with a marriage ending message."

Shakespeare looked around and saw a small card sitting on a nearby table and picked it up with a latex glove he pulled from his pocket. Handwritten, most likely by the florist, he read the text:

TICK TOCK
LITTLE TIME ON THE CLOCK
HAVE YOU TOLD YOUR DEAR WIFE
ABOUT YOUR SECOND LIFE?

"I see what you mean," said Shakespeare. He dropped the card into a second evidence bag. "Any chance your wife knew what was going on?"

"What, you mean she might have killed Samantha?" Tate thought for a brief moment. "I wouldn't put it past that cold hearted bitch. She'd kill anything that got between me and my money."

"Is that the brain or the heart talking?"

Tate sighed, waving his hand like an eraser. "Forget I said that, I may hate the bitch but she's no killer. Did she know I was cheating on her? She accused me of it enough when I wasn't, so no, I don't think she knew. She'll claim she always suspected if you ask her, but like I said, she's been accusing me of it for years, and I only met Samantha a year ago."

"Could Samantha have told anybody about you?"

Tate shook his head. "That was part of the arrangement. She'd be cut off if she told anyone."

"Therapist, boyfriend, mother?"

"No, like I said, a peep and it's over."

"Do you have an address for her?"

"Yeah, it's on my phone." He pointed to the jacket. "Other inside pocket."

Shakespeare fished it out and handed it to Tate who turned it on and entered a code to unlock it. He hit some buttons and handed the phone to Shakespeare. "Here you go."

Shakespeare wrote Samantha's contact info in his pad and as he started to hand the phone back to Tate, it vibrated with a new text message. By instinct he hit the prompt to view it.

TICK TOCK
LITTLE TIME ON THE CLOCK
WHEN TWO STAR CROSSED LOVERS MEET
IT WILL SIGNAL THEIR DEFEAT

He showed the message to Tate, but didn't let him touch the phone, it now evidence. Tate paled.

"What does it mean?"

"I have no clue."

"Clearly the flowers and this message are linked."

Tate nodded.

"And you have no idea who's sending these."

He shook his head. "No clue."

"Any idea who the 'star crossed lovers' are?"

"How should I know?"

"This was sent to you, so it's supposed to mean something to you. Samantha's dead. Are you seeing any other women on the side?"

Tate emphatically shook his head. "Absolutely not."

"And it says 'their defeat'. Who are they?"

"How the hell should I know! I have no clue what the hell is going on here. I'm the victim, remember?"

"Your wife might beg to differ." Shakespeare flipped his notebook closed and placed it in his pocket. He held up the phone. "I'll be keeping this, to see if we can trace that text message."

Tate waved his hand. "Fine, can I at least cancel the account? I get a lot of confidential phone calls to that line."

"I can't stop you, but I'd prefer you didn't, just in case they try to contact you again."

Tate nodded. "Any idea when I can get out of here?"

"I'm not a doctor, but you're free to go as far as the NYPD is concerned."

Shakespeare stepped out into the hallway and closed the door. As he turned, Mrs. Tate shoved a phone in his face. "Here, he wants to talk to you."

Shakespeare took the phone. "Hello?"

"Shakespeare, what the hell is going on?"

Shakespeare tried not to laugh. "Hey, LT, why, what do you hear?" *He had to admit, the woman was fast.*

"Apparently you were rude to one of the richest and most powerful families in the city?"

"You know me, LT."

"Yeah, I do. Nod your head while I'm talking, then say it won't happen again. Who do these people think they are? For Christ's sake, I have enough on my plate, I don't need to be wasting time with spoiled rich people."

Shakespeare's head bobbed through the tirade. Finished, he said, "Okay, sir, it won't happen again."

He hung up and handed the phone back.

"I hope you learned your lesson!" She stormed off, an entourage of three staff scurrying to keep up.

"Anything you care to share with the press?"

Shakespeare turned toward the voice and smiled. Aynslee was young and eager. He remembered what that was like. He was never her league of handsome, but he once had the gung ho attitude. *I wonder what she'll be like when she's my age.* Would the spirit be drummed out of her like so many others? He hoped not. The world needed more people like her. Go getters that, when knocked down, got back up, that recognized an opportunity, and were willing to grab it.

"Nothing I can share, but"—he took her aside, out of earshot of her crew—"when you go in there, see if you can pry a few lovers out of his closet. I need to know if he's a serial cheater, or just a monogamous one."

Aynslee smiled. "I'll throw on the charm, see if he takes the bait."

Shakespeare planted a kiss on the top of her head, patting her shoulder. "Just show him that smile, and he'll be putty in your hands." Her smile grew into one he pictured a daughter of his own might have given him if he had just told her he was proud of her. "I've gotta run. Keep me in the loop."

"Absolutely."

Shakespeare rushed toward the elevators, fishing his phone from his pocket to call Frank. The only logical explanation that fit the case so far was that the star crossed lovers were Frank and Sarah. And if that were the case, their meeting would trigger someone's defeat. And the only someone he could think of were those trying to solve the crime. And the only way he could see himself defeated, was if he wasn't able to rescue her alive. Which meant one thing.

Frank must, under no circumstances, meet Sarah.

EIGHT

"You're sure she's okay?"

"Yes."

She shivered despite the heat, the voice sounding disembodied over the cellphone speaker. She fed the lubricated tube down the naked woman's throat and began pushing the enriched supplement directly into her stomach. She definitely wouldn't be hungry after this feeding. She had already hooked her up to an IV to rehydrate her, and had just finished administering a drug that would evacuate her bladder and bowels over the next hour.

"When will you be finished?"

"In about an hour."

"Very well. When you have finished your task, proceed through the red door to your right. Your payment will be waiting."

"Okay, thanks."

The phone went dead, and she was thankful for it. She had participated over the past seven years of med school in many experiments, had dealt with comatose patients like this one, but never in this type of atmosphere. It was always a hospital environment. But this? She looked around, not sure what to make of what she was looking at. Three large shipping containers, like those you might see on a cargo ship, stood in the center of the warehouse, a warehouse that was nowhere near any of NYU's campuses. And definitely nowhere near the Psyche campus.

She was told the Psyche Department needed a doctor for one evening for a comatose patient they were doing experiments on, trying to determine what level of awareness they might have despite their condition. The email she had received had sounded fascinating, and the payment of five hundred dollars for coming at the last minute, their regular doctor having fallen ill, was too good to pass up.

Everything in the email had looked fine, it had been CC'd to the proper department heads, it had come from a professor in the Psyche department that she had heard of. The payment was unusually high, in fact, the payment in itself was unusual. Quite often these types of requests to help out other departments were expected to be donated. But if it wasn't on the up and up, why would they have mentioned it in an email also sent to her department heads? And if there was a problem with it, wouldn't they have responded, refusing her permission?

It all had seemed perfectly legitimate, until she had responded indicating she was available, and gave her contact information. That's when she was told to come to this warehouse. From the outside, the warehouse looked fairly rundown, but inside it was clean, the necessary facilities were here, and there was a patient: female, mid-twenties, naked, covered by a sheet on the table waiting for her. Fortunately it was quite warm in here, a little too warm to her liking, but it was most likely for the patient's sake.

Her cellphone had rung the moment she entered, and what was required was explained. Some of it wasn't exactly the most pleasant of tasks, but it was nothing she hadn't done before, and she knew it was nothing she wouldn't do again. She did wonder however why they didn't get an experienced nurse, but then perhaps they were concerned in case something went wrong.

"But why is no one here?" she had asked.

"Because we can't risk the patient being exposed to the staff conducting the experiments while this type of discomfort is being inflicted. We do not want our voices, our smells, our touches to be associated with this."

It's a psyche thing. It did all make sense, in a macabre sense. If the patient were awake, which they weren't, but she assumed the hypothesis here was that they *were* aware, then having tubes shoved down your throat and up your orifices would definitely not be a pleasant experience.

It all made sense.

Then why did she feel something was wrong?

She waited for the medicine to kick in, and completed her gruesome tasks of evacuating the bowels, and cleaned up, her job done. She hadn't heard from her employer for almost an hour, and curiosity had gnawed at her the entire time she had worked.

What is in the containers?

Finished, she checked the patient's vitals one last time, looked about, and finding no one, walked toward the closest container. She found the opening blocked by some type of wood structure. She circled around to the farthest container, and opened the latch then pulled open the door, surprised at how quietly it slid out. Inside she found a small room, perhaps four feet deep, with an ordinary door you might find in any house the only thing of any significance, the walls, floor and ceiling all covered in what she assumed was painted drywall. *But black?* It was odd, why would they paint such a small room black. She reached for the door and found it locked.

Disappointed, she stepped from the container, closed the outer door, and slid the latch in place. She stepped quietly toward the second container and was about to open it when she began to have second thoughts. Where were the staff monitoring the experiment? They had to be in here, hadn't they? If she opened the door, did that mean she'd lose her payment? *But I have to know.* With 'curiosity killed the cat' playing through her mind, she unlatched the door to the second container, and pulled it open.

This was a raw container with no small room at the front, instead the complete interior was exposed, the floors and ceiling merely metal. As her eyes adjusted, the only light coming through the door, she saw something at the far end. As she stepped inside to investigate, the shapes began to take form. She pulled out her cellphone and activated her flashlight app, and gasped. In one corner lay a man in a golf outfit, in the other a nun.

What the hell is going on here?

The door behind her slammed shut, the clunk of metal on metal as the latch was closed barely heard over her blood curdling scream.

"What are you doing here?"

"Is that any way to greet a guest?"

He frowned, confused but excited. "Come in." He held the door open and bowed slightly, his hand arcing into his small apartment.

"My, I love what you've done with the place."

He surveyed the mess and shrugged. "If I had known I was going to have company, I would have cleaned up." He watched her walk into the place as if she owned it. And shivered. This woman scared him. She was so cold, almost emotionless, and the things he had done for her were unforgiveable. But she somehow had a control over him he couldn't explain. She was irresistible. An unstoppable force of sheer will, sheer dominance.

When he had met her several months before, he was quickly smitten. She was way out of his league, but for some reason she had paid him particular attention. Concerned with his performance in the production, constantly asking him questions, personal questions, questions he had never been asked before, questions he couldn't believe he answered. Then she had invited him to a "session" as she called it. These became more and more frequent over the coming weeks, these sessions almost like something he'd see on television. They were always at fancy hotels. She'd have him lie down on the bed. She'd sit on a chair, and begin asking him questions in a quiet, calm voice. After a few minutes he would feel himself drifting off to sleep.

Then he'd wake up, and she'd be riding him, naked, and he couldn't resist. He began looking forward to the sessions, and had quickly fallen in love, a love that went unrequited, it clear to him she had no interest in him beyond the sessions and the sex. But he could live with that. He would do anything for her, anything to have her.

Which was why when she began asking him to do strange things, "favors" as she called them, he didn't think twice. He didn't care if he broke into someone's apartment, planted cameras, sent text messages, or helped her move bodies. She had complete control. She had his heart, and his mind.

But today she was here, in his world. This had never happened before.

And it excited him.

He felt a stirring in his loins as she patted the couch she now sat perched on, inviting him to join her. He felt himself drawn forward, as if she had lassoed him and were pulling him in like a steer. He sat down beside her and she smiled.

"Turn around for me."

It was a command, not a request. And he followed it. He turned, his back to her, and immediately felt her hands on his shoulders, gently squeezing, kneading the knots from a hard day's work.

"You did well today."

"Thank you."

"Close your eyes."

He closed his eyes, sighing as she pulled him back into her, her hands now over his shoulders, massaging his chest. He felt completely relaxed. And aroused. He knew what was coming, and he couldn't wait. She made gentle cooing sounds as her hands explored his body, and he felt his breathing get more ragged. He wanted to turn around and take her, right there, right now, but that wasn't how it worked. She was always in control, she was always on top, and he was always unaware of how it started.

In fact, this was the first time he could ever recall this part of their lovemaking. He always woke up with her on top of him, as if waking from some sort of trance. He often wondered if she were hypnotizing him, and if she were, he could care less. But today it was different, the anticipation of what was going to happen was incredible, his heart raced and he forced himself to keep his hands at his sides, his eyes closed as she explored.

"You did *very* well today."

"Thank you."

"In fact, that was the last task I had for you."

He felt a pit form in his stomach. *Does this mean it's over?* "What do you mean?"

"Shhh," she said, her hands travelling up his body, her left hand resting on his face gently, her cool skin soothing his uneasiness. He felt her other hand leave his body for a moment, but the fingers of her other hand caressed his lips, and he couldn't resist opening his mouth slightly and licking a finger that strayed inside. "Everything is going to be okay."

He relaxed again as he felt her other arm return to massaging his chest, then his neck. She gently pulled back on his chin, his head now in her lap.

"Open your eyes."

He opened his eyes and looked at her. She smiled down at him, something she had never done before. He returned the smile.

"I love you," he sighed.

"I know."

He felt something cold and hard slide across his throat, followed by a sharp pain.

"Shhhh, it's okay, I will take care of you."

He smiled, all his fears gone, the warm pulse of blood now flowing from his neck no concern. She leaned down and kissed him, her tongue intertwining with his as he felt his world slowly turn black.

And he would have it no other way.

"Anything unusual?"

Trace shook her head as Shakespeare climbed into the passenger seat, the entire car rocking with the effort. "Not really, just a low-middle income high-rise. Somebody's got money though."

"What makes you say that?"

"Saw a high priced piece of snapper go in there about an hour ago, then come back out fifteen minutes later."

"Just fifteen minutes? She must be good."

"Or he's the one minute wonder."

"No time for the bam, just the wham?"

"So inconsiderate, no 'thank you ma'am'?"

"Rome is burning, my dear, no time for pleasantries."

"If men stop thanking their whores, I shudder to think what's next." A mounted officer slowly sauntered by on his horse, eyeing them through the windshield. Trace flashed her shield and he gave them the two finger salute, moving on. Trace looked up at the building. "So, do we wait for backup?"

"Nope, there's no time to waste."

"Suits me."

They both exited the vehicle and casually strolled toward the building, just in case their suspect happened to be looking out the window. Once inside, Trace made a beeline for the stairs, Shakespeare headed for the elevator.

"This way's quicker," said Trace, stopping when she saw Shakespeare heading in a different direction.

"Sure I could make it up the stairs"—he jabbed the button for the elevator—"but once I got there—" He paused, his eyes looking up in thought. He looked at Trace. "Picture a whale, on a beach, gasping for air. It isn't much use to its buddies, now is it?"

Trace walked over to join him as one of the elevators chimed its arrival. "So, we're buddies now, whaleboy?"

Shakespeare chuckled, regretting his analogy. "Repeat that one at the precinct, and they just might not find the body."

This time Trace laughed as the doors opened and they stepped aboard. "Careful, after what happened two weeks ago, you might just get sent for a psyche eval."

Shakespeare felt as if all happiness had been sucked out of him, and Trace clearly picked up on it, her hand darting to squeeze his arm.

"Hey, I'm sorry, I shouldn't have said that. Gallows humor, you now."

Shakespeare nodded. "Yeah, just a little too fresh." He took a deep breath and watched the numbers climb toward their destination.

"You going to be okay?" Her voice was soft, gentle, caring. He thought of Louise and how he wished she were here right now, just for one of her silent, no questions asked hugs she gave him when she knew he was down. He nodded as the elevator chimed and the doors opened.

Exiting, they both drew their weapons and approached the door, taking up positions on either side. Shakespeare rapped on the door, three quick, hard sets of knuckles. "NYPD, open up, we have a search warrant!"

Nothing. This time he pounded on the door with the bottom of his fist. "NYPD, open up!"

This time they heard the clicking of locks. From other doors on the floor. The first one opened ten feet to their left. Trace glared at the woman as she poked her too curious head into the hallway. "What are you, stupid?

Get your ass back inside!" yelled Trace, shaking her head. The woman's head disappeared, and her door slammed shut.

"Okay, I'll go get the super."

Shakespeare put a hand out to stop her. "Hear that?"

"What?"

"Somebody calling for help, very weak. Must be in trouble."

Trace smiled. "Yeah, I think I hear it too."

Shakespeare stepped back and turned his shoulder to the side, preparing to be a human battering ram, when Trace reached out and tried the knob. The door opened. Trace looked at Shakespeare and smiled. "Little trick I learned, around when I was five."

Shakespeare pushed the door open and stepped inside. "No respect for her elders," he muttered. He had to admit, he was enjoying working with Trace, and he just might ask the LT to make it permanent. He'd have to propose to her first, after all, he'd be asking her to spend the next several years at his side, and that was a lot to ask of somebody almost twenty years his junior, and of the opposite sex. And then there was his reputation.

He rounded the corner and saw pretty much what he expected. A filthy, single, mid-twenties male apartment, clothes, pizza boxes and beer bottles everywhere, with a body adorning the couch. They quickly cleared the apartment then turned their attention to the bloody corpse.

"Is he smiling?"

Shakespeare nodded. "Seems like he died happy." He pointed at the deep slice across his neck. "Just like the other two vics."

Trace nodded and checked his pulse. "This guy's still warm!"

Shakespeare felt the man's wrist. "Very warm. As in 'I just died in the last hour' warm."

Trace looked about the apartment and paused, swatting Shakespeare's arm with the back of her hand. "Look." She pointed with her chin toward the tiny kitchenette. Shakespeare followed her gaze and saw a vent in the ceiling exposed, its grate sitting on the counter.

"Another camera?"

Trace stepped over and hopped bum first on the counter, swinging her legs up and then turning around so she was on her knees. She pushed herself up so she was now standing. Shakespeare immediately stepped over, nervous she might lose her balance. "Careful."

She leaned over and looked in the hole, then reached inside, pulling out a piece of paper. She rebalanced herself on the counter and read the paper, frowning. She handed it to Shakespeare who took it then extended his hand which she accepted and jumped down. "Take a look."

Shakespeare opened the paper and felt his heart pound a little harder.

TICK TOCK
LITTLE TIME ON THE CLOCK
IT IS TIME TO TEND
TO THE LAST LOOSE ENDS

"Well, now we know Sandy was involved, but as an accessory, not a primary." He shook his head. "Call it in, I'm going to start the search." He snapped on his latex gloves as Trace called in the murder. Soon the place would be crawling with techs, but not soon enough.

Are Frank and Sarah loose ends too?

John "Johnny" Walker took the key from the super and unlocked the door, motioning him back, as he and his partner, Terry Curtis, drew their weapons. No one had answered the door, not that they expected anything different, what with the resident, Samantha Alders, dead. Trace had pulled the plates off the security footage from when Alders had arrived at the hotel, and a quick DMV check had found her address. According to the super there were no roommates, and she had only moved in less than a year ago. Walker pushed the door open.

"NYPD executing a search warrant!" he yelled as he stepped inside, Curtis quickly following. No response. He stepped deeper into the impressive apartment, scanning for any movement that might give someone away, finding none. As he cleared the kitchen and living area, Curtis cleared the bathroom and bedroom.

"Clear!" he heard Curtis call from the bedroom, reappearing moments later. "Quite the spread."

"Yeah, I guess if you spread 'em for the right people, you too can have a place like this."

"Hey, I'd let Tate do me if it meant living in a place like this. Have you seen my shithole?"

"Yeah, but that shithole has a wife and two kids waiting at it."

"So? She wouldn't be jealous. Tate isn't competition. Now, if I had to bump uglies with Mrs. Tate, then she might get jealous."

Walker looked at Curtis. "I think you've thought this through entirely too far."

Curtis shrugged. "Gotta explore all my options."

"Stay away from me."

"Don't worry, I'm way too expensive for you."

"I'll start in the bedroom, you start here."

Curtis nodded and headed for the kitchen as Walker entered the bedroom. *Always start in the nightstands.* There was a large king sized, four poster bed, bookended with two nightstands that looked like they cost more than he made in two weeks. He opened the nightstand that had the alarm clock on it, it most likely to be her regular side of the bed. He found an assortment of sexual accoutrements he hoped would make the women in his life blush. *Sex with the old man wasn't that hot?* Shoving the tools of the trade aside, he found a small pink book tucked in the back of the drawer. Pulling it out, he knew immediately what it was.

A diary.

But, how many times had he seen diaries with one or two entries? He yanked the simple lock open, breaking the mechanism, and flipped through the pages, discovering hundreds of days' worth of entries. He flipped to the back, and began to read the mostly short entries, it more of a calendar of what she had done that day, rather than her deep, personal thoughts. *Boring!*

"Find anything?"

Walker looked up at Curtis. "A diary." He tossed it to Curtis who snatched the slightly wide throw from the air.

"Anything juicy?"

"Nope. But go through it anyway, see if there's anything interesting."

Curtis looked at the first few pages. "Damn, I was hoping for some dirty stuff to keep me awake." He shook the diary at Walker. "This is liable to put me to sleep."

"Better you than me. Find anything?"

"Nope. It's like this girl had almost no personal life. The place is decked out, top to bottom, but no personal items, no photos, no letters. I did find one thing odd."

"What's that?"

"There's a docking station for a laptop out there, but no laptop. Did Shakes mention one being at the scene?"

Walker shook his head. "No, apparently it was wiped clean, so perhaps whoever cleaned up the scene took the laptop."

Curtis thumbed through a few more pages of the diary. "Hey, look at this!"

"What?"

Curtis flipped the diary around. "The last entry says she was returning home for a while."

"So?"

"So, isn't this"—he waved his hand around—"home?"

"That's odd. Parents maybe? Did you see an address book?"

"Nope. Probably keeps everything on her phone or computer. I'll check again though."

"Well, if she was returning home, then whoever was expecting her should be missing her by now. I'll check and see if a Missing Persons report has been filed."

Curtis nodded and headed into the living area as Walker fished out his phone, trying to remember when he stopped thinking of his parents' place as home.

Frank didn't want to screw anything up, not on this case, not with him so intimately involved, not with Sarah so near death. The 'star crossed lovers' had to be him and her. It gave him butterflies to think of it. *Lovers.* He had never had a girlfriend. And Sarah was as good as any to start, and maybe even end, with. The thought of her made him all the more determined to do his job. And he finally had a break. He had discovered the cameras were sold by the same supplier, and that supplier was cooperating without waiting for a warrant once they heard just a few details of what was going on. *Some people actually have a conscience, and don't worry about lawsuits.* He hoped to have the information before the night was through, which might help.

Unless that Sandy guy bought them.

He shivered at the thought. Sandy had always seemed like a nice guy, and had prepared his coffee probably a dozen times over the short period he had worked there. Had he started working there to target him? Or had he picked him after working there? He stopped, struck by a troubling thought.

What coffee shop am I going to go to now?

Could he go back to that place? He loved that place, it had been part of his life for years, and it was something he didn't want to lose. *I'm going back.* There was no way he was going to let some criminal, especially some dead criminal, change his life. He slammed his fists against the seat, sealing his decision. In fact, he'd go right now if it weren't for the deadline he was working.

The computer beeped, demanding his attention. He had run a program to hack the cameras, and at last he had his first result. The password for the first camera, the one found in the apartment downstairs. He read it and felt the color drain from his face.

FRANK

He looked over at the other computer still working away at the camera from his apartment. He slid his chair over and opened the software he had downloaded from the manufacturer's website to use the camera, and typed in his hunch.

BRATA

The software popped up with all the settings. He was in. He pulled the IP addresses assigned to both cameras, and began his trace. Within minutes he had found the website the cameras had streamed to. It was password protected as well. And he didn't have a warrant.

Sarah!

He typed every combination of his name he could think of for the user ID and password, with no success. Then on a hunch, he tried something different.

User Name: SARAH
Password: PAXMAN

He had access. But it was illegal access. He was about to click on a link to view the uploaded video, but hesitated. *What if you screw up the case?* Yanking his phone off his belt, he phoned Shakespeare. It only took one ring for his gruff voice to answer.

"Hello, Detective, it's Frank."

"What've you got for me?"

"I've got the website for the cameras, but it's not public, it's password protected."

"Did you get in?"

"Yes, but without a warrant, I can't legally look at anything."

"I don't give a damn—" Shakespeare stopped speaking. Frank waited a few seconds, unsure of what was happening."

"Are you still there?"

"I have an idea. I'll call you back in a minute."

The line went dead and Frank waited, wondering what possible idea Shakespeare could be thinking of, when the phone rang again.

"Gather up anything you're going to need, and meet me at WACX right away."

Shakespeare hung up the phone before Frank could say a word, leaving him to wonder what was going on.

Then he smiled.

Shakespeare pulled into the underground garage at WACX and parked as close to the elevators as he could. He climbed out and saw a squad car nearby flash its lights. He walked over as Frank and the officer climbed out.

"Hi, detective, I don't have a car, so Officer Richards here offered to drive me. Plus, I figured with the nature of the equipment I've got, it might be best to have an armed escort."

Shakespeare nodded at Richards. "Thanks for the help."

"We aim to please." Richards leaned in and popped the trunk. Shakespeare circled the car and whistled at the sheer volume of equipment.

"Did you leave anything at the office?"

Frank blushed slightly. "I didn't want to have to go back since I don't know what kind of setup they have here."

"What're you guys doing, anyway?"

Frank and Shakespeare looked at Richards without saying anything. He raised his hands. "Okay, okay, I get it, not a word." He reached in and grabbed two large duffel bags and hauled them out. Frank and Shakespeare followed suit, and they all headed for the elevators.

"What floor?" asked Richards as he gently placed the two bags on the floor.

"Twenty-third," said Shakespeare, panting slightly, the size of the items he had chosen apparently inversely proportional to their weight. He rested them on the railing in the elevator, and looked at himself in the mirror. He was flushed, sweat trickled down his forehead, and his hair was already damp. *You fat bastard, you need to start doing something about this.*

The elevator chimed its arrival and they were greeted by a smiling Aynslee which warmed his heart, caused Frank to look away, probably afraid of what his face might reveal if he looked too closely at her figure, and Richards to stare, mouth agape. "You're Aynslee Kai!"

She smiled at the young Officer. "Yes I am, and you are?"

"Officer Richards," he gushed. "Brent."

The boy was obviously star struck. And blocking the doors. "Let's go, this isn't The Dating Game. We can all get to know each other later."

Aynslee laughed and took one of the pieces of equipment from Shakespeare. He was about to protest but she swung around so quickly with it, that he didn't have time. He was also grateful for the lighter load.

The four of them strode deeper into the depths of the station's offices, it still abuzz with a full staff.

"Doesn't anybody go home around here?"

Aynslee looked over her shoulder at him. "We have a morning shift for the morning and noon news broadcasts, then we have an evening shift for the supper and late night broadcasts. I'm on in about an hour to anchor the eleven o'clock news, then I'm done for the night."

She knocked on the door of a large, windowless room, then opened it. Inside, what Shakespeare could only describe as a stereotypical computer geek, skinny, pale, pimply face, messy hair, jumped out of his seat, grinning through his braces. *The poor kid!*

"Hi, *Ayn*slee." The long, drawn out way he said the first syllable of her name, combined with the nasally voice and awkward elbows pointing out, hands on his ribcage, not hips, a slight sway to the side with his legs, made the boy look like an italicized letter 't', and made Shakespeare think he was being punk'd. *Revenge of the Nerds, anyone?*

"Reggie, these are the policemen I told you about." A quick round of introductions later and Frank along with the resident nerd were setting up the new equipment, chattering back and forth like an episode of Star Trek. Shakespeare turned from the spectacle when Aynslee took his arm.

"I have to go on air in a little bit. I'll be back around midnight." She glanced at the two uber dorks, smiling. "If you don't want to hang out with these two, you can come and watch the broadcast from the control booth."

Her voice sounded almost hopeful. He glanced at the two. "Frank, how long will you need?"

"Not sure, Detective, hopefully no more than an hour."

"Come get me when you're in, I'll be at the control booth."

"Will do."

Shakespeare followed Aynslee to the control booth and was introduced to the room. When word spread of his arrival, more and more people peeked into the booth to introduce themselves and thank him for saving Aynslee's life. It was nice to be appreciated, but at the same time he was getting a little self-conscious and a little sweaty from standing for almost twenty minutes of handshakes in the closed environment.

Thankfully the show interrupted the pleasantries, and he was able to settle into a chair and watch the principals arrive, Aynslee throwing a wave and a smile at him as she took her seat at the anchor desk, her makeup touched up and her hair freshly fluffed. She looked stunning. He wondered if she had parents that sat at home every night watching her broadcast. He could run her name through the system and find out, but he had sworn he'd never do that outside of business. He knew cops who ran girlfriends and ex-girlfriend's new boyfriends, especially if there was a child involved, all the time, but he had never done it. He felt it was an abuse of the position. He'd have to just ask her one day.

The newscast started, and he found himself transfixed, almost mesmerized by her voice, her look. *She's so good at this!* He had to admit he hardly ever watched the evening news anymore—he was usually sawing lumber by then. But he remembered local news always being amateur hour, but not here, not today. Aynslee's delivery was smooth, the feed he was watching looked professional, and when they cut to the first commercial break, he had to stop himself from clapping. There was only one way he could describe his feelings about the entire experience. He was proud. Proud of seeing this young woman who had been through so much, such a short time ago, take life by the horns once more, and attack it with a vengeance.

"Okay, Aynslee, we've got a breaking item that we're going to go live to."

"What is it?"

"Shaw's at the Waldorf, he's got a breaking story on Richard Tate."

Shakespeare saw her jaw drop then quickly recover. He wasn't as quick. *Is my case about to go public?* He leaned forward as the countdown from five began.

"Welcome back, we now go live to the Waldorf Astoria, where our Crime Reporter Jonathan Shaw is standing by with this breaking story."

His eyes flew up to the monitors to watch the feed. "Good evening, Aynslee. I'm here at the Waldorf Astoria with an update to our shocking news story from earlier today. As reported earlier, Richard Tate, the flamboyant millionaire, some say *billionaire*, real estate developer, was taken to hospital earlier today with what had been described initially as a heart attack, but now has been characterized as a *panic* attack. What this reporter has just learned, is where this *panic* attack occurred. Right here at the Waldorf Astoria. Sources have confirmed that Richard Tate was found lying in the hallway, unconscious, when paramedics were called and he was rushed to the hospital. What caused the attack is not known at this time, however police are now looking for an unknown companion, described as an extremely attractive blonde, twenty-something female, who was apparently a regular guest of Mr. Tate's at the Waldorf." Shakespeare's eyes darted to Aynslee who was looking at him with a quizzical look on her face. He shrugged his shoulders, indicating this was all news to him. "This is Jonathan Shaw, WACX news, reporting live from the Waldorf. Back to you, Aynslee."

Shakespeare left the booth, pulling his phone out and calling Trace who immediately picked up.

"Trace."

"Looks like the press are getting a little closer than I'd like to the Tate story. According to the breaking news report I just watched, the word is out that he was at the Waldorf when he had his panic attack, and that apparently *we* are looking for a young blonde companion."

"Really? Nice of them to let us know."

"Indeed. I guess it's better than them knowing we already found her. You still at Sandy's?"

"Yup, just finishing up."

"Okay, I'm following up some leads here, I want you to take a photo of our three vics down to the Waldorf, and see what you can find out. Now that the story is public, the tongues might start wagging. Threaten them with interfering in a police investigation if they try to stonewall you."

"I'll hit the door men and bellhops first, leave the managers 'til last. Their first call will be to their lawyers."

"Good thinking. See if anybody has seen Henwood there before, how often Alders was there, and see if our friend Sandy ever made an appearance. And check on Vinny, I sent him to the room after I talked to Tate, so he may have something. Shake every damned tree there until something falls out. Good luck."

Shakespeare snapped his phone shut and headed to the computer lab. When he opened the door, his jaw dropped.

"What the hell is that?"

NINE

Trace showed her badge to the officer manning the door to the biggest suite she had ever seen. As she entered she whistled at the size, but gagged at the gaudiness of it all. This was definitely not her style. The blue was off-putting, just too regal for her tastes. *You can never go wrong with earth tones.* Her mother's voice echoed in her head. *Dusty rose never hurts either.* She had tried a couple of dusty rose throw cushions on her chocolate brown couch and immediately regretted the forty dollars she had spent on them, the effect akin to a Valentine's Day chocolate rather than a touch of class. Fortunately she had been able to re-gift them to an old high school girlfriend who was getting married.

That signaled the end of her dusty rose phase. And royal blue would never enter her apartment.

She stepped further in and found Vinny in the bathroom.

"Find anything?"

Vinny looked up and nodded. "Get that light for me," he said, waving at the switch to her right with the bottle of luminal he had just finished spraying the marble walls of the large soaker tub with. She flicked the switch, immediately plunging them in darkness. Large glowing blue stains could be seen everywhere—in the tub, on the fixtures, all over the walls.

"Holy shit!" whispered Trace.

"Somebody definitely died here, in this tub."

"They weren't killed somewhere else, then moved?"

"No." Vinny quickly snapped photographs of the area, then pointed at one part of the wall. "See the spray pattern? That's arterial. You don't get that from a dead body, you only get that from a live body. And you can't fake it either by throwing blood at a wall." He stood back to survey the area. "No, somebody definitely died here."

"I wonder if our friend hadn't have done what he did, would we have found something similar in the first crime scene."

Vinny nodded as he flicked the light switch back on. "I think so. Whoever did this either didn't know our techniques, or didn't care."

"What about the bedroom? Shakespeare said Tate woke up and there was blood everywhere?"

Vinny shook his head. "Nothing on the bed, almost nothing in the bedroom, just a couple of drops here and there, most likely falling off of him and onto the carpet as he made his way into the bathroom. Lots of blood evidence around the sink, most likely from someone cleaning themselves up, Tate probably."

"But he said the bed was soaked in blood, apparently he slipped?"

"My guess is the vic was drugged, carried into the bathtub, had her throat slit, then the killer held a sheet over her throat, soaking it in blood, put it on the bed, then placed Tate on top of it. His normal movements would cover him in the blood, probably wiped some on him just for good measure, then when they did the cleanup, just pulled the sheet, the mattress cover, bagged them, and put a new cover and sheet on the bed."

"And the body, any theories on how they moved that?"

"I've got theories comin' out of my ass, but nothing I can prove. I'd review the security tapes."

"I'm already having them pulled. Probably used one of those big luggage carts I saw downstairs. Load the body in a trunk, put it on the cart, wheel it to the parking lot, and you're free and clear."

Vinny nodded. "Could be." He peaked around the corner to make sure none of the rest of the crew was within earshot. "How's the kid doing?"

Trace shrugged her shoulders. "No idea. He's with Shakespeare at the news station, apparently they're pulling some video feeds from those cameras and he didn't want to wait for a warrant."

"Ballsy. Could screw up the case."

"So? I'd rather have a perp get off a *kidnapping* rap on a technicality, than have a solid *murder* case."

Vinny sighed. "Yeah, I guess you're right. Effin' system drives me nuts sometimes."

"You're preaching to the choir. Violate a guilty man's rights in a case like this, big deal. If he turns out to be innocent, then throw the book at us. Don't let a guilty man go free because we were trying to save a life. These goddamned judges should spend a few years in our shoes before they ever sit on the bench."

"Some DA's I know could stand a few years in the trenches as well. They're so quick to make a damned plea bargain, they let violent criminals off with a wrist slap so they can keep their dockets clear."

"Ahhh, if only I were Queen for a day, I'd straighten the whole damned system out."

"You'd have my vote."

"Oh well, what ya gonna do." She looked at her watch. "I'm going to go check out those tapes."

"Any luck on the canvas?"

"Not much, they confirmed that Tate and Alders were regulars here, almost every Saturday night. No one recognized Angela Henwood or Sandy Thorton."

"But it establishes a pattern, doesn't it?"

"Yup. Anyone who wanted to target Tate would know exactly where he was, with no security, once a week."

"Assuming Tate was the target."

Trace looked at Vinny. "What, you think Alders was?"

"Well, she's dead, isn't she?"

Trace paused for a moment. "Well, yeah, but I thought we were working under the premise that Alders was killed to frame Tate, assuming of course Tate is telling the truth?"

"Well, you may be working under that assumption, but I can guarantee you that Shakes has got both possibilities running through that mind of his."

Trace smiled. "Wow, I think that's the first nice thing I've heard you say about him in years."

Vinny smiled out of half his mouth. "Yeah, well just don't tell him I said so."

"Oooh, I don't know about that. That would be like lying to my partner."

"Don't you have some video to review somewhere other than here?"

Trace laughed and left Vinny and his crew to finish their investigation, her mind now contemplating a completely new theory.

Frank and Reggie looked up from the monitors at Shakespeare. Frank shook his head. "I'm not sure, but"—he pointed at one of the monitors—"I'm pretty sure that's Sarah."

Shakespeare approached the monitors and leaned in for a closer look. On the screen was an image shot from above, not an overhead shot, but from an angle as if the camera were positioned like the other two they had found in Frank's building. It showed a long, narrow room, featureless, save a lone, naked woman, huddled in one corner, apparently asleep.

"How can you tell? You can't see her face."

Frank shrugged. "I don't know, I just know."

Or you just want it to be her. Shakespeare didn't blame the kid, but the worst thing you could do in this business was jump to conclusions. This could be an entirely different victim for all they knew. If this was a serial killer situation, they quite often went after similar looks, and young and plump was definitely in abundance in this day and age.

"I'm in."

Shakespeare looked at the station's resident geek. "In what?"

"The historical archives."

"You mean what these cameras have been taping is stored there?"

"Yup." He hit a few keys and pointed at one of the monitors showing an empty room and a time code from Friday night. It ticked by in real time.

"Anyway to speed this up?"

"Yup, but we're probably looking at two days of footage, and there's three cameras."

"Can you edit that down?"

"Are you kidding me?" The geek guffawed painfully. "This is a TV station, of course we can."

Shakespeare pointed at Frank. "Okay, I want you to go through that footage, and pull together anything of interest. And if you get any hint of a location, or someone else involved that we don't know of yet, you let me know right away."

"Where are you going?"

"NYU. Right now everything keeps pointing there."

"Back it up!" Trace pulled her chair closer to the monitor, her finger poised in the air. "Now stop." The security tech from the Waldorf stopped spinning the control on his specialized keyboard, and let it play forward. The image clearly showed Richard Tate entering the room, alone, at 5:55pm. The tech spun the control a few times, the time code jumping ahead, showing only a few people in the hallway, but none approaching the door, until 6:13pm when a tall, well-dressed blonde woman, clearly their second victim, entered.

"Okay, that matches up with what we know. Now let's see who arrives."

The control spun, and it wasn't until 6:58pm that anyone else approached the door. "Wait a minute, is that a masseuse?"

The tech nodded. "Looks like it to me." He pointed at the fold-up table she had. "No logo. She's not from the hotel, that's an outside company."

Trace made note of the time. "Okay, move it forward." The door opened and the masseuse disappeared. "Someone's still alive and awake in there!" *But who?* Could the killer have been hiding in the room? It was a definite possibility. She had seen the room; it was huge, separate bedroom, two bathrooms, large closets with doors, an entrance area, sitting area, living area. It was essentially a large apartment with everything except a kitchen. More than enough places for someone to have hidden. And according to Tate's statement, he had passed out within minutes of Samantha arriving, and this was almost an hour later.

The tech spun the wheel, sending the footage leaping ahead. An hour later the door to the suite opened again, and out walked the masseuse, table under her arm, heading toward the elevators, apparently completely calm.

Trace stared at the screen as the woman disappeared from site. *But that makes no sense!* "Are these time codes correct?"

"Yup, there's no way to fake these."

She racked her brain for all it was worth. Tate arrives. Fifteen minutes later Alders arrives. Forty-five minutes more and a masseuse arrives. An hour later that masseuse leaves, completely calm. *That means they were alive and well long after Tate said.* But why would Tate lie? Then it occurred to her.

"Do you guys have any problems with prostitution here?"

"Of course not."

Yeah, right! "I'm not looking to get you guys in trouble, but how unusual is it to have an outside masseuse come in for a little, how shall I put it, rub and tug?"

The man blushed slightly and he lowered his voice. "I see it all the time. Our girls would never do this, so some guests order in, shall we say, questionable girls. There's no way to tell, and the front desk isn't going to stop them, because most of them are legitimate. We have no way of knowing."

Trace waved her hand at him, cutting him off. "Okay, I get it, you guys are completely innocent." She took a deep breath and let it out slowly. "So, Tate arrives, his date arrives, they order up a third participant, get their little massage à trois on, then she leaves." She nodded. "Okay, I can see why he wouldn't want us to know about that, so he messed with the timeline by omitting his additional guest."

"Makes sense."

Trace twirled her fingers in the air. "Okay, let's roll it forward and see what we've got."

Hours spun by on the clock, and it wasn't until the next morning, 9:47am, that the door burst open and Tate himself rushed from the room, and toward the elevator. "That's Tate leaving, that matches up." Minutes later a bellhop, fully decked out in a Waldorf uniform, a hat perched atop his head, pulled low hiding his face, pushed a luggage cart with a large case down the hallway. He stopped in front of the Tate suite, swept a card through the lock, and opened the door. He backed in, pulling the cart inside. *Just like I thought!* A few seconds of spinning, and the time code jumped to 11:39am, the door opening again, the bellhop backing out, pulling the cart. As he walked under the camera, he glanced up slightly, in what looked like an attempt to stretch, and she caught a clear look at his face.

Sandy Thorton!

"Do you recognize him?"

The tech shook his head. "No, but we've got a huge staff. I can run him through personnel if you want."

Trace shook her head. "No, I've already got that happening with a better photo."

The tech spun the control forward and several hours later, at 2:23pm, Tate reappeared, entered the suite, and less than ten minutes later reemerged, collapsing on the floor. Minutes later he was surrounded by staff, then paramedics.

"Okay, send me a copy of that footage." She handed the tech her card. "Also, I need you to see if you can tell where that bellhop came from and went." She unclipped her cellphone from her hip. "And I'll need to see if there were any phone calls made from that room. Maybe they hired the masseuse using the room's phone."

The tech nodded as Trace called Shakespeare.

"Hey, Shakes, I've got some news for you."

"Go ahead."

"Tate lied about the timing. I've got footage of a masseuse showing up a few minutes after Alders gets there, then leaving an hour later, completely calm."

"You think she's the killer?"

Trace thought for a moment. *That hadn't occurred to me.* She decided to go with her gut. "No, Tate said he passed out almost right away, and this one was let in. Why would Alders order a masseuse if Tate was passed out cold? And wouldn't she be wondering why he was out cold?"

"Good thinking. If Tate's drugged, we have to assume Alders was too, so who let the masseuse in?"

"Right. Either it was the killer, already hiding in the room, and if so, why would he let a masseuse in, unless she was in on it—"

"Which doesn't really make sense."

"—or, more likely, the masseuse was invited to participate in their evening of debauchery—she was an outside masseuse, not hotel—then left, and after that Tate and Alders pass out from something they drank."

"So Tate lies because he doesn't want to admit to hiring a prostitute."

"Right."

"Makes sense. I'll go back and question him on that. What else?"

"I have a clear shot of Thorton, dressed as a bellhop, entering the room after Tate leaves the next morning, then leaving about two hours later, pushing a luggage cart with a large case."

Shakespeare whistled. "Well, that definitely links him to the case."

"Yup."

"So, now there's only one question."

"What's that?"

"How did they drug Tate and Alders?"

"Maybe they dosed the liquor ahead of time?"

"Could be. Check the footage and see who went in there before Tate arrived."

Trace's heart suddenly shoved against her chest in excitement. "You know, another thing just occurred to me."

"What's that?"

"What if we have it all wrong?"

"Come again?"

"Listen, what if everything Tate said is a lie?"

"Go on."

"Tate says he was drugged, wakes up the next day, flees, comes back, has a panic attack, right?"

"Yes."

"Well, what if it played out like this? They have their threesome, masseuse leaves, he and Alders make a night of it, something goes wrong, he kills her, calls somebody he knows, and they send in a cleaner of sorts, he leaves, Sandy the cleaner comes in, scrubs the crime scene, and then Tate returns?"

Shakespeare grunted on the other end of the line. "It's a possibility, but there's a few holes."

Trace felt her chest tighten slightly. "Such as?"

"One, why leave? If he did it, why not call in the cleaner, and help him? Or, call the cleaner, and leave and not come back? Second, who left the note? How would he have known about the Tick Tock messages? Third, how would someone like Tate know a cleaner?"

Trace felt a little crestfallen. "Yeah, okay, you're right. It was just a thought."

"And keep them coming. I prefer my partners to not only be able to think outside the box, but to actually do it. Never hold back an idea, you just may hit on something sometime."

She felt better. *Partner?* She could live with that.

"Anything else?"

"Not yet."

"Okay, keep me posted, I'm going to have some video sent to your phone. You're not going to believe the shit we're looking at."

"And I'll send you the clips from here showing the time codes for when you talk to Tate."

Shakespeare pulled a U-turn and headed for the hospital only three blocks away. He phoned Frank and told him to feed any footage they found to both him and Trace. Minutes later he was parked and in an elevator riding up to Tate's floor. He looked in Tate's room but found it empty. He went to the Nurse's Station and showed his badge. "Any idea where Richard Tate has been moved to?"

The woman looked up from her paperwork and shook her head. "Sorry, dear, I just got on, but I assume he went home after checking himself out."

"He did what?"

"He's at home with his own medical staff probably. Can't blame him. If I had his money, I wouldn't spend a night here."

Shakespeare spun on his heel and headed for the elevator. He called dispatch for Tate's home number, and had them put him through. A man's voice answered the phone almost immediately.

"Tate residence."

"This is Detective Shakespeare, Homicide. I need to ask Mr. Tate some additional questions."

"Ah, Detective Shakespeare. My name is Lawrence Cannon; I'm one of Mr. Tate's attorneys. I've already spoken to your lieutenant about you questioning my client without his lawyer present—"

"To which I'm certain my lieutenant reminded you was completely legal since he was not a suspect."

"—and he assured me it wouldn't happen again."

"Since he is *now* a suspect..."

There was a pause. *Don't fuck with me, lawyer boy.*

"My client was drugged, the tests confirmed that. It appears you are fishing, Detective."

"I have video evidence that appears to indicate he lied in his statement. I'm willing to come over there right now and clear this up, or we can do this down at the station. Whichever you would prefer."

"Here would be preferred. But we aren't at his residence in The Hamptons, we're in his suite at Tate Tower." Shakespeare whistled to himself. *Fancy.*

"I'll be there in fifteen minutes."

He hung up the phone before Cannon could say no, and climbed into his car. His phone vibrated and he checked the attached clips Trace had just sent him, making notes in his pad with who entered and exited the room, and when. He shook his head. *This isn't making any sense.*

Why would a man like Tate kill his glorified hooker?

"There's gaps."

Frank nodded. "I noticed that. Looks like every twelve hours they shut her camera off for an hour or so."

Reggie nodded. "I wonder what they're doing in that hour."

Frank shuddered to think. Sarah was naked, alone except for two visitors, both of who appeared after the blackouts, one left within minutes somehow, perhaps a door they couldn't see, the other remained for some time, then the video showed them both falling asleep, and what looked like a nun walking out through some exit directly under the camera.

Reggie looked at Frank, waving at the feed. "If there's a door, why doesn't she just walk out?"

Frank frowned. "And what do you think is on the other side of that door?"

Reggie blushed slightly, apparently realizing the idiocy of his question. "Yeah, I guess you're right. What I don't get is the nun. What the hell is a nun doing there?"

Frank was stunned at the naiveté of the questions. "Well, I think it's safe to say it isn't a real nun."

Reggie's head bobbed. "Yeah, I guess that makes sense." He snapped his fingers. "Or, she's being held in a church, and the nun is trying to help her?"

Frank exploded. "What the hell kind of fucked up church would do something like this to an innocent girl?" He took a deep breath. "Sorry, this is personal for me. She was with me when she was taken, and I just don't want to see her killed. I've seen more dead bodies in the past two days than I care to ever see again."

Reggie turned back to the screen, sufficiently chastised. "Sorry, just trying to help. My mom keeps telling me to work on that brain-mouth filter."

Frank's phone vibrated with an email. He opened it and read the text, then the attachment, and immediately forwarded it to Shakespeare and Trace. Erring on the side of caution, he phoned Shakespeare, just in case he didn't know how to open an attachment, or missed the call.

"Hello, Detective, it's Frank."

"What've you got for me?"

"I just sent you an email I got from the camera supplier. He said they were all part of a batch of ten cameras, ordered and shipped directly to the NYU Psych Department."

"Was there a name?"

"No, sorry, just the department and address."

"Okay, good work, kid, keep the info coming."

Frank shoved his phone back on his hip as Reggie nodded at the screen. "Look at this. A new file just appeared." Reggie clicked on it, launching the video. "What the hell is this?"

Frank typed into his phone furiously, recording the text appearing on the video, then bolted from the room.

Shakespeare pulled his car in front of Tate Tower, the latest and apparently flagship property of the Tate Empire, his name emblazoned across the top several stories, as well as at ground level. The man had an ego, there was no doubt about it, but you couldn't argue with success. And Shakespeare appreciated success through hard work. Success through lying, stealing, getting bailed out—no. Put your nose to the grindstone, work your ass off, solve your own problems, and reap the rewards. Sometimes that reward was a life of luxury like Tate had earned, sometimes it was a happy family living in a humble home, with a job you hated. It was up to the individual to decide what was important to them, then make it happen.

Shakespeare climbed out and flashed his badge to the valet.

"Not a scratch."

The young man nodded, and gently pulled the car away as Shakespeare entered the opulent lobby, an impeccably dressed doorman holding the door open for him. Shakespeare nodded at the man, noting his neat appearance, his attention to personal grooming, and the pride he appeared to have in his job. This was a perfect example of taking responsibility for your own happiness. Would this man ever be rich? No, most likely not, but he probably went home at the end of the night tired but happy with how he did his job, a little richer with the good tips he earned because of doing that very job well, and hopefully into the arms of a loving wife and child. That was being rich.

That was something Shakespeare wished he had.

He had lost the pride, but he had it back, he was rebuilding his career, his reputation, and had at last found love. *Better late than never.*

As he entered the lobby, another man approached him. "Detective Shakespeare?"

He nodded.

"Please come with me, Mr. Tate and Mr. Cannon are waiting for you."

Shakespeare followed him to the elevators, then travelled in silence to the penthouse level, more than one hundred stories in the air. The elevator opened to a private reception area, several numbered doors available. PH1 appeared to be the correct choice, as the man rapped twice on the door. It opened and a suit appeared that had to be a lawyer.

"Detective Shakespeare, I'm Lawrence Cannon." Shakespeare nodded to the man who had just led him up, then shook Cannon's hand. "Come inside, Mr. Tate is waiting. He is still under medical care, therefore only has a few minutes.

"That's all I will need."

Shakespeare followed Cannon inside, then into what looked like a reception area. Tate was sitting in a large, plush chair, his feet up, a bathrobe on, a blanket covering him, and a nurse hovering nearby.

"Mr. Tate"—Shakespeare nodded—"I won't take much of your time." Shakespeare fished out his cellphone, cued up the first video Trace had sent him, then held out the phone with one hand, as he read the time codes from his notes.

"Here we have you arriving at five fifty-five. Is that correct?"

"Sounds right."

"And here we have Ms. Alders arriving at six thirteen. Is that correct?"

"Yes."

"And here we have a masseuse, not from the hotel, arriving at six fifty-eight. Is that—"

"No!" Tate had a lot more color in his cheeks than just a minute ago. "That's not right, I don't remember a masseuse."

"Detective, we both know that our client was drugged, the tests proved that. We also both know that this particular drug can affect short term memory retroactively, therefore is it really any surprise that my client would not remember a masseuse who arrived shortly before he was drugged."

Shakespeare nodded, but in no way convinced. "Oh, I'm sure that it's possible he doesn't remember. But she did stay an hour and left quite calmly." Shakespeare turned to Tate and fired his final salvo. "Do you often hire rub and tug prostitutes when you are entertaining your girlfriends from sugar daddy websites?"

"This interview is over."

But Shakespeare had what he wanted. The look of shock on Tate's face told him everything he needed to know. Tate didn't remember the masseuse, and wasn't in the habit of hiring one. Now the question was, who did hire her? Could it have been him, on a whim, and he just didn't remember? Could it have been Alders, or could he have hired the masseuse for Alders, and it was all innocent? There were many possibilities, but finding that masseuse could answer quite a few questions.

Aynslee watched Frank bolt past her, toward the elevators. She rushed to the computer room and found Reggie sitting alone, Shakespeare nowhere to be found. "Where're our guests?"

Reggie whipped around and gave her a toothy grin. "Hi, *Ayn*slee."

Aynslee waited a moment. "Our guests?"

"Oh, sorry!" Reggie looked up at the ceiling, then, as if pointing at a rewind of his life's video, he nodded. "The detective said he was going to NYU, and Frank didn't say where he was going, but I can guess."

"What do you mean?" Aynslee was getting tired of having to pry. *You're a reporter. This is what you do.*

Reggie pointed at one of the screens. "This video just popped up on the site. We watched it, then he ran out."

"Show it to me."

Reggie clicked to start the video and she gasped at the text that appeared, line by line:

TICK TOCK
LITTLE TIME ON THE CLOCK
IF FRANKIE WANTS TO SAVE HIS FRIEND
HE WILL COME ALONE IN THE END

After a few moments an address appeared that she jotted down. She pushed the paper toward Reggie. "Google this for me."

He nodded and popped over to the website, entering the address. Seconds later a full satellite view with the streets appeared. "That's a warehouse district, isn't it?"

Reggie shrugged his shoulders. "Could be, I don't really know the city that well."

"Weren't you born here?"

"Yeah, but I don't get out much."

I never would have guessed. Aynslee decided not to respond, instead dialing Shakespeare.

"Ah, one thing, *Ayn*slee."

She looked at him as her phone rang. "What?"

"Well, that's a different address than before."

"Hello?"

Aynslee, Reggie's statement catching her off guard, didn't reply to Shakespeare.

"Hello, anyone there?"

Aynslee came back to reality. "Detective, it's me, Aynslee. We've got a problem."

"What is it?" She could hear in his voice the evening hadn't been going well. She was just about to add to his problems.

"Frank and Reggie found another video on the site. It just shows text. Let me read it to you: Tick tock, little time on the clock, if Frankie wants to save his friend, he will come alone in the end."

"Let me speak to him."

"That's just it, as soon as he read this, he took off."

"What!"

"The worst part is that there was an address after the message, but Reggie is positive"—she looked at him to make sure, and he nodded emphatically—"that it is a different address now, than it was when Frank looked at it."

"What? How is that possible?"

Aynslee looked at Reggie. "The detective wants to know how that's possible."

"It's really quite simple. It's probably an Apache server and you can have files redirected by view count or time of day or user id or—"

She raised her hand, cutting him off. "Take my word for it, it's possible."

"Damn! So the kid took off to save his girlfriend, and we have no way of knowing where he went!"

Aynslee felt her chest tighten as she thought of what had happened to her just two weeks before. "We have to find him before he gets to wherever he's going. Reggie, is there any way to get that video back?"

"I'll try, but hacking isn't really my bag. I can do the basics, but this is beyond what I do. I'm just a tech. Frank was the expert, he's been trained in this."

Aynslee returned the phone to her ear. "Did you hear that?"

"Tell Reggie that I'm going to try and get another tech sent out ASAP and to keep going through the video in the meantime, sending me any clips he thinks I should see."

"Where will you be?"

"I'm heading to NYU. Too many things pointing there."

"Can I come along?" She already knew what the answer would be.

Shakespeare chuckled. "No, you most definitely cannot."

Shakespeare ended the call with Aynslee and immediately dialed Vinny. *What the hell was the kid thinking?* But he already knew the answer. He was thinking with the wrong head. *Or he feels responsible.* That was definitely a possibility. The kid had taken things hard. And personally. He knew how he'd feel if he was in the same position, if he had just found out that a girl he liked was confirmed kidnapped. He pictured Louise. *If I were him, there's no telling what I'd do.*

The phone picked up. "What can I do for you, Detective?"

Vinny's voice snapped Shakespeare back to reality. "We've got a problem. The kid saw another message, and this one had an address."

"Don't tell me—"

"He took off."

"Do we know where?"

"No, the message was actually a video on the website he hacked. The address on the message changed the second time it was viewed, so right now we have no idea where he went."

"Are you kidding me? Is that even possible?"

"Trust me, the WACX geek tried to explain it. It's possible."

"What do you need from me?"

"I need a tech you can trust to get over to the studio and hack that damned computer so we can find out where he went."

"Consider it done."

"Can you trace his cellphone?"

"Yeah, but we'll need a warrant for that one for sure. I'll take care of it."

"Okay, thanks. I'll get Trace to check the cab companies."

"Damn, I hope we find that kid before he gets himself killed."

"You and me both."

Shakespeare ended the call and slammed his fists into the steering wheel. He was not about to lose another colleague. *What were you thinking, Frank?* He turned his car toward the NYU campus security office and hit the accelerator, the car surging forward, his back pressed into the seat as he weaved through the relatively light nighttime traffic. His father's voice echoed through his head. *Take it easy on the gas, she's reliable, but still an old horse.* He lifted his foot. Slightly.

"Okay, what have we got?" he asked aloud, triggering the beginning of a mental technique he had used for years. By vocalizing the case to himself, usually in a car since he loved driving, he could organize his thoughts. "We've got the first victim, Angela Henwood, found in her apartment, dead, most likely abducted, perhaps even killed, before Frank and Sarah were even taken. She's an NYU student. But why? What's the motive? Means and opportunity are easy. But what motive? Maybe she's random?

"Frank and Sarah are then drugged and abducted, we assume by Sandy, at the coffee shop. Frank is placed in Henwood's apartment. Why? To begin the game? Were they random targets? Couldn't be. Henwood is in Frank's building, and Frank goes to that coffee shop every day, so he was the target. Sarah was just an unfortunate bystander? She normally would never be there, so Sandy had to change his plans. But why?

"Because the game had already started, and couldn't be stopped! Henwood was supposed to be in the box, not Sarah, but because Sarah was with Frank, and they needed Frank for some reason, they took her too, killed Henwood, set Frank up for the murder to put him in a panic, probably just to up the ante in the game from him being concerned about a missing night and a missing date, to him being worried about having committed murder?"

He stopped at a light. *It's thin. And it all hinged on when the first victim died.* He grabbed his phone from the passenger seat and dialed MJ. After a few rings a groggy voice answered.

"This better be good."

Shakespeare looked at his watch. *Yoikes!* "Sorry, MJ, it's Shakespeare."

"What is it?" He heard a little more life in MJ's voice. "Another vic?"

"No, I just need to know if you narrowed down the TOD on Henwood."

"Yeah, the file's on your desk."

"Humor me. I haven't been at the office most of the day, and probably won't get there until tomorrow."

"Pulling an all-nighter?"

"Looks that way."

There was a pause. "Shakes, what's going on? You know you can trust me."

This time it was Shakespeare's turn to pause. "Umm, what do you mean?"

"I mean two murders in Frank's building, one in his apartment, Vinny giving me a bullshit story about why an out of place chair with duct tape was being ignored, Frank jumping at the sound of a fly farting, and you and Vinny actually working together. Something's up."

Shakespeare sighed. "Listen, MJ, you have to trust me that I'm doing the right thing."

"I never doubt that with you."

Shakespeare felt a slight surge at the words from his friend. "Thanks, MJ. As to what's going on, the less you know the better. If I need you, I'll tell you, but for now, I need everything on the QT."

"Okay, Shakes. I just hope you know what you're doing."

"So do I, my friend, so do I." A horn blared behind him and he looked up at the green light glaring at him. He waved at the driver behind him and pressed the gas. "So, TOD on Henwood?"

"Between noon and six p.m. Friday."

"Thanks, MJ. Sweet dreams."

"Love you too."

Shakespeare laughed and tossed the phone on the passenger seat. "Okay, that firms things up. She was dead before Sarah was even in the picture, so Sarah was a crime of opportunity, or a crime of necessity. They needed Frank. He was normally alone, but Friday night, the night they actually needed him, he wasn't alone. So they took her too. But they didn't kill her. Why not?"

Shakespeare thought for a moment. This was obviously planned out, planned well. There were planted cameras, Rohypnol to purchase, that strange room that Sarah was in, websites, throwaway cellphones. This wasn't random, but she was. "They were going to take someone else." He nodded to himself. *That must be it.* "They were going to take someone else, but they had to take her." Shakespeare raised his finger, an idea forming. "And rather than kill her, they decided to use her, to involve Frank even more!"

He heard laughing to his left and turned to look. A group of teenagers in the car beside him at the intersection were giggling. He slowly lowered his finger.

"Yo, Dude! When you start talking to yourself, that's a sign you need to check into Bellevue!"

Shakespeare fished his badge off his belt and held it up, silencing the car. "Riddle me this, smart ass, what weighs two-hundred-fifty pounds and doesn't need to chase you because he's got a gun?"

The passenger who had made the comment suddenly looked terrified, his face sagging, his eyes wide. "Y-you?"

Shakespeare nodded. "Now move along before I call in your plates and have a black and white look for an infraction." He waved his hand for them to move on, the light now green. The car slowly pulled away and took the first turn available to get out of sight. Shakespeare continued on, the incident already forgotten as his thoughts retuned to the case.

"Okay, so they target Frank, probably because he's NYPD. This is a high-tech operation, so they target a tech. He's young, so it's more fun for them?" *Maybe.* "Or maybe Frank isn't random at all. Maybe they chose him specifically." *The shooting!* When Frank was shot in the vest two weeks ago, his name and file picture had been splashed all over the newspapers due to the huge national interest in the case, and its aftermath. His name, photo, where he worked, what he did—it was all there. All there for the public, and any nut bar, to read. And with his photo, all they needed to do was sit on the lab, wait for him, then follow him. They could find out his habits, where he lived, what apartment—it was all too easy. Frank fell into their lap. "That has to be it."

"But what about Henwood? Her living in the same building? That's too big of a coincidence." *But if it wasn't a coincidence, then what was it?* "The resident of the apartment was supposed to be some old woman. Instead we find a young girl living there, apparently alone." *But where did we get that info?* "Jackie St. Jean. She's the one who said it was Henwood. She's the one who said Henwood lived there." Shakespeare's jaw dropped as his mind whirled. "If none of it's true, then Jackie St. Jean is in on this."

Shakespeare slammed his brakes on as he noticed the red light he was about to barrel through. He checked his rear view mirror, then stared blankly at the light ahead of him. "Holy shit! If St. Jean isn't a witness, but a participant, we can't even rely on the ID!" He grabbed his phone and dialed Trace.

"Hey, Shakes, what's up?"

"Where are you?"

"Just finishing up at the hotel."

"Did you ever confirm Jackie St. Jean's identity?"

"Huh?"

"Her ID. Did you ever check it?"

"Yeah, but all she had was a student ID, but she was a witness, so, you know." There was a pause. "Why?"

"Listen to this and tell me what you think: if we assume Frank was targeted, then Henwood living in the same building is one hell of a coincidence."

"Riiight…?"

"Soooo, who's the only person who told us it was Henwood that lived there?"

Shakespeare waited for the bulb to go off. "Holy shit! You mean she wasn't a witness, she was the killer?"

"Not necessarily the killer, but definitely a participant."

"If it's true, she's got balls of steel."

"Agreed. We need to find out if NYU even has a student named Jackie St. Jean. And Angela Henwood for that matter."

"Okay, I'll start waking people up and try to find out."

"I'm on my way there now to talk to their Public Safety office and see what I can shake loose. Call me when you have something."

Shakespeare tried calling Frank, but only reached his voice mail. He left a message, but knew it would do no good. Tossing the phone aside, he continued his analysis. "So where were we? Jackie St. Jean. Let's assume she's involved somehow. They pick Frank from the paper, they kill or kidnap a little old lady from his building that no one will miss, kill Henwood, set up Frank, send St. Jean over there to plant the story that Henwood actually lived there, making her look like an innocent victim." He paused. "But why do they need to make her look like an innocent victim? Why not just kill the old lady, set Frank up with Henwood in the apartment? They've already framed him, they've already got him on video. Why make Jackie, or whoever the hell she is, go to the apartment?"

Shakespeare growled in frustration. *This is making no sense.*

Trace had one clear shot of the masseuse's face as she entered the hotel. At one point she had looked up and the security camera had a clear image. *We need to find this girl.* She emailed the photo to Walker and Curtis, who she knew were still working, and sent a text asking them to check the rub and tug parlors that accepted out calls in the area, none of which would be closed at this time of night, this their prime time. She received a text message a few minutes later from Walker.

> *You're lucky I'm just single and not single and sexy, otherwise I'd be busy at this hour.*

Trace chuckled and replied:

Don't worry, you're sexy to someone. I think I saw Curtis checking out your ass last week.

The reply was almost immediate:

I thought I felt my ass burning. We're starting our canvass now. Will call as soon as we have something.

Trace sent a quick acknowledgement then launched her phone's browser to look up NYU's campus security phone number. Within minutes she was talking to the night supervisor. "This is Detective Trace of the NYPD. I need to know if you have a student there named Jackie St. Jean."

"I'm sorry, ma'am, but I can't give out that information over the phone. You could be anybody."

Trace rolled her eyes. "Listen, this is life or death. My partner, Detective Shakespeare will be there shortly but time is of the essence. I'll give you the number for central dispatch, and they will forward your call to me if you want to be sure."

"Did you say Shakespeare?"

"Yes."

"Yeah, I was talking to him just a little while ago. Okay, what was the name?"

"Jackie St. Jean." She spelled the name for him, as she knew she wouldn't have known how to just from hearing it. She could hear some very slow keyboard work on the other end, the letters spoken aloud as each was typed with excruciating deliberation. At last, she heard the final letter and then a blow by blow description of each mouse move and click.

"Okay, here we go. Jackie St. Jean. Yes, she's a student here, or rather was a student."

"What? When did she leave?"

"Just a second, this is odd."

"What?"

There was no reply for several moments. She was about to ask again when he finally started speaking.

"Why are you looking for her?"

"She's a witness in a murder we're investigating."

"From when?"

"What do you mean from when?"

"When was the murder?"

"Saturday, why?"

"Because according to our records, Jackie St. Jean was reported missing two years ago, and was never found."

TEN

Walker knocked on the door, then eyed his watch. "I hate these types of calls."

Curtis nodded. "Your daughter has been missing two years, and two policemen show up at the door in the middle of the night. I know what I'd be thinking."

Walker knocked again, this time a little harder. Their canvas of the massage parlors had been reassigned, the news that Jackie St. Jean was a missing person taking higher priority. "I guess if it is her, then it would be good news."

"Right. Hi, Mr. and Mrs. St. Jean. We found your daughter, she's a murderer!"

"Shhh, I think I hear someone coming."

"Who is it?" a man's voice asked through the door.

"NYPD, Mr. St. Jean." Walker held his badge up to the peephole. "We need to talk to you about your daughter, Jackie."

"Kathy, it's about Jackie!" they heard the man yell, his voice indicating his excitement as he unbolted, unchained and unlocked the door. He yanked it open just as his nightgown clad wife rushed into the small entrance.

"Did you find her?" she asked.

"May we come in?" asked Walker.

The anxious parents quickly moved deeper into the small apartment. Walker followed, with Curtis bringing up the rear, closing the door behind them.

"Well?" asked Kathy St. Jean. "Did you find her?"

"Please have a seat," said Walker, motioning toward the couch.

"Oh no!" Kathy's eyes filled with tears as she turned to her husband. "Ronnie, she's dead, our little baby is dead!"

Walker shook his head and waved his hands. "No, no, it's nothing like that."

The distraught parents took their seats, and Walker sat across from them while Curtis held back, discretely surveying the apartment. Walker pulled out his phone and brought up a photo from the Bureau's surveillance camera. "We had a possible sighting of your daughter on Saturday." He handed them the phone with a picture of the woman claiming to be their daughter in the interrogation room. "Is this—"

"Oh my God!" exclaimed Kathy, "That's our Jackie!"

"Are you sure?"

"Yes, absolutely! She's changed her hair, but that's her, no doubt about it!"

Walker looked at Ronnie. "And you, sir, is it your daughter?"

He stood up and went to a nearby table with a baker's dozen of framed photographs filling its surface. He grabbed one and brought it back to the couch. He sat down, held the photo up facing Walker, with the phone flipped around. "You tell us, Detective. Is this our daughter?"

Walker looked at the two pictures side by side and frowned. There was no doubt, these two people were one and the same.

"Did you say Saturday?"

Walker turned to Kathy. "Yes, why?"

She turned to her husband, her hand squeezing his arm. "The phone call."

Walker glanced at Curtis who had stopped and turned to face the conversation. "What phone call?"

"Saturday afternoon I received a phone call. No one was there, but I just had a feeling it was Jackie. When I asked if it was her, they hung up."

"Was there a number on the call display?"

Kathy nodded, reaching over and grabbing the cordless phone from its cradle. She scrolled through the numbers and handed it to Walker. He dialed the number in his phone and waited. It rang once then picked up with a message from the phone company indicating the number was a phone booth and the call couldn't be completed.

He handed the phone back and turned to Curtis. "Phone booth." He stood up, ending the interrogation. It was clear what the next step was.

"What now?" asked Kathy.

"We'll try to track her down. If we find anything else out, we'll let you know."

"But if she's been out there all along, why hasn't she contacted us?"

"There's any number of reasons ma'am, and I wouldn't want to speculate." He headed for the door, Curtis already waiting. "And if you receive any more phone calls like the previous, call me." He handed them his card.

"There's something you're not telling us." Ronnie stood in the doorway, his arm around his wife. "What is it?"

"I can't say at this time."

"It's been two years. Please, we need to know." Tears welled up in his eyes. "That photo. It looked like she was in an interrogation room. She looked scared. She looked—" He paused. "She looked sad."

Kathy buried her head in her husband's chest, her body suddenly racked with sobs. Walker knew nothing he did or didn't tell them would help. And telling them their daughter might be involved in one or more murders, certainly wouldn't help.

"I'm sorry, sir, but I just can't say any more." Walker lowered his voice. "She's alive. That's the important thing. Now just give us time and we'll try to find her."

Ronnie nodded, and turned back into the apartment, his wife still sobbing into his chest. The door closed and Walker turned to Curtis.

"Glad that's over."

"Uh huh."

"Notice anything unusual?"

"No, none of the usual slip-ups evident. Photos all seemed to predate the disappearance, no mail lying around, no birthday or Christmas cards to Mom or Dad."

"Yeah, they seemed genuinely upset. I think they truly were shocked their daughter is alive."

"What now?"

"I'll let Shake 'n Trace know about the ID, and then we need to see if there're any surveillance cameras on that phone booth."

"Shake 'n Trace. I like that."

"They won't."

"That's why I like it."

Frank paid the cabby and climbed out, looking about. Pedestrian traffic was light, so were the cars. In any other city at this time of night the streets might have been deserted. But not New York. Its citizens might sleep, but the city certainly never did. Yes, there were still revelers on the streets, walking one off, but the bustle was from the businesses. Deliveries were made, garbage hauled away, cleaners swept and polished, laundry services picked up and delivered, while machines swept streets and vacuumed sidewalks, erasing the previous day's grime away. All while the majority of the city slept, and while the notorious New York traffic slept as well. Deliveries during the day were almost impossible. Overnight was the time to do it.

But Frank noticed none of it, the activity occupying the periphery. His eyes scanned everything, looking for a clue as to what he should do next. For the past hour he had been sent instructions with new addresses to go to, and each time he had arrived, he had ended up hailing another cab as the next set arrived. He had realized if anyone wanted to trace him through the cab companies, they'd have one hell of a time. Which was why he had started to use his credit card on the last several pickups. When it had occurred to him, he had stuffed his cash into his sock, just in case whoever he was going to meet might check his wallet. He'd at least then have an excuse for using the credit card instead of cash, and might survive that part of their encounter. But would Shakespeare think to check his credit cards?

Of course he would.

Frank knew Shakespeare's reputation, both new and old, and he was relying on his old reputation, the one where he was considered the best damned detective in the Bureau. His phone vibrated with another message.

TICK TOCK
LITTLE TIME ON THE CLOCK

IF YOU WANT TO SEE YOUR FRIEND
FOLLOW THE MAP TO THE END

Another vibration and a set of GPS coordinates arrived. He input them into his phone and soon had an address. Flagging a cab, he gave the cabby the address and sat back in the seat, his eyes heavy.

How much longer is he going to keep this up?

Jackie stood at the portal, awaiting her final instructions from her master. The sound of his voice still terrified her, but by obeying him since her death, recently she had been chosen from his minions to serve him, the opportunity providing a slight taste of the world she was once part of so long ago. In fact, until yesterday, she had no idea how long it had been since she had died and been punished for her sins.

Two years.

Two years since she had died. Two years of suffering in Hell. Two years before her master had granted her some slight reprieve, granted her the honor of serving him. And she was eternally grateful. To serve her master meant to be rewarded, and after two years of living in her own personal hell, the sounds of those around her and their suffering, the loneliness broken only by the occasional visitor that only seemed to add to her suffering, the rewards, no matter how small, how confusing, were to her a little taste of Heaven, a Heaven she knew she would never experience, her sins apparently too great.

Her suffering she could stand, but her poor parents, and what they must be going through. She knew the worst nightmare of any parent was outliving their child, and hers had been forced to live that nightmare. Which was why, after the police released her, she had done one thing, one thing her master had forbidden, but something she couldn't resist.

She had phoned home.

The sound of her mother's voice on the other end had been heartbreaking, especially as she couldn't answer her, she couldn't say anything, her master having told her they would be eternally damned if spoken to by someone from the other side. She had silently cried as her mother asked several times if anyone was there, then almost balled when she heard her mother ask, "Jackie, is that you?" She had immediately hung up and cried, her heart shattering all over again at the thought of the pain her parents had been suffering.

But would her master know? Was he all knowing, all seeing like God was supposed to be?

"Are you ready to serve your master again?"

His voice sent shivers down her spine, her heart slamming against her chest.

"Yes, my master." She waited. Would he say anything, would he know what she had done?

"You did well on your last task. Are you prepared for your next?"

"Yes, my master."

He didn't know!

"Very well, you may proceed."

"Thank you, my master."

She reached forward, shaking both from fear of displeasing her master by failing at the task at hand, but also from the excitement of knowing he hadn't caught her. She turned the handle and opened the portal, stepping inside.

"Greetings, Sarah Paxman. Are you prepared to serve your master?"

"What?"

Sarah lay stretched out along the wall farthest from the entrance, her head resting on the palm of her right hand. As the door opened, she immediately drew her legs up into a ball, attempting to preserve her modesty as best as possible. She sighed slightly as a young woman, about her age, stepped in, rather than a man. But she wasn't sure she had heard what she said. *Serve your master?*

The girl walked toward her, then sat down not five feet from where she was huddled in the corner. "I said, are you prepared to serve your master?"

This one was different. Her other visitors had never mentioned *him*. And what did she mean by 'serve'? "I don't know what you mean. Who are you?"

"Jackie."

"Yes, but *who* are you?"

The girl smiled. "I serve our master, and he has given me the task of offering you this opportunity to serve him."

She didn't like the sound of it. What could she possibly do for the devil? Whatever it was, it couldn't be good. And no matter how horrible a future, how horrible an eternity she was facing, she wouldn't do anything truly bad.

"Serve him in what way?"

The girl's head bobbed in approval, as if Sarah had already agreed to whatever it was she was about to ask.

"Very good." The girl leaned forward. "You have a friend."

Sarah somehow knew exactly who she was talking about.

"Yes."

"His name is Frank."

Oh, God, please let him be okay.

"Yes."

"He will be coming here shortly."

Her chest tightened and a pit formed in her stomach. "Wh-what do you mean?"

Jackie leaned back and frowned. "What do you think I mean? I mean he's about to die, and he's about to be delivered here."

"But he didn't do anything!"

Jackie grunted. "That's what I thought, yet"—she waved her hands at their prison—"here I am."

"Wh-what did you do to get here?"

"Nothing I thought was all that bad until I arrived here."

The room shook suddenly, and a roar filled the chamber. The girl in front of her yelped and covered her head, as if protecting herself from a pending assault. "I'm sorry, Master, I know I have sinned and deserve to be punished. I only meant I didn't know when I first arrived." The shaking subsided, and after a few moments, Jackie slowly uncovered her head, looking back at Sarah, tears streaking her face.

Sarah didn't say anything, too terrified herself to even move, her hands and feet having shoved her body tightly into the corner. But she felt sorry for the girl cowering in front of her. She reached out to touch her, but the girl scurried away. "No, no touching, no physical contact. It's forbidden."

Sarah nodded and withdrew her hand. "How will he die?"

Jackie shook her head. "I don't know. All I know is he will die, and he will be brought here."

Sarah's eyes filled with tears. *Poor Frank. He doesn't deserve this.* But then again, neither did she. She could never see herself believing the life she had led deserved this sort of punishment for eternity. Then again, she hadn't been here long, and clearly Jackie had felt the same way when she first arrived, but now seemed to be a servant to their keeper.

"Why are you telling me this?"

"Because my master wants to give you an opportunity to prove your loyalty to him."

"Why?"

"If you are loyal, if you can be trusted, then you can leave."

Sarah's heart leapt. *Leave?* That couldn't be right. Leave Hell? Leave eternal damnation? "Do you mean leave here"—she nodded at the walls surrounding them—"and go somewhere else, like Heaven?"

A roar of laughter filled the room, its volume vibrating through the floors and Sarah's bones. Jackie cowered again, awkwardly laughing as well. "No, don't be crazy. We're never going to Heaven."

"Then what do you mean?"

"I mean you can serve our master in our former world from time to time."

She felt a surge of excitement. A chance at seeing the world again, of seeing, hearing, smelling people, traffic, subways, life. She smiled slightly. "That would be nice." Then she frowned. "But what would I have to do?"

"Whatever he asks."

"What has he asked you?"

"Nothing much. Nothing bad like killing or hurting anyone. I'm not allowed to tell you what. But trust me"—she leaned in, lowering her voice—"it was worth it. Just to see the world again. After you've been here as long as I have, you'll do anything for that. I just wish I had been lucky enough to have had the opportunity as early as you."

Sarah thought about it. A chance to see the outside world. If it was something truly bad, she could refuse. But if it was something benign, then why not? She knew this place was probably filled with millions of people who would do whatever it was she'd be asked to do if she didn't, so what additional harm could she possibly be doing?

She nodded. "What do I have to do?"

"First, you have to prove your loyalty to our master."

"And how do I do that?"

"Easy. When your friend arrives, convince him of where he is."

Sarah felt a lump form in her throat. "You mean he's coming here? I mean, right here, in this room?"

"Yes."

"But why?"

Jackie waved her hands quickly, as if sweeping away the words. "Ours is not to question why."

Ours is but to do and die? A harrumph echoed in her mind. *I'm already dead.* "And why do I need to convince him he's dead? When I arrived he"—she pointed at the ceiling—"convinced me pretty quickly."

Jackie nodded. "Me too." She wiped her suddenly tear-filled eyes. "I guess this is a test. Master wants *you* to convince him."

"But how?"

"You need to convince him he's dead. Master said that when he arrives, he will try to convince you that both you and he are still alive, and try to take you through the portal. If you do—" She stopped.

"What?"

Jackie looked at her. "If you go through the portal without permission, you will be torn limb from limb, over and over, for eternity." Her voice cracked. "At least here there is no physical pain. I-I don't think I could take that."

Sarah shook her head. "But what if I can't convince him?"

"If he goes through the portal, he will suffer unbearable pain for eternity."

Bile filled her mouth as she pictured Frank in agony.

"But what if I can't?"

Jackie smiled, reaching behind her back. "If all else fails"—her hand came from behind her back and Sarah gasped—"you use this."

Sarah's eyes filled with tears as she shook her head. "No, no, I can't."

"You must."

Sarah continued to shake her head, but she knew the woman was right. *It's the only way.* A sense of calm swept over her. She had the power. The power to save him, to save the man she loved from an eternity of agony.

Aynslee watched as the new NYPD tech, Bryan, attacked the keyboard. It didn't take long before he had what he was looking for, but unlike Frank, he didn't seem willing to share anything. She watched, frustrated, as video after video displayed, each quickly replaced by the next, as he made notes on another screen, hiding them each time.

"Whoa."

She leaned in. "What?"

Bryan looked at her then back at the screen. "Umm, nothing."

"Come on, how about a little quid pro quo here? We're letting you use our equipment so you can bend a few rules and possibly save some lives. The least you can do is let me know what 'whoa' means."

Bryan frowned, then pointed at the screen. It appeared to be some sort of directory listing. "What about it?"

"We've been looking at files in this directory"—he pointed at one of the cryptically named folders—"all of which seem to be related to the case we're currently working on."

"And?"

"Woah!" This time it was Reggie.

"What?" Aynslee was getting frustrated.

Bryan pointed at the other directories. "I just managed to access the root of their system, something I don't think they expected us to be able to do." He pointed at a folder and clicked on it. "Some of these directories contain videos as well. He clicked on a file and it opened a video, showing what appeared to be the same long room Sarah was held in. But this time, it was definitely not Sarah. This one had a much slimmer, but still naked, woman.

"Oh my God, you mean there's more than one victim?"

Bryan nodded, closing the video and pointing at the directory listing. "And not only that, look at the date."

Aynslee leaned forward and gasped. "That's two years ago!"

"It gets worse." A few clicks and they were looking at the list of directories again, along with the dates they were created.

"Worse how?"

He pointed at the first directory.

"They go back ten years."

"Hey, Shakes, Walker here, I don't think we're going to get much until morning."

Shakespeare looked at his watch. 3 a.m. "Yeah, you're right. What's the status?"

"We've got calls into every voice mail in the area where we could see cameras that might have a shot of the phone booth, but almost nobody is open here."

"Okay, you two get some sleep then follow up in the morning. I think tomorrow is going to be non-stop craziness."

"Okay, Shakes, but remember, you need some sleep too."

Shakespeare yawned as if on cue. "Yeah, tell me about it. Okay, goodnight."

He ended the call as he pulled into the NYU Public Safety parking lot. It looked deserted. He turned off the engine and climbed out, shivering as the cool air snapped at his body. *They better be here.* He went up to the door and found it locked. To the right there was a buzzer. He pressed it. After a few moments, he heard a burst of static then a voice. "Security."

He leaned into the speaker. "NYPD, Detective Shakespeare, I'm expected."

"Come on in."

A buzzer sounded and he pushed the door open. He walked into the empty office, looking about, but found no one. Something tweaked in the back of his mind. The door. He turned around, not having heard the door close behind him, and found a young woman standing there, tears on her face.

"Are you okay?"

She nodded, then paused. Tears gushed and she shook her head. "No, I'm not okay."

Immediately Shakespeare assumed rape. It was a university campus after all. A young girl thinks she's going out with a nice guy, one thing leads to another, she thinks he'll listen when she says they've gone far enough, and testosterone combined with alcohol and a libido that demands to be talked about publicly with his friends, takes over. Minutes later it's rape, and she's usually too scared or embarrassed to come forward, blaming herself for putting herself in the situation.

He showed her his badge. "Maybe I can help. Did somebody hurt you?"

She shook her head. *Denial?*

"It's not me, it's my roommate. She's missing."

"Not you again!" Shakespeare spun toward the voice, finding a short, rotund woman glaring at the girl, her ruddy cheeks flaring even more. "I thought I told you there was nothing we could do before forty-eight hours?"

The girl nodded and turned toward the door. Shakespeare held up a finger. "Wait for me. I want to talk to you before you leave, but I need to talk to security first."

The girl's head bobbed up and down, a look of hope spreading across her face as her eyes opened wider and a slight smile tried to break through. She looked about and found a chair. Sitting down, she pulled her knees up and hugged them, her flip flop covered feet now on the seat.

"Detective Shakespeare? I'm Officer Stewart. Follow me." He followed the woman down the hall and into an enclosed office. She closed the door and waddled around her desk, dropping into the seat that creaked in protest. "That girl has been there all damned day. She won't go away."

"What's the story?"

"Claims her roommate went out to meet someone yesterday, never came back this morning. Happens a thousand times a week, but most don't bother phoning us for a couple of days. Usually ends up the roommate met a guy, or forgot to tell someone they were visiting the parents for the weekend. You know, innocent stuff."

"She seems pretty upset."

"They all do."

Shakespeare nodded. "I suppose." He clapped his hands against his legs. "So, what have you got for me?"

"What do you mean?"

Shakespeare frowned. "I called ahead about several students here?"

Stewart shrugged her shoulders. "Hey, I just got on shift. The outgoing shift said you were coming at some point tonight, that's all I got."

Shakespeare sighed. He hated dealing with amateurs. "Okay, I need everything you have on three students: Angela Henwood, Jackie St. Jean and Samantha Alders."

"Why?"

Shakespeare flushed with a burst of anger. "Because two are dead, and one is missing," he said curtly.

The woman bristled, leaning back in her chair, crossing her arms. "Have a warrant?"

Perhaps a little too curtly.

"There's no time for a warrant. We have a kidnap victim who we believe could be killed at any moment."

"That may be, but there are privacy laws that I can't just break. I could lose my job."

"She could lose her life!"

"I have three kids to feed. There's no way I'm putting my job at risk."

Shakespeare shook his head in frustration. "But I was talking to somebody earlier who said they'd give me the information. Scott Powell."

She shrugged her shoulders. "Well, his shift is over and now I'm the night supervisor, and no rules get broken on my watch."

Shakespeare sprang up, his heart pounding, face flushed. He leaned on her desk and glared at her. "If this kid dies because of your delay, it's on your conscience." He stood up and headed for the door. "And hug your kids as often as you can, lady, because someday, somebody might make the same decision you just did, and they may die."

He stormed from the office and down the hallway. He shoved the door and burst out into the cold of night, sucking in a lungful of the crisp air then slowly exhaled it. *I can't believe what just happened!* When a life is at stake, you bend the rules, break them if necessary. Who gets hurt by looking at the files of two dead girls and one missing girl?

"Excuse me, sir?"

Shakespeare spun on his heel to find the girl from earlier standing in the doorway, he having forgotten her. He took a deep breath. "Sorry, I forgot you were there."

"That's okay." She looked at him closely. "You don't look very happy."

Shakespeare waved his hand. "You have no idea."

"Does that mean you won't help me?"

Shakespeare shook his head. "No, no." He shivered. "But let's get in my car so I can warm up. I may have a built-in Arctic layer, but I still get cold."

She giggled and followed him to his Caddy. He held the door open for her, then he climbed in the driver's side, firing up the engine. Heat from the still warm engine began to fill the interior and Shakespeare sighed. He pulled out his notebook and turned to the young girl who had curled one leg up under her and now sat facing him.

"Give me a minute, I need to phone in for a warrant." A few minutes of details fed to the poor bastard on the nightshift at the DA's office had him a promise of a warrant in the morning, noon at the latest. *Believe it when I see it!* They were waiting on warrants for Tate's city and country homes, which he didn't expect to get, for permission to track Frank's phone, along with Frank's, Tate's and Sandy's phone records, video footage along where St. Jean may have made a phone call, cab company and masseuse company records just in case they weren't cooperative, and finally for permission to hack the webcam sites so anything they found at the television studio might in fact be admissible in court. And they were all coming, hopefully, this morning.

He turned his attention to the young girl beside him. "So, what can I do for you?"

"Can you help find my roommate?"

Shakespeare held up his hand. "First, what's your name?"

"Antoinette Ayers."

He smiled at her. "And I'm Detective Shakespeare. You're a student here?"

"Yes."

"And your roommate?"

"Yes, she's a med student and I'm drama."

"Med and drama. And you're roommates?"

She smiled slightly. "I know, odd couple, but it works out well. With her long hours, I get the apartment to myself and can practice."

"So you live off campus?"

"Yes."

He handed her the notebook and paper. "Please write down the complete address and your phone number." She quickly complied and handed him back the notebook. Shakespeare read the address. "Just off campus I see. And you think she's missing?"

"Yes. She went last night on a medical call, and said she'd be back in a couple of hours. That was over twenty-four hours ago."

"And you're aware that NYPD requires a person to be missing more than forty-eight hours before you can even file a report?"

"Yes, I called them first, but they wouldn't do anything. So I thought I'd try campus security instead, since she's a student here."

"And they told you the same thing."

She nodded.

"How do you know she didn't just meet up with some friends, or go visit her parents?"

"Well, this morning the hospital called where she does some of her training, looking for her."

Shakespeare frowned. He knew med students. They wouldn't miss a shift unless they were dead or dying. "And her name?"

"Alexa Ryan."

"Okay, I'll tell you what. I'll put the paperwork in today to speed up the process a bit."

Her eyes opened wide and she jumped across the seat, hugging him and sobbing. "Oh thank you, thank you, thank you!" she cried. "I've been so worried, especially with all the disappearances here lately."

Shakespeare pushed her away gently, still holding her by the shoulders as he looked directly into her eyes. "What do you mean, disappearances?"

"You mean you don't know?"

Shakespeare let go of her shoulders and shook his head. "No, enlighten me."

"Three students from my drama department are missing." She paused. "Well, one is officially missing, I guess, the other two I just assume are missing."

That makes four. Maybe this kid is just a little paranoid. "What makes you think that?"

"We had an important dress rehearsal for a play this morning and three people didn't show up."

"Hung over?"

She shook her head. "No way, this is the type of thing the Prof fails you for. Two were leads in the play, one was the set designer."

He returned to his pad, pen poised above the page. "And their names?"

"Ross Brennan, he's playing Romeo."

"As in Romeo and Juliet?"

Her head bobbed furiously. "Exactly, you see, he would never miss the rehearsal!"

"And the others?"

"Mrs. Bryant. She's actually a senior student, I mean, old, like you."

He raised his eyebrows and her hand darted to her mouth. "I'm sorry, I didn't mean to say you're old, I meant—"

He raised his hand, cutting her off. "Don't worry about it. I *am* old." *Especially compared to you.*

"And the set designer?"

"She I know has been missing since Friday afternoon because apparently she didn't show up to finish the set, so the others had to do the work and were complaining about it this morning."

"Her name?"

"Oh, sorry. Angela Henwood."

ELEVEN

Frank watched the cab pull away into the empty street. This was the warehouse district. There wasn't going to be any more cabs to hail if he was sent to another location. He looked at his phone's GPS. He wasn't at the coordinates, but he was close. He began to walk toward the location indicated on his screen, and soon found himself standing in front of one of the warehouses. Large freight doors spread to his left, and to his right, one normal sized one with a small glass window in the top half crisscrossed with embedded steel mesh, its glass covered from the inside, blocking the view. His phone vibrated.

TICK TOCK
LITTLE TIME ON THE CLOCK
OPEN THE DOOR
THEN LIE ON THE FLOOR

He debated risking a text message to Shakespeare, but his instructions sent a few minutes after the initial message were crystal clear. No contact with anyone. And they'd know if he tried. He had had a lot of time to think about that part. How would they know? There was the possibility he was being followed, but he hadn't noticed anything, and there certainly weren't any vehicles in sight now. He had settled on his phone being hacked. When he was drugged, there would have been plenty of time to plant a piece of software on his phone that could send copies of his text messages to another number, could track his GPS location, could even allow them to listen in on his conversations. For Sarah's sake he hadn't risked it. And for the same reason, he decided not to test his theory now.

He grasped the handle in front of him and turned the knob. Pulling on the door, it opened silently. He took a tentative step inside, but could see nothing but an inky blackness. Not even a ray of light from the street lamps, or the constant glow of light pollution from the huge city, broke the solid sheet of nothingness in front of him. He stepped inside further, the door closing behind him, the quiet hiss of a hydraulic door closer doing its job. Now he was completely enveloped in the black soup.

He listened. There was nothing. Not even a drip of water, the scurry of a rat, the creak of a chain. Nothing.

The snap of something hard tapping on concrete sounded in front of him, followed by another, then another. *Footsteps!* As they neared, his heart raced, his chest tightened, and his ears roared in fear. He was unarmed. He didn't have a vest. He was alone. And no one knew where he was. *What was I thinking?* The door was right behind him, only a few steps away. He could find it in the dark, he was sure of it. He took a step backward, but it didn't help. The terror still gripped him, and the steady, rhythmic steps continued to get closer. *How can she see me?* And he twigged. *She!* It was high heeled shoes he was hearing. Not a man's steps, but a woman's. *A woman is doing this?* It made no sense. He knew enough to know female serial killers were rare. But did she think she could take him by herself? If she was armed, he might have no choice. But what if he jumped her? Maybe he could take her by surprise, then he might be able to save Sarah.

The steps stopped. It seemed like she was only feet away. If he reached out, he was sure he would touch her. He reached for his phone in his pocket and raised it in front of him. He swiped his finger across the screen, lighting up the area in front of him.

He gasped. "How can you be here?"

She smiled then he felt someone grab him from behind as the woman in front of him, a woman who couldn't possibly be there, stepped forward, disappearing once again in the dark as his phone clattered to the floor. A foul order filled his nostrils as whoever had him from behind held a cloth over his face. He reached to grab the hands but he felt his legs kicked out from under him as the person behind lowered him slowly to the ground, his hands instinctively grasping for the floor he slowly dropped to. By the time he was lowered, he felt someone's knees drop on his shoulders as whatever was held over his mouth started to take effect. As he drifted off, one thought consumed him.

How can she *possibly be here?*

"Do you have her password?"

Antoinette shook her head. "Sorry, no. But she said she got an email giving her the details."

Shakespeare looked around the small apartment, a single common area including kitchenette, with one bathroom but two separate bedrooms. He found it interesting the drama student's room was the neat one; the med student's strewn with clothes and piled high with books and papers. He waved his hand at Alexa's room. "Is this normal?"

Antoinette giggled. "This is actually pretty good."

Shakespeare's eyebrows shot up. "And she's going to be a surgeon?"

Antoinette giggled again. "I know, crazy, huh? I keep telling her if she can't keep her bedroom tidy there's no way I'm ever going to let her operate on me.

Shakespeare nodded. *She's liable to leave the scalpel inside. Or worse.*

"And she told you nothing about where she was going?"

"No, just that she'd be picked up somewhere and taken to the location."

"Picked up?"

"I think that's what she said, but I might be confused. I'm really not thinking straight."

"So then even if we get the email, it may only tell us where she was picked up, not where she was going."

Antoinette's face sank. "I never thought of that."

"Does she have a cellphone?"

Antoinette nodded and gave the number to Shakespeare who jotted it down in his notebook. He flipped it closed and headed for the door. "Here's what's going to happen. I'm going to have somebody come by in the next little while to take her computer. We'll see what we can find off of it. You go about your normal daily routine, and if you hear anything, you call me right away at the number I gave you."

She nodded. "Shouldn't I stay here?"

Shakespeare shook his head. "No, just get some sleep now, and in the morning if she's not back, leave her a note, telling her to call you right away, and leave my number. Make sure you tell her the police are involved, or she might not take you seriously and just go to bed first." He put his hand on her shoulder. "We'll do everything we can to find her, okay?"

She gave a weak smile then leaned in and gave him a quick hug. "Thanks, Detective." Shakespeare patted her back and she pulled away.

He opened the door and stepped into the hallway. "You try to get some sleep now. And don't forget, someone will be by to get the computer within the next few hours."

"Okay, good night."

"Good night."

Shakespeare headed for his car, his stomach rumbling. He felt a little woozy and could sense that telltale sign his blood sugar was dropping. *Better get some food.* He climbed in the car, phoned in the computer pickup, then headed off campus, quickly finding an all-night diner. He opted for the three-egg breakfast special since it was so close to morning, then began sending text messages. It had taken him years to embrace the technology, but once he had, he realized how convenient it was. He had tried one of those fancy iPhones but his thumbs just couldn't type on it, so he had remained with the full keyboard of the Blackberry. He sent instructions for Vinny to pick up Alexa's computer, Trace to go to sleep if she wasn't already, and a message to Louise to tell her he was alright, and to apologize for worrying her. And for probably waking her with his text.

He polished his plate and returned to his car, then drove to the NYU Medical campus parking lot. Parking as far from the entrance as he could, he set the alarm on his watch, put the seat back, and within minutes was sound asleep.

Trace pulled her car to a stop, looking at the deserted street. *I definitely should be calling for backup.* She debated for a moment, then grabbed her phone and requested silent backup—the last thing she needed were lights and sirens here, she just wanted a couple of uniforms to watch her back.

She looked at the warehouse. *Could this be it?* She hadn't waited for the warrant. She had some good connections with the cab companies, one of whom happened to be working the night shift, and they were generally cooperative as long as they knew the warrant was going to be arriving shortly. It didn't take long to find the cab that had picked up Frank, it the only pickup in front of the studio within half an hour of when he left. The drop off was on Seventh. The cabby was still on duty and she had had a chance to talk to him, confirming as she had suspected that Frank had said nothing beyond his destination, and had paid in cash. The key tidbit was mentioned as an afterthought by the cabby that just may be the break they needed. When he had left Frank on the curb, he had carried on down Seventh, picked up a fare, and in his rear view mirror had seen Frank hail another cab. He had thought it odd at the time, which was why he had remembered it. This cab too was traced, and this time Frank had used his credit card. Several more pickups were traced to the same credit card, and half an hour later they had a final destination.

And now she waited.

She knew Shakes had told her to get some sleep while waiting for the warrant, but she had so much coffee and adrenaline flowing through her system, there was no way she was going to sleep. She eyed the coffee sitting in the cup holder and shook her head. She needed to lay off for an hour or two, then she'd crash hard and get the rack time she needed. *Unless I find the kid's body in there.* She said a silent prayer, then opened her door as she saw a blue and white turn the corner behind her.

The patrol car turned off its headlights as it approached and pulled in behind her. The two officers climbed out, quietly closing their doors, and approached Trace. She flashed her badge. "Detective Trace, Homicide."

The driver nodded. "Richards and Scaramell."

"Thanks for coming. We think one of our techs might be in trouble, and we've traced his last location to this building"—she tossed a thumb over her shoulder at the warehouse—"almost two hours ago."

"Who's the tech?" asked Scaramell.

"Frank Brata."

"Really! I drove him to the lab yesterday, or Saturday I guess." Scaramell looked at his watch. "Christ, I hate third watch."

Trace nodded. "I've been up almost twenty-four hours. Let's go before I fall asleep." They fell silent as they approached the door. Trace looked through the window but could see nothing, it apparently blacked out from inside. She put her hand on the knob, and made eye contact with each of the officers. They both nodded, their guns drawn. One stood directly behind her, the other next to her at the door.

She turned the knob and yanked the door open, bursting into a jet black, empty space, yelling, "NYPD, nobody move!"

Her voice echoed into the darkness. Two beams of light cut through the black as the two officers turned on their flashlights. She turned to the officer on her left. "Can I borrow that?"

He flipped the flashlight over and handed it to her. She played it across the wall, and quickly found a panel of switches. She walked over and began flipping them, the sound of halogen lights firing up, and with a flicker, the entrance was flooded with light. She flipped the remaining switches as fast as she could, now that anyone in the warehouse had a clear shot at them.

In seconds the warehouse was flooded with light. And empty.

"Well, this was a bust."

"Look!"

Trace looked to where Richards was pointing. She stepped over to a broken cell phone lying near the entrance. She pulled a pair of latex gloves from her pocket and carefully picked up the phone. The display was cracked, and when she tried to activate it, nothing happened.

"This was a *real* bust. Wait." She pointed to the floor near where they had found the phone. "Looks like some foot prints." She pointed at another set of drag marks, leading from the door and further down toward one of the large doors. "Looks like someone was dragged here."

Richards walked over to the door and knelt down. "Tire treads. A car was here recently."

Trace followed the trail ending near the rearmost tire marks. "Looks like he was loaded into the trunk." She snapped a photo of the tread marks and emailed them to Vinny. He might be able to figure out what type of vehicle left them. Within moments her phone vibrated with a reply from Vinny. *Get me a measurement of how far apart the treads are.* She turned to Richards. "Can you get me a measurement from tread to tread?"

"I've got a tape in the car I think. I'll check."

Within minutes they had a measurement and she sent it to Vinny. His reply indicated he was on his way to the lab.

She turned to Richards. "Okay, secure the scene, I'll have the crime scene guys come over and see if they can find anything else."

She headed for the door, now even more worried about Frank.

I hope the kid is okay.

She made a quick call to the Bureau and was pleased when Harold Nonkoh, a new and eager detective, answered. His determination to prove himself, and get off the nightshift, meant he would most likely track down any information she needed far faster than anyone else that may have picked up. In fact, he probably leapt for the phone while the others stared at the case board to see who was next in the rotation.

"Hey, Harold, this is Trace, I need a favor."

"Sure, what can I do ya for?"

"I need you to run an address for me. Get me the usual, who owns it, who rents it, any history. You know the drill."

"No problem. What's the address?"

She read the address off her pad. "Got it?"

"Yup."

"Okay, this is urgent. One of our techs is missing, last seen here."

"Holy shit! Okay, I'll get back to you as soon as I can."

"Thanks, Harold, you're the best."

"Tell my wife that. She seems to think that the nightshift means I'm an idiot."

Trace chuckled. "She'll say a lot worse if she hears it coming from me."

"Too true," he laughed. "I'll get back to you shortly."

Trace ended the call and sat in her car, waiting for the crime scene guys to arrive. She closed her eyes and leaned her head back, the caffeine and adrenaline wearing off as she crashed into the oblivion of sleep.

Aynslee moaned as Eldridge kissed her neck, his tongue flicking her gently, his hot breath sending surges of pleasure through her body. She had waited so long, and at last he was here, with her, in her bed, their bodies intertwined as they explored each other, their passion and intensity growing ever more fervent with each passing moment, with each new caress. He squeezed her breast and she moaned again. With a shove she pushed him on his back and stared at him playfully, a sly smile spreading on her face as she held his arms over his head, straddling him. She began to kiss down his neck, then his chest, his moans of anticipation becoming louder and louder.

"Oh, Aynslee."

She smiled as she kissed his washboard abs, continuing to move lower.

"Oooh, *Ayn*slee!"

She stopped. *Something's wrong.* She looked up Eldridge's chest and saw Reggie smiling back at her. "Oooh, *Ayn*slee, wake up!"

Suddenly reality roared into focus as she woke. She opened her eyes and saw Reggie looking down at her, a shit-eating grin spread across his pimply face. "What were *you* dreaming about?" he asked, his tone suggesting he knew damned well it wasn't about sunshine and lollipops. *Well, maybe lollipops.* She smiled to herself, then remembered who she had been dreaming about, and a cloud replaced her good mood. She looked at Reggie who was still leaning over her, entirely too close. She waved him away as she sat up on the couch in her office.

"What is it?"

"Bryan found something *big*!" His emphasis on big shot her eyebrows up.

"Big?"

He waved to her. "Come on, you've gotta see this."

She stood up, straightened out her clothes and gave her hair a shake, then followed Reggie to the computer room. He opened the door and she found Bryan on the phone.

"Yes, files going back ten years. They look like notes on experiments. Very detailed. They almost read like notes a shrink might make. I don't know, this isn't my area, but this is some weird shit."

He paused a moment as he listened to the other end of the line and nodded. "I've copied everything already and uploaded it to the lab's secure storage. You should be able to look at it now. There's a lot of stuff there including extensive video archives. I've just glanced at some of the stuff, but it looks like some sick shit. People imprisoned for extended periods. You have to look at this. It's going to take weeks to go through, if not months. There's years' worth of stuff here." Again he paused. "Four seem to still be active." He nodded again. "Okay, I'll head back to the lab now." He hung up the phone and started packing up the gear Frank brought earlier.

"What's going on?"

"I'm done here."

"Yes, but what did you find? Reggie said you found something big?"

Bryan paused and stared at the floor, as if debating what to say. "Listen, I'll tell you this much. I found files that looked like case studies, going back ten years, looks like about one a year. Four of those file sets are still active."

"What do you mean?"

"I mean, there are four sets of files still being updated on a regular basis."

"You mean—"

"That it looks like four people are still being held captive, including Sarah."

Aynslee stood for a moment as her mind processed this information. "Was there any clue on where they're being held?"

Bryan shook his head. "They all seemed to be in the same type of room as Sarah was in. Is in."

"What about in the case studies? Any addresses?"

Bryan packed up the last of the equipment. "Look, I just quickly scanned a couple. My job was to pull the data while it was available, before they discovered the breach. We were never supposed to see these files, just the files for Sarah. They didn't count on Frank. He's brilliant. Nothing is going to keep him out of a system he wants to get into." He hooked the straps for the equipment over his neck, balancing two large cases over each shoulder, then grabbed two more with his hands and stepped toward the door.

"Do you want a hand with that?" asked Aynslee, trying to figure out a way to stall him.

Bryan shook his head. "No, I'll manage." He headed out the door, then turned toward Reggie. "Oh, umm, just so you know, I noticed the key logger you guys are using." He stared directly at Reggie for a moment, as if trying to telepathically send him a message. Aynslee looked at Reggie's void expression, the brain waves apparently deflecting off the blank slate. Then his eyes shot open and his head bobbed excitedly, a smile spreading on his face.

Bryan headed to the elevators as Aynslee looked at Reggie. "What was that all about?"

Reggie beckoned her back into the office, closed the door then sat at the computer, furiously typing away. Within moments he had a file open and pointed. "We have key logger software on these machines for security purposes."

"And just what exactly is that?"

"Every keystroke is recorded."

"Meaning?"

"Meaning, I have all the website addresses, user IDs and passwords that they were able to hack."

Aynslee plopped down into the chair, a smile on her face. She pulled the chair closer to the computer screen as Reggie began to work his magic.

Thank you, Bryan!

Trace woke, her phone demanding attention on the passenger seat. She grabbed it and pressed the keypad, holding it up to her ear. "Trace."

"It's Vinny, did I wake you?"

She stretched one arm out to her side and arched her back. "Yeah, I was just crashing here at the scene while I wait for your boys to arrive." She looked out her windshield and noticed the Crime Scene truck parked in front of her. "Oh, looks like they're here already." She looked at her watch. "Christ, I've been asleep two hours!"

"It's been a long damned weekend, and it's not over yet." She heard him take a deep breath, ending in a yawn. "Okay, here's what we've got. Your vehicle is a 2011 Cadillac Escalade. Which of the several thousand in the city is yours, I have no clue."

"Okay, at least it narrows it down. Hopefully we'll come up with something else that will lead us to where it was going."

"Hopefully. If he or they have Frank, I—" Vinny stopped. And Trace knew why. Another death in the family was something none of them could take right now. And if they were to believe the last message, Sarah would die alongside Frank, making it three deaths in less than two weeks.

A thought popped into Trace's head. "Crazy question, Vinny, but is the Escalade lojacked?"

She heard Vinny suck in a quick lungful of air. "I think they are!" She heard him type furiously at his keyboard. "Yes, it was an option. If we can find out which Escalade it is, and they have the option, we can track it!"

Trace closed her eyes and let her head drop against the headrest. "So we might still have a chance." Her phone beeped. She glanced at the call display and saw it was from Nonkoh. "Got another call coming in that I have to take."

"Okay, I'll update Shakes on where we're at."

"10-4." She hit the button to take the other call. "Trace."

"Hey, there, it's Harold, I've got some info for you."

Trace retrieved her notebook and paper. "Shoot."

"Okay, the warehouse you're at is owned by some company called Abaddon Incorporated."

"Never heard of it."

"Me neither. I Googled it and found lots of video game references on the web, but no companies."

"So a shell."

"Most likely."

"What address are they registered at?"

"You'll love this." He paused, most likely for effect. "Look to your right."

"Huh?"

Nonkoh laughed. "It's one door down. They own the warehouse right beside the one you're in now."

"You're shittin' me!"

"Nope. I'm running a trace to see if they own anything else, buildings, businesses, you know, the usual. I'm also trying to find out who the principals are behind the business. Hopefully have more soon."

"Okay, thanks for the update. I'm going to check out next door."

She jumped from the car, waved at Richards and Scaramell, who were sitting on the hood of their cruiser, sipping from steaming thermoses. "Let's go!" They capped and tossed their thermoses in their car and trotted over to join her as she strode quickly toward the warehouse less than one hundred yards away. "Just found out that the owners of that warehouse"—she jerked her thumb at the crime scene—"is owned by the same company that owns this next one."

They approached the door and drew their weapons. She listened for a moment, then knocked on the door. Nothing. She tried the handle but it was locked. Looking at her watch, she growled. She knew it would take hours to get a warrant, and Frank might not have hours. *Time to take a page from the Book of Shakespeare.* "Did you hear that?" she asked, cocking an ear and looking at Richards.

He nodded. "Sounded like someone calling for help."

Scaramell leaned in closer and put his ear to the door. "Sounds like people crying and screaming."

Richards raised his eyebrows at the rookie. "No need to get that specific. Keep it simple in case you're questioned."

Scaramell shook his head. "No, I'm serious. Listen."

Trace and Richards both put their ears against the door. Scaramell was right, she could hear something on the other side. And it didn't sound good. She stepped away from the door. "Exigent circumstances."

Scaramell positioned himself in front of the door, and with a deep breath and a lunge, he kicked at the door near the lock. It groaned, but didn't break. Scaramell jumped back, shaking his leg. "Fuck me, that hurts!"

Richards chuckled. "That only works in the movies, rookie. I'll get the ram for this *metal* door frame."

Trace watched as Scaramell shook off the shock to his joints. "Don't worry about it, Hollywood makes it look so easy. Christ, they've got dainty little actresses tossing two hundred pound men around like they were bags of feathers."

Scaramell chuckled. "Yeah, but did I have to learn that lesson in front of my Training Officer?"

Trace smiled. "We all fuck up in front of our TO. That's why it's sometimes fun to be a TO." She pointed at the door. "Look, hinge side, you've got at least two, usually three, and sometimes four hinges, each providing support." She pointed at the handle side. Only one point of support, maybe two, close together, unless they've got top and bottom locks, then you'll probably need a ram." She pointed at the plate surrounding the handle. "Kick here, full force, and on most doors you'll be dealing with like apartment doors, the wood on the other side of the door frame will shatter, since it's weak from being bored out for the locking mechanism. Usually one good kick will get it open. Use the ram if you need to be sure you get in on the first try, and to get out of the way if tactical or your partner needs to get in right away. If you're there, off balance and in his way, you lose vital seconds."

Scaramell nodded. "Makes sense. And since this has a metal frame, kicking it won't shatter the wood since there's no wood."

Trace slapped him on the back. "You got it. We need to use blunt, possibly repeated force, to try and bend this damned thing open. We're just lucky it opens inward. If it opened outward, even if wood, it can be a challenge."

Richards returned with the ram. Scaramell grabbed one side, Richards the other, and on a three count, sent the ram sailing into the door. It shuddered, but didn't open. The next swing showed clear evidence of a gap forming, and on the third swing, it tore open, the ram pulling the officers slightly inside as its momentum continued with the door. They quickly stepped back and tossed the ram behind them and drew their weapons and flashlights. Richards led the way, followed by Trace then Scaramell. Inside it was almost completely dark except for an odd orange glow deeper inside that cast long, faint shadows toward them. The screams and cries they heard earlier echoed through the darkness. Trace immediately went to the right of the door, feeling for the lighting panel, hoping for it to be in the same place as the other warehouse, their designs looking identical. She smiled when she felt the familiar switches, and began flipping them.

The clunk of industrial lighting echoed through the warehouse, accompanied by flickers as the halogen heated up, throwing a white glow over what was definitely not an empty building like its twin next door. In the center of the large open space stood three shipping containers, lined up side by side. They could only see the backs of the farthest two, but the nearest caused Trace to pause. The container was lined up with its partners, however had what looked like some sort of heating unit above it, attached to what looked like might be a stage lighting kit hanging from the ceiling, speakers, lights and the heating elements all attached. The doors of the container, facing the back of the warehouse, were open, and some sort of long, framed walkway, covered on all sides in black, led to the very back of the warehouse, joined to the wall there.

"What the hell is that?"

Richards shrugged his shoulders. "I have no freakin' clue."

Scaramell pointed near the far wall. "Is that a door?"

The three cautiously approached the far wall where the enclosed structure ended. Trace opened the door, the other two covering her. The light from the warehouse poured inside, confirming a walkway, or hallway, leading from the container to a door to the outside, painted black itself.

"Look," said Richards, pointing at the interior side of the door Trace had just opened. "No handle."

Trace frowned then pointed at Scaramell. "You stay here and watch our backs."

He nodded as Richards took up a position behind Trace. They stepped inside, and Trace opened the other door, revealing the back of the building and a large paved area shared with other warehouses. She tried the handle on the outside. "Locked."

"Must need a key to get in," said Richards.

"But not to get out." She shook her head. "That doesn't make sense. Look at this place. This has to be some sort of prison. The video footage showed them in long rooms. Those could be these shipping containers."

"What video footage?"

Trace remembered the uniforms weren't in on the details, and had no time to bring them up to date. "Never mind, no time." She looked at Scaramell. "Give me your flashlight."

He handed it over and she flicked it on, walking deeper into the walkway, Richards several paces behind her. She touched the walls. It felt like stucco. Rough stucco. She shone her light on it, then tapped.

"Sounds like just straight framing and drywall," said Richards.

Trace nodded. "Yeah, and this stucco is so rough, you wouldn't want to bump into it in the dark, it's liable to scrape you."

The sounds of the people crying and wailing was getting louder. And it was getting hotter. She could see the end of the hall only yards away. The floor ramped up, and the walls opened to attach to the frame of the container, giving it an eerie, unsettling openness that if it weren't for the flashlights, she might find disconcerting. She could only imagine walking along this corridor, in the pitch black, with the screams and heat, how horrifying that must be.

Did anybody walk this? What was the purpose?

They stepped into the back of the container, the walls of it framed and drywalled as well, the rough stucco and black paint continuing. But directly in front of them was a door with a simple, brass knob. Trace reached out to open it, when Richards stopped her. "Better let me. We don't know what's on the other side of this."

Trace nodded and stepped back, painfully aware she had neglected to put her vest on. Richards grabbed the knob and pulled the door open, his weapon pointing straight ahead. A dim glow greeted them, and Richards stepped inside, followed by Trace.

A gunshot cut through the screams and Richards dropped. Trace dove to the side and rolled as a second shot rang out. She took aim and fired twice, directly in the chest. The shooter, standing at the far end of the room, collapsed. Trace climbed to her feet and rushed over, kicking the gun away from the body. She spun as she heard footsteps racing toward them. Scaramell burst into the room. Trace pointed at Richards.

"Check on him and call for a bus!"

She turned to the body lying in front of her. It was a woman, naked. She rolled the body over to see the face and gasped. Lying in front of her, with two bullet holes to her bare chest, was Jackie St. Jean. She was still alive, her eyes barely able to focus on Trace, but her life was quickly slipping away. She whispered something and Trace leaned in.

"What did you say?"

"Don't worry."

"About what?"

"There is no death here. No escape. I will be reborn."

Trace had no idea what she was talking about, but knew she only had moments. "Where is Frank Brata?"

"He's already here."

Trace spun her head in both directions, confirming what she already knew—they were alone.

"What do you mean? There's no one else here. Do you mean he's in another one of the shipping containers?"

The girl looked confused. "Wh-what do you mean?"

"You've been held prisoner. You were kidnapped two years ago and held here."

She shook her head. "No, you're wrong. I died two years ago. This is my punishment."

It was Trace's turn to look confused. "Listen, it's not too late. You can help save Frank. Just tell me where he is."

"He's already here," she repeated. "And so are you, you just don't know it yet."

Trace shook her head. "What do you mean?"

"You crossed the portal." St. Jean squeezed her hand. "Don't worry, your new master will explain everything." She sighed, and her eyes slowly closed, her chest falling one last time.

Trace turned to check on Richards. "How is he?"

Richards coughed. "I'll be fine. She caught me in the vest."

Trace looked about. The chamber was long and narrow, just like in the video footage forwarded to her phone. The heat was almost unbearable. A dim, flickering orange glow emanated from around the edges of the ceiling, and the cries they heard outside could be heard inside. She thought about what St. Jean had said when it finally clicked.

"Holy shit!"

"What?" asked a still struggling Richards.

"I know where we are!"

"Where?"

"Hell."

TWELVE

Reggie pulled the fourth report off the printer and stapled it together. Grabbing the other three, he rushed to Aynslee's office, the drumbeat of his heart exciting him with the prospect of pleasing her, of working with her as an equal, instead of a lowly tech fixing her computer, a mere tool for her brilliant mind. Her brilliant, beautiful mind. He sighed and closed his eyes slightly, staring at the ceiling, a dream state taking over.

He tripped over his shoes.

The packages of papers flew out of his hands as he reached to break his fall. He hit with a thud but quickly sprang to his feet, looking around to see if anyone had witnessed his embarrassment. He was alone, everyone else either not in yet, or their heads buried behind the dull blue cubicle walls. He picked up the four packages, and continued to Aynslee's office, remembering to keep his eyes on where he was going, his mother's voice echoing in his head. *Terry, darling, you've got brains, but absolutely no coordination.* She was right. But what he really needed was to coordinate his way out of the same bedroom he had been in since he was born, and into an apartment of his own. How would he ever hope to get a girl as incredible as Aynslee, if he lived with his parents? A lovely, romantic evening out, she hints at more to come, a quick drive home, and then what? *Shhhh, you'll wake my mom?*

He arrived at her office door and found it slightly ajar. He pushed his head in and found her once again asleep on the couch, the morning rays of the sun shining through the window and landing on her face, her dark brown hair glowing. Her brief blonde experiment he had to admit looked hot, but her natural hair looked beautiful, radiant. He stood there for several minutes, staring at her, at her gorgeous face, hands, feet. At how cute she looked, her hands tucked under her head, her knees curled up into a fetal position, how her chest ebbed and flowed with each breath.

He stared at her chest.

Then blushed and turned away. *What are you doing?* He cleared his throat. "Ummm, Aynslee?"

She stirred slightly.

"Aynslee, I have those reports."

This time she did wake, her eyes fluttering open like rose petals, her hand rising to shield her eyes from the sunlight. "What was that?"

"I have the reports. I was able to print them, for the four active files."

She swung her silky smooth legs off the couch and tucked her dainty feet into a pair of high heels sitting neatly on the floor, then stood. She took the files from him and sat behind her desk, rubbing the sleep out of her eyes. She retrieved a mirror from her drawer and checked her hair and makeup. He wanted to tell her out loud, but he stopped. *There's no need to check. You're beautiful. You're perfect. You're everything any man could ever want.* He felt almost sick to his stomach, his chest tight, his palms sweating profusely. She was his dream. And he knew that was all she would ever be. A dream. Impossibly out of his league. Impossibly out of reach. *I'm such a loser.* Tears welled in his eyes and he quickly tried to blink them away, turning his head away from her.

He felt a hand on his shoulder. "Reggie, what's wrong?"

It was her, her voice gentle, as if she actually cared. He felt worse.

"N-nothing, just tired I guess. Thinking of those people on the videos."

She squeezed his shoulder gently. It felt electric. It was a feeling he hoped he would never forget. He wanted to reach up and place his hand on hers. His sweaty, sticky hand.

"I understand. It can be quite upsetting to see others suffer." She let go of his shoulder, her hand taking a little part of his heart away with it. "Which one is Sarah's?"

This caught him off guard. "Huh?"

"Which one is Sarah's? There's no names on these, just notes and the address."

He pointed to the top printout. "It's that one, the first I printed off." A slight smear of sweat remained when he removed his finger. He resolved to start using his Drysol regularly, it being the only thing that had ever worked to stop the sweating.

Aynslee nodded and grabbed her jacket and purse. She gave him a pat on the arm and smiled. "Thanks, Reggie, for pulling this for me. I know you didn't have to."

He blushed. "Anything for you, Aynslee."

She smiled. "Call Mike and Steve and tell them to meet me at this address," she said, shaking the file. She strode from the office and he stepped out into the hallway, watching her head for the elevators, the sway of her hips and the billowing of her long hair almost making him forget his task. He returned to the lab, retrieved the address from Sarah's file, looked up Mike's number, and phoned him.

Finished, he leaned back in his chair and relived the few minutes in her office. He could still feel her hand on his shoulder, on his arm. Her voice, caring, soothing. Almost as if he mattered to her. He sat in the chair in the lab, staring at the ceiling and spinning in place, his fingers interlaced across his chest, his eyes half closed and an ear-to-ear smile stretched across his face. How long he sat there, spinning a fantasy love tale, he didn't know. His mind replayed their conversation over and over, her tone, her caresses, her question about the file.

And then it hit him and his foot fell, stopping the spin.

He had dropped the papers. When he left his office, the file on top was Sarah's. But when he picked them up, what order were they in?

And where was she now going?

Alone.

Trace sat in the passenger seat of her car, feet on the ground, leaning over with her elbows on her knees, sipping a bottle of water. This was her first shooting, and she didn't know how she felt. It was a righteous shoot, of that there was no doubt—the suspect had shot one officer and was trying to shoot her. She did the right thing. And she'd do it again. *But she was just a kid!* She felt a tightness in her chest and tears well up in her eyes. *No! This was not your fault!* She took a deep, slow breath in through her nose, filling her chest and abdomen with the brisk morning air, then slowly let it out her mouth, her lips pursed, and wiped the tears away with the back of her hand.

"You okay?"

She looked at the shoes as they walked up to her then raised her head. "Yeah, LT. Just getting used to the idea."

He nodded and squatted in front of her. "I remember my first shoot. Nasty son of a bitch that deserved every one of the four bullets I put in him. But when I saw him just lying there, the adrenaline rush over, I went out to my squad car and balled my eyes out for twenty minutes."

Trace smiled through half her mouth, trying to imagine the tough as nails LT blubbering. "Can't picture it, LT."

He chuckled. "Well, let me tell you something I've learned over almost thirty years as a cop. Everyone reacts differently to their first shoot. And no one ever feels good about it, whether it's their first or tenth. You just learn how to deal with it. You learn that it wasn't your fault, you were doing your job." He stood up, groaning. "I'm too old for this squatting shit." She stood up and he put a hand on her shoulder, looking her directly in her eyes. "This was a clean shoot. You've got nothing to worry about from IAD."

She nodded and unholstered her weapon. Removing the clip, she cleared the chamber, then handed it to him. He took the gun and clip without saying anything, just placing them in an evidence bag he retrieved from his pocket. Her phone vibrated on her hip. She looked at the call display then at the LT. "I better take this." He nodded as she answered.

"Hey, Walker, you're up early."

"And you're up late, if I'm not mistaken."

Lieutenant Phillips gave her another pat on the shoulder and strode toward an unmarked unit that had just arrived. Trace recognized the IAD assholes climbing out. *First things first.* "What can I do for you?"

"Our warrants and the first of the footage have arrived for that phone call St. Jean made."

Trace's pulse raced at the mention of the name. "Shit, I'm sorry, Walker, I guess no one's told you, we found her."

"Really? When?"

"Just about an hour or so ago."

"And she's not here for questioning yet?"

Trace sat back down in the passenger seat. "No, and she won't be." She took a deep breath. "Jesus Christ, Walker, I had to shoot her."

There was silence on the other end, then Walker spoke, his voice gentle. "Are you okay?"

Trace shook her head, tears welling up again as guilt gripped her heart like a fist. "I-I don't know."

"How did it go down?"

Get a grip! Trace took a deep breath and wiped her eyes. "She shot a uniform, then tried to shoot me. I put two in her chest, just like we're trained to do."

"Listen to what you just said. 'Just like we're trained to do'. Remember that. This sounds like a clean shoot, you've got nothing to worry about, and nothing to feel guilty about."

"Yeah, that's what the LT said."

"And he's right." He paused. "Did I ever tell you about my first shooting?"

"No."

"Bronx, fifteen year old kid, robbing a liquor store, firing his gun at anything that moved as he came out, including me and my partner as we pulled up. My partner got it in the neck. I emptied my gun into the kid, then watched my partner die in my arms as the kid lay twenty feet away, dead, his eyes staring at me the entire time."

"How'd you handle it?"

"I hit the bottle for three months, almost got kicked off the force. It wasn't until a detective investigating another case that I had been witness to came looking for me that I smartened up. He smacked me across the face and told me to stop feeling sorry for myself. He said he had read the case file and talked to the witnesses, and it was clear there was nothing else I could have done. The kid shot and killed a cop, and had a long history of doing bad. The gun had been linked to three other shootings including a homicide, and I had done the world a favor by removing him from it. He hauled me out of my apartment and to a diner, filled me with coffee and pie, and I reported back for duty the next day, sober. It took somebody else to tell me I had done nothing wrong. Somebody I could trust. Not a buddy, not a family member, but someone I respected."

"Who was it?"

Walker laughed. "Detective Justin Shakespeare."

Trace smiled. She could picture it in her head. Shakes' solution to everything—pie. "He's full of surprises."

"Yup. That was ten years ago. He's never mentioned it since, and neither have I, but that man saved my career, and probably my life, by hauling me out of a bottle, and back into the world."

Trace pushed her shoulders back and took in a lungful of air. "Yeah, I guess you're right. It will take some getting used to." She suddenly stood up, determined to move forward. "So, I guess there's not much point in you going through that footage now."

"Not sure if you'll want to stick to that statement after I tell you what we found."

Trace stopped in her tracks. "What do you mean?"

"We have a clear shot of her making the phone call to her parents, then ten minutes later being picked up by someone driving a black Escalade."

"Black Escalade!" Trace's heart slammed against her ribcage in excitement. "Please tell me you got a plate."

Walker chuckled. "Not only do I have a plate, I have a name."

"Who?"

"You're never going to guess."

Trace twirled her hand to urge him on, despite him being on the other side of the city. "Who?" she pleaded.

"Richard Tate."

Aynslee, driving one of the station's floater vehicles, made the final turn according to the GPS. She came to a stop several hundred feet short, and looked about. There were a few people in sight at various warehouses, mostly arriving for their morning shifts. Her warehouse however appeared deserted. She looked at her watch. *Where are those guys?*

Her phone rang, startling her.

She grabbed it and saw it was Mike. "Where are you?"

"We're going to be late. Reggie gave us the wrong address."

"What?"

"Yeah, I guess he dropped the files and mixed them up. We were on our way to the address I guess you thought you were going to when he called. We'll be there in ten minutes."

"Okay, I'm going to take a look around and I'll meet you out front."

"Don't do anything stupid, Aynslee."

"Moi? Stupid? You know me better than that!"

"Riiight, you know I know you."

She laughed. "Just get your butts here pronto."

She hung up the phone and climbed out of the car. She walked nonchalantly toward the warehouse, holding her phone to her ear, pretending to be listening intently. Instead, her eyes scanned every inch of the building and its surroundings. She could see nothing out of the ordinary, except for the entrance door being blacked out, which, if she thought about it, might be completely normal around here.

A gust of wind carried a candy bar wrapper across the street and past her, directly toward the warehouse. Reaching into her purse, she tore off a piece of paper from her note pad, then pretended to read it. Loosening her fingers, the page blew from her hand, toward the large warehouse doors. She made a production of having dropped it, and walked briskly after it. The wind had done its job, and she was now bending over directly in front of the large doors, retrieving her paper. She stood by the door, phone to her ear, staring at the paper.

In truth, she was desperately trying to prevent her jaw from dropping. On the other side of the large doors, she was certain she was hearing people screaming in agony, crying for mercy. She slowly walked away from the door, toward her car. She dialed Shakespeare's number, praying he would pick up. As she walked by the smaller entrance, she jumped as the door swung open, the morning light, still low on the horizon, revealing nothing but the barrel of a gun, pointed directly at her. She dropped her phone and turned to run when two shots rang out.

Shakespeare rubbed the sleep out of his eyes as he held the phone to his ear. A quick glance at his watch showed him it was a little after six in the morning. "Hello?" he repeated. "Aynslee, are you there?" He knew who it was from the call display, but she had yet to answer. *Had she pocket dialed?*

Two unmistakable cracks followed by a scream came over the earpiece and he shot straight up in his seat, adrenaline surging through his veins forcing him wide awake. "Aynslee!" He held the phone tight to his ear as he adjusted his seat back into a driving position and started the car. He could hear footsteps, their crisp double tap sounding like woman's heels as they rapidly got louder then stopped. A burst of static filled his ear as apparently the phone was crushed under someone's shoe.

Shakespeare immediately dialed the studio. "Good morning, WACX, how may I direct your call?"

"This is Detective Shakespeare, NYPD Homicide. I need to get a location on one of your reporters, an Aynslee Kai."

"I don't think we can do that, sir, it's called Freedom of the Press. I can forward you to our legal department if you'd like?"

Shakespeare sensed another battle with the arrogant voice on the other end, but calmed himself, his last annoyed response not having worked out. "Listen, I'm a friend of hers. Perhaps you heard what happened to her a couple of weeks ago? Well I'm the cop that saved her life."

"Oh, you're the one! I just have to say that all of us—"

Shakespeare cut her off. "Listen carefully, time is critical here. She just called me, and I heard gunshots. She's in trouble. I need to know where she is so I can send police."

The momentary silence at the other end suggested he had gotten through to the girl. "I'll put you through to the news director."

A few clicks and beeps and a man picked up the phone. "Jeffrey Merle."

"Hi, this is Detective Shakespeare, NYPD Homicide—"

"Detective, how are you! What can I do—"

"Listen carefully. I just got a call from Aynslee. There were gunshots. I need to know where she was going."

"Gunshots?" Muffled orders were yelled, the phone evidently pressed against his shoulder. "Detective? Just hold on. She's not supposed to be on a story. In fact, I haven't seen her since the broadcast last night. She should have just gone home. I'm trying to find out now."

"Talk to your lab geek. She was helping me with something late last night. He might know something."

"Just a second." This time the orders weren't as muffled. "Get me Reggie, now!" Moments later Merle returned to the phone. "Let me put you on speaker." A click was followed by the hiss of a speakerphone. "Can you hear me, Detective?"

"Yes."

"Reggie is here."

"Reggie, this is Detective Shakespeare."

"Hi, Detective."

"Do you know where Aynslee went?"

"Yes, I have the address in my office. I sent her to the wrong location, she was supposed to go to Sarah's, but instead she's gone to some other one. Her camera crew should be there any minute."

"Shit! Call them off, they could be heading straight into a trap."

"Is it Mike and Steve?" asked Merle.

"Yes."

Shakespeare heard a chair creak and footsteps fade from the speaker, then Merle's voice yelling, "Tracy, get in touch with Mike and Steve and tell them to pull over. Tell them *not* to go to their location, it's a trap!"

There was a pause.

"Don't just stare at me, pick up that phone and dial. They could be about to get shot!" The voice started to get louder as he approached the speaker again. "Reggie, get me that address!"

"Yes, sir!" Shakespeare heard a crash and a grunt, then another impact, this time against glass, followed by another grunt, then silence.

"You still there, Detective?"

"Yes."

He heard a knocking sound. "I just reached them, sir, and they've stopped. They said they're just around the corner from their destination."

"Okay, thanks."

The woman who had just spoken yelped and there was another banging sound. "Christ, Reggie, you've got to learn to coordinate those feet!"

"Sorry." There was a pause and Shakespeare readied his pad and pen. "Here's the address."

Merle read it off to Shakespeare who jotted it down then punched it in his phone's GPS. "Shit, I'm only five minutes from there."

"Good luck, Detective."

"Thanks." Shakespeare put the car in gear and roared out of the parking lot as he called dispatch for backup. His chest was tight as he pictured Aynslee. After what the poor woman had gone through over the past two weeks, he couldn't imagine how much more she could take.

At what point does even the strongest of us break?

MJ cracked his knuckles as he began to go through the pile of emails and paperwork that had arrived since the night before. He quickly scanned each email, deleting the standard announcements and the odd spam that creeped through the filters, forwarded the jokes and personal email to his home account, then started through the much reduced list. The third email caught his attention.

He took a bite of his BLT bagel and opened the attachment. His chewing slowed, then stopped, as he read the file. He grabbed the phone and dialed the sender to confirm the findings, his bagel forgotten.

"Carl, MJ. Are these results you sent me correct?"

"Hey, MJ, which ones are you talking about? I've sent out a dozen already."

"Alders, Samantha." MJ stared at the screen, his mind racing with the implications of what he was reading.

"Oh yeah, thought you'd get a kick out of that one."

"Is it correct?"

Carl chuckled. "Absolutely, I double checked it. I knew as soon as I saw the results, you'd be asking. Definitely not what we were expecting."

"Okay, thanks." MJ hung up the phone and quickly dialed Shakespeare.

If this is true, it changes everything!

Trace sat in her car, sipping water, waiting for IAD to finally ask to question her when she heard something over Richard's radio that caught her attention. She jumped out of the car and motioned with her hand for him to give her his radio. He handed her the mike.

"Dispatch, this is Detective Trace. Who's the primary on that last call?"

"The request for backup came from Detective Shakespeare, Homicide."

Any fatigue she may have had was wiped away in one moment. "Give me that address."

She wrote it down as did Richards. She handed the mike back and rushed to her car. She started it up, the powerful engine roaring to life. As she peeled away from the curb, everyone, including IAD and the LT, turned. In her rear view mirror she saw Richards and Scaramell jump in their squad car and pull out as well.

She was only minutes away, and right now, as far as she knew, her partner was heading into a 'shots fired' situation alone, without any backup. And from what she had learned about him over the past few days, she knew he wouldn't wait.

Hang on, Shakes, we're coming!

Shakespeare raced around the corner, past the parked news van, and eased off as he approached the warehouse. He parked behind a car with a WACX sticker on the rear bumper that he assumed must be Aynslee's. He looked about and saw no one in the vicinity.

Including backup.

He climbed out of the car and approached the blacked out entrance. He held his ear to the door, listening for any hints of what he may face on the other side, and what he heard shocked him. It sounded like dozens, perhaps hundreds, of people screaming and crying. He turned the handle, and the door pushed open. He couldn't say he was surprised. This had 'trap' written all over it. The faint cries became louder as he stepped inside.

He was greeted by darkness and a faint orange glow deeper in the warehouse. Other than that and the light pouring in from outside, he could hear nothing. He pulled a pocket flashlight out and played it around, finding no one. He went to the left, shining the flashlight along the wall, looking for a lighting panel. What he found a few feet in wasn't what he had been looking for, but it would do. He pressed the three buttons and the roar of three motors kicking in drowned out the cries from deeper within.

Three slivers of light appeared, then rapidly expanded as the automatic garage door openers he had activated hauled the huge doors up, flooding the warehouse with light. A black Escalade was parked at the second door, the tread marks on the dusty floor indicating it had entered through the closest door and circled to face the next door for what he presumed would be a quick getaway. One set of fresh footprints led from the driver side door deeper into the warehouse where three large shipping containers stood. One had a large stage rig above it holding what appeared to be speakers and heating elements. The cries were much louder now, and clearly coming from the speakers.

Just a recording.

He looked back to the door he had entered through, and found a jumble of footprints leading toward the closest container. With nothing else obvious in sight, he followed the prints deeper into the warehouse, toward a door in a long black structure attached to the nearest container. He opened it, and stepped inside. To his right was what looked like a door to the outside. He opened it, and left it that way, flooding the corridor with light. To his left, about fifty feet in was what he assumed to be the container entrance. He quickly walked toward the container, his gun drawn. The hallway widened to the width and height of the container, and he found a simple, plain door, and nothing else.

His phone vibrated on his hip, causing him to jump. He reached down and sent the call to voice mail. He gripped the handle when the phone vibrated with a text message. The debate raged in his head for a moment. *It might be important.* He grabbed the phone and read the message from MJ.

URGENT YOU CALL ME IMMEDIATELY!!!!

The phone vibrated again. He stepped back from the door and turned his back, taking the call. "What the hell is it?" he asked in a harsh whisper.

"It's about our second victim. I just got the results back—"

A scream rang out from the other side of the door, a scream he recognized as Aynslee's. The phone still in his hand, he tore open the door and rushed through, his gun leading the way.

And gasped.

Aynslee stood at the far end, a gun held to her head by the last person he expected to have ever seen. He raised the phone to his ear.

"Let me guess," he said, his gun trained at the head of the person standing in front of him. "It's not Samantha Alders."

THIRTEEN

Aynslee could barely focus. Her mind was shutting down from the shock of yet another situation where she could die. *Maybe I'm not cut out for this business.* Her thoughts angered her, and she began to focus. She knew she was meant to be a reporter. Tough as nails. And she was in the middle of a great story. And if she didn't get her wits about her, she'd miss it.

She took a deep, slow breath, the cold steel of the weapon pressed against her temple a constant reminder of her situation. But it was a situation she was back to, the roar in her ears gone, her eyes now fully open.

And a smile of relief spreading across her face as she saw Shakespeare standing in front of her, gun in one hand, pointed directly at the woman who had taken her captive, and a cellphone in the other. She flinched as the woman beside her spoke.

"Turn off the phone."

Shakespeare pressed a button and put the phone in his pocket, placing his now freed hand on his gun.

"Drop your weapon, Samantha, and we can all walk out of here alive."

"Alive?" She laughed. "None of us are alive. You crossed through the portal, old man, you're as dead as I am, as dead as she is."

The woman lowered the weapon and Aynslee breathed a sigh of relief just as she was shoved into a corner. She fell unceremoniously to the ground, and saw a flash of concern from Shakespeare. She made eye contact and nodded she was fine. She returned her attention to the woman Shakespeare had called Samantha.

"Listen, you're confused. You're not dead. You're as alive as I am right now."

Samantha shook her head. "No, I died three years ago." She flicked her gun at the walls around them. "Don't you know where you are? Don't you know why you're here?"

Shakespeare stared at the woman, confused. "What do you mean, you died three years ago?"

"Are you deaf *and* dumb? I'm dead. I was killed three years ago in a car accident. For my sins, I'm being punished for eternity. This was my own personal hell for almost two years until my master sent me on a mission."

"A mission?"

"To deliver the soul of Richard Tate by fulfilling all his sinful desires."

She's clearly whack. Aynslee slowly straightened herself into a seated position with the corner at her back, facing the woman. If things were to go wrong, she might have time to tackle her before she could get a shot off at her. As if Shakespeare could read her mind, he took a step to his left, Samantha turning slightly to follow him, exposing more of her back to Aynslee.

A shot rang out and Samantha screamed, then dropped to the ground, blood rushing from a hole in her chest. Shakespeare spun around, the shot having come from behind him, only to find the door he had come through closing. He ran for the door, but it was closed tight before he could reach it, and much to Aynslee's horror, there was no handle. He pushed on the door, then slammed it with his shoulder to no avail, the framing solid.

Aynslee stood up and rushed over to him, throwing her arms around his shoulders, relief sweeping over her. But not tears. Not this time. They weren't out of this yet, and she didn't want him having to worry about her.

Samantha gasped, then laughed. Aynslee spun toward the noise, slowly backing away. "She's alive!"

Shakespeare hurried over and kicked the gun that lay beside her toward Aynslee. She stooped over to pick it up.

"Do you know how to use that?"

She shrugged her shoulders. "Point and shoot?"

"That's what I thought. Just leave it where it is. Backup should be here any minute, and the last thing I need is you shooting them, or worse, them shooting you." He glanced at the sealed doorway. "In fact, come over here with me."

Aynslee hesitated. *I've already watched one person die in the past two weeks, and that was enough.* Shakespeare seemed to read her mind and his tone softened. "On second thought, just sit in the corner here and watch the door. Tell me if you see it opening."

She nodded, grateful for the reprieve. Sitting down, she glued her eyes to the door, but quickly found them wandering to Shakespeare and Samantha, as he turned her over so he could see her face. She gasped in pain and Aynslee's hand flew to her mouth as she saw the amount of blood that had pooled under her captor.

"Where is Frank?"

"You've accomplished nothing," the woman whispered.

Aynslee slid closer.

"You're dying, do the right thing. Tell me where Frank and Sarah are.'

Samantha managed a weak laugh ending in a cough, blood trickling from her mouth. "I'm already dead. And so are you."

"How are we dead? Is this container booby-trapped?" Both Aynslee and Shakespeare looked about.

"You crossed the portal. Only the master lets someone cross the portal."

"Who's the master?"

"You will hear from him soon when he lists your sins, and why you have been condemned to this place."

"A warehouse?" Shakespeare gripped the woman's hand. "Listen to me, you're not dead. You've been held captive in this warehouse for three years. I'm a cop, she's"—he jerked his head toward Aynslee—"a reporter. We are alive and well and living in New York City. And so have you been. We've had officers at your apartment."

The woman coughed again and blood sprayed across her chin and blouse. "You are so naïve." She reached up and gripped Shakespeare's arm. "Obey the master. If you do, this is your torture for eternity. Disobey, and you will be torn, limb from limb, for eternity." Her arm dropped and her eyes closed. "Obey the master," she whispered before her entire body relaxed and her breathing stopped.

Shakespeare stood and pulled out his phone and held it to his ear.

"Did you get all that?"

MJ nodded to no one. "Yes, I got it. Started taping as soon as I heard it going down." He paused. "Is she dead?"

"Yes, but she seemed to think she was already dead."

"Strange. Some sort of brainwashing, I guess. I wonder who 'the master' is."

"No idea, but she seemed terrified of him, and at the same time, almost adoring. Some sort of Stockholm Syndrome thing, maybe."

MJ leaned back in his chair. "I'm sorry you had to shoot her."

"What? I didn't shoot her!"

MJ leaned forward in his chair, his elbows hitting the desk hard. "What? Then who did?"

"No idea. Someone came through the door and shot her. My back was to them so I never saw them. Aynslee, did you see them?"

He heard a faint, "No."

"Aynslee's there? The reporter?"

"Yeah, she was being held by Alders. Speaking of, who was our second vic?"

"She showed up in IAFIS as Hillary Banks. Has a few convictions for prostitution, mostly rub and tug stuff with massage parlors."

"So *that* explains it!"

"Explains what?"

"The footage at the hotel. We saw Tate, then Alders, then the masseuse go in. Then we saw the masseuse leave, then Tate leave. Alders never left, so we assumed she was the body transported by Sandy."

"But it was actually the masseuse, and not Alders who was dead."

"Right, so she must have killed the masseuse, set up the scene, slaps a fake tattoo on the back of the girl's neck, put on the masseuse's clothes, then left. Tate wakes up, thinks it's Alders, rushes out, Sandy cleans up the scene and plants the body to torment Frank some more, and Tate comes back, not knowing what the hell is going on."

"So Tate was telling the truth, he's not involved. He was framed just like Frank!"

"Looks that way. Now we need to find out where the hell Frank is. And where the hell my backup is."

"Frank's missing? Shakes, you really need to tell me what's going on."

"Yeah, I'll bring you up to date later. Wait, I think I hear something. I'll call you back."

MJ heard the line go dead. *Frank is missing?* He knew something was going on he wasn't being told about, but this was getting ridiculous. With Frank missing, that meant two of their own.

And by the sounds of it, they had no clue where either of them were.

Trace whipped around the corner, the squad car driven by Richards now in front, she having waved them ahead earlier so lights and sirens would be leading the way. It had only been five minutes, but it seemed like an eternity. There had been no word from dispatch that any backup had arrived yet, and Shakespeare was alone, with shots fired on the scene. She hit her brakes then accelerated through another turn, taking it a little wide and finding herself racing almost headlong into a large SUV. She jerked the wheel to the right, regaining her lane as the SUV swerved to avoid her. She looked in her rear view mirror to make sure they were okay and gasped.

A black Escalade!

She didn't believe in coincidences. A black Escalade, at this time of the morning, leaving the scene they were approaching? She honked on her horn and flashed her lights at Richards, then stuck her arm out the window, swirling it in the air, indicating they should turn around, then pointed at the Escalade fading in the distance. The patrol car decelerated rapidly, then pulled a U-turn, her message received. She gave them the thumbs up as she blew by them. She continued toward Shakespeare's backup call, blasting past what looked like a news van, and fishtailing around the final turn. Two other units down the road screeched to a halt in front of a warehouse, their occupants jumping out, guns drawn, as she raced up, squealing to a halt mere feet from the gaping delivery doors that stood open to the world.

She jumped out, holding up her badge. "Detective Trace, Homicide. That's my partner in there so don't shoot first and ask questions later." She grabbed her backup weapon from the trunk, then led the way into the warehouse, motioning for them to spread out to either side. They pressed deeper into the massive shell, its only contents apparently another Escalade sitting empty, facing the middle door, and three shipping containers, set up almost identically to the warehouse she had just left. She found her mind wandering to the other Escalade. *Maybe it was just a coincidence?*

She motioned for the officers to her left to check the two farthest containers, then proceeded toward the long, framed structure leading from the back of the nearest container, to the far wall. The door leading into it was ajar, as was the door inside leading to the rear of the building. She poked her head into the structure, her gun leading, and found it empty, the black, rough walls highlighted by the sunlight pouring in the open door, raising her eyebrows as she recognized what the paint job and plaster work were trying to accomplish. *Coal.* She pointed at one of the officers then at the door to the outside, and he nodded, taking up a covering position, protecting their rear just in case someone decided to return. Trace and the other officer raced forward, deeper into the structure, and finally to the door leading into the container.

She gripped the door handle then thought better of it. She took up a position on one side, and waved the officer to the other side. She knocked on the door. "Shakes, you in there?"

There was a muffled, "Yes!" The voice was unmistakable and she breathed a sigh of relief.

"Is it okay to open the door?"

"Yes, go ahead, we're okay in here."

She gripped the handle and pulled the door open, then poked her head around the side. A woman was down and most likely dead judging by the pool of blood. That woman reporter was sitting near the corner, looking pretty damned worn out, and Shakespeare stood facing the door, gun in one hand, cellphone in the other, and dripping in sweat.

She smiled and stepped inside. "Holy shit is it ever hot in here."

Shakespeare holstered his weapon and wiped his forehead. "You've got a gift for stating the obvious." He pointed at the body. "Meet Samantha Alders." Trace's eyebrows shot up and Shakespeare nodded. "Yeah, I had a similar reaction when I walked in here and found her with a gun pointed to our friend's head. Alders killed the masseuse, then walked out of the room wearing her outfit."

"So she's the killer?"

"One of them, at least. She and Sandy must have kidnapped Frank and Sarah, planted Angela Henwood's body in the apartment, killed the masseuse and set up Tate. Something strange is going on though. She kept referring to 'the master'. I think there's someone orchestrating this whole damned thing."

"'The master'? That's the same thing St. Jean said."

"Probably whoever shot Alders."

Trace stopped. "You mean you didn't?"

Shakespeare shook his head. "No, somebody shot her through the open door behind me, then closed the door before I could get to it. I didn't see them, and neither did Aynslee."

Trace walked over to Aynslee and knelt down in front of her. "You okay?"

She nodded. "Just tired of being the story, rather than covering it."

Trace chuckled and stuck out her hand as she rose. Aynslee took it and Trace pulled her to her feet. "Let's get out of this heat and do all the formal stuff outside."

Shakespeare strode toward the door and pointed to the uniform standing there. "You take control of the scene. CSU should be here soon, and if you don't want your chestnuts roasting, you might want to set the entry point at the far end." The officer chuckled and hauled out his pad, rapidly writing down what he saw, and who was there. Shakespeare showed him his badge so he could write down the number, then headed for the cool air pouring in from outside with Aynslee and Trace in tow.

"Did you see that?"

"I'm sitting here, aren't I?"

"What do you think?"

"I think Aynslee would hand us our balls if we didn't follow them."

"That's exactly what I was thinking." Mike fired up the van and hit the gas, turning the lumbering beast toward the black SUV and the cop car now in pursuit. He caught a glimpse of them as they both turned the corner several blocks down. As he rapidly closed the distance, Steve grabbed the camera and began rolling. Mike turned the corner, and slammed the brakes on as he nearly rammed the back of the SUV, the cop car having overtaken it and blocked its path. The SUV backed up straight at them, and Mike pressed the brake into the floor, yelling, "Hang on!" as the SUV hit the front of the van, rocking them hard.

Mike gasped as the airbags deployed, shoving him into the back of his seat and momentarily depriving him of oxygen as the bag pressed into his face. The airbag rapidly deflated and he heard Steve cursing, then the passenger side door opening. He reached for his door and found the handle. Pulling it, the door opened, and he tried to get out, but found the seatbelt pinning him to the seat. He reached down and popped it, then climbed out to the sound of the SUV crashing into the passenger side of the police car, the officer still trapped inside. The driver had jumped out and was running around the rear of his car, gun drawn, pointing at the tinted driver side window.

"Turn off the vehicle or I will shoot!"

The backup lights for the SUV came on and the vehicle started back toward their van. Mike jumped out of the way, looking for Steve. As he hit the ground, the SUV crashed into the van, shoving it back several feet. Mike caught a glimpse of Steve's legs on the other side of the van, some distance away, apparently safe.

The first officer shot at the driver side tires, quickly deflating them, as the officer still trapped in the car emptied his weapon into the engine. The first officer then placed a shot in the top left of the driver side window, shattering it. Inside the driver covered his head, then slowly raised his hands.

"Turn off the engine!" ordered the cop. The man reached forward and pressed a button, the powerful engine cutting off. "Now slowly open the door and come out with your hands up."

The door opened, and the man stepped out as the trapped officer rushed over to join his partner. He grabbed the driver and threw him to the ground. Within moments he was handcuffed and searched, then hauled to his feet just as Steve came around with the camera focused on the driver's cut covered face. Despite the blood there was no hiding who this man was. It was a face Mike would recognize anywhere.

Richard Tate.

Aynslee looked through the two way mirror at Richard Tate. He had minor cuts all over his face that paramedics had tended to, and now sat with what was surely one of many lawyers under his employ. Shakespeare, Trace and a man she only knew as Vinny stood in the room with her, staring in silence. Her phone vibrated with a call from the station. She answered it. "Aynslee Kai."

"Aynslee, you've gotta see this!"

"What is it, Reggie?"

"There's live footage streaming to the server, you've gotta see this!"

She placed the phone on her shoulder and turned to Shakespeare. "Reggie says there's live footage streaming onto the server."

Shakespeare turned to Vinny who was already dialing his phone. "Bryan, check the server, apparently there's some live footage streaming." He hit the button to put it on speaker so the entire room could hear."

"Just a second." They could hear some keystrokes, then a gasp. "Holy shit, you're not gonna believe this."

"Can you send us the feed here?"

"Sure, go to your display in the pit, I'll send it straight there."

Trace grabbed the handle and almost ripped the door off as she rushed out, Vinny and Shakespeare following her, Aynslee bringing up the rear. She raised the phone back to her ear. "Thanks, Reggie, we're about to see the footage now." She hung up and followed the other three into what looked like the office area where most of the detectives had their desks. To one side there were white boards, timelines outlining various cases in progress, and several large flat screens. The one in the middle suddenly flickered and a display of the same chamber she had been in, or one strikingly similar, flashed on the screen. As if one, the room gasped. On the display was a naked girl, huddled in the far corner, and a fully clothed man stood, facing her, his back to the camera.

"That's Sarah Paxman!" exclaimed one of the female detectives.

The man on the screen looked over his shoulder and directly at the camera. "That's Brata!"

Shakespeare, Vinny and Trace stood silently watching as more of the squad gathered around the screen. "What's she got behind her back?" asked one, pointing. Aynslee leaned in but couldn't see anything, however the girl definitely had one hand behind her back, the other trying to cover her breasts.

"I don't see anything," said Vinny.

"Neither do I," said Trace. "But I can tell you one thing, if I was her, I'd be using both hands to cover my ta-tas, not just one."

Aynslee and the other women in the room nodded. She looked again and had to agree. The girl was clearly trying to maintain her modesty, but with only one hand.

What's behind your back?

Frank stood in the room, blinking at the brightness. He had woken in complete darkness only moments before, finding the door he had just opened by feeling the walls around him. As his eyes focused, he realized he was standing in a room much like what he had seen in the video footage. He turned his head to look where the camera should be if this were the same room. He didn't see anything, but the design of the ceiling left a dark, six inch gap all around the room, the camera most likely recessed inside.

"Frank?"

Frank spun toward the voice. "Sarah!" He rushed to the other end of the room where she lay, relief washing over him, the sight of her alive and well lifting a weight off his shoulders he didn't realize he had been carrying. As he neared her he suddenly became aware of what should have been obvious. *She's naked!* The primal part of him demanded he stare, to take in her naked, vulnerable form, but the civilized man quickly won out and he averted his eyes. He unbuttoned his shirt and took it off. He turned back to her, and holding the shirt up so he could only see her head, moved closer and then dropped to his knees, gently draping the shirt over her shoulders, covering most of her naked flesh. She moved her hand covering her breasts and placed it over the shirt, holding it in place.

"Thank you," she whispered, apparently so embarrassed she couldn't make eye contact.

"Are you okay," he asked, gently, wanting to reach out and hold her, to comfort her, but not sure if he should. He barely knew her. They had spent perhaps only hours together, and what they had done, he couldn't remember. *I wonder if she remembers.*

She nodded, then shook her head. "No, no I'm not. But I could be worse."

"Well, it's over now. Let's get out of here before they come back." He reached out and offered her his hand. She looked at it then at him.

"We can't leave."

Frank's eyes narrowed. "Why not?"

"You don't know where you are, do you?"

"Well, no, but I'm sure we can figure a way out of here, then get to a phone and call for help."

She smiled weakly at him, as if she pitied him. "There's no leaving here."

Frank wasn't sure what to say.

"You mean there's no way out?" He pointed at the open door at the other end of the room. "Have you figured out where that leads?"

She shook her head. "No. All I know is its some type of portal. Only *he* can let anyone pass."

"Who's 'he'?"

Her eyes filled with tears and poured down her face. "The Devil," she whispered, as if afraid someone might hear.

Frank chuckled. "The Devil? What are you talking about?"

Sarah reached out and grabbed Frank's arm, his shirt slipping down her chest, she apparently not noticing. "You're dead, Frank. Just like me. We're in Hell."

Frank tried to comfort her with a smile. "No, we're not dead. We were drugged and kidnapped. You're being held here, where I don't know because I was just abducted again myself, but we're alive."

She shook her head, a deep sadness spreading across her face. "He will explain it all to you soon, but I must convince you of the truth first."

Frank couldn't believe what he was hearing. It was all so ridiculous. She sounded as if she were brainwashed. *How can she think she's dead and in Hell?* He finally took a moment to observe his surroundings. The room was filled with a dull, pulsating, orange glow. He could hear faint screams and pleads from hordes of people on the other side of the walls. And it was hot. He wiped his forehead, then looked down at his glistening chest. Very hot. The room was featureless with no amenities, and he found himself suddenly fighting the urge to urinate.

He looked back at Sarah. *If I were held in a hot, featureless room, lit by what appeared to be fire, surrounded by screaming people, and told I was in Hell, maybe I'd believe it too.* He had to convince her she was alive. He stepped toward the door. "Look, I'll prove it to you. I'll go get help, and bring them back."

"No!" she screamed, jumping up, his shirt now at her feet, her body fully exposed, both arms held out in front, one with its hand held up, pleading for him to stop, the other pointing straight at him, gripping a gun. "If you go through the portal, you will be damned for eternity," she cried. "You'll be torn limb from limb, over and over, suffering for eternity in agony!"

Frank didn't hear a word she said. He just stared at the weapon, frozen in terror, the memories of his shooting fresh in his mind. And the fact he wasn't wearing a vest painfully at the forefront.

Sarah's eyes filled with tears. Here he was. The man she barely knew, but had grown to love over the past few days. A romanticized creation of her own mind, of an evening she couldn't remember, and a lifetime they would never know. Her life was over, and so was his. But what type of afterlife he would lead, she now knew was up to her. And she was determined he wouldn't face the eternity described to her.

"You need to accept where you are before you can be saved."

Frank just stared at the gun, saying nothing.

"We died that night, at the coffee shop. Do you remember? Do you remember that night?"

Frank slowly shook his head, then his eyes finally moved from the gun to her. "No. No, I don't remember."

"And neither do I. It's because we died. Something happened. Somehow we were killed. I must have died right away, because I've been here longer than you. You must have somehow survived a few days longer. Maybe we were hit by a car or something, I don't know."

Frank shook his head. "No, we weren't. I've been trying to find you. Me, Shakespeare, Trace, Vinny. All of us have been looking for you." He took a step toward her, reaching out his hand. "Give me the gun, Sarah, and we can leave."

Her heart broke. There was no way he was going to accept his fate, accept what had happened to him. And she knew Jackie was right. This was the only way to convince him. If she shot him, and he didn't die, then he would know he was already dead. It was simple to say, but to actually do it, to squeeze the trigger, to inflict so much pain and fear on the man she loved. Could she do it?

Torn limb from limb, for eternity.

She squeezed the trigger.

The shot was deafening, the confined chamber making it painfully loud. Frank staggered back, his eyes wide in shock. He fell through the door, landing beyond the portal. She rushed over and pulled him back inside, just in case. He lay there, gasping, a hole in his shoulder oozing blood onto his bare chest and the floor he now lay prone on.

"Why?"

"Why?" she cried. "Because I had to convince you! Because you needed to know you were dead!"

"How does shooting me prove anything?" he asked, his voice weakening.

She knelt beside him, her hand on his chest. "Because the dead can't die."

"But we're not dead. What can I do to prove it to you?"

Her chest tightened and she felt sick to her stomach. *I've failed.* She knew he would never accept it, not even his own death would convince him. But there was another way. One final way she could convince him. And it wouldn't involve hurting him anymore. She stood and looked down at him, her breaking heart painful in her chest.

"There's only one other way I can think to convince you."

She raised the gun to her head and squeezed on the trigger.

"Sarah, no!"

"Jesus Christ, she's going to shoot him!"

Shakespeare wasn't sure who said it, he was already racing out of the room the moment the gun made an appearance. He rushed down the hallway toward the interrogation room and tore open the door, just as he heard someone from the squad room yell, "She shot him!" He slammed the door behind him and leaned on the table, knuckles pressed against the wood. Tate looked up, startled. His lawyer opened his mouth to speak when Shakespeare pointed a finger directly at him, glaring. "Don't you say an effin' word." He turned to Tate.

"You've got one chance to tell me where Frank and Sarah are, otherwise I'll make sure your life is a living hell once you're on the inside."

"You have no right to threaten my client like this."

"Shut the fuck up!" roared Shakespeare. "Two lives are at stake here. We're watching live footage right now of them, and Sarah has just shot Frank. Judging from what we heard come out of the mouths of St. Jean and Alders, she's most likely been brainwashed just like them!" Shakespeare rounded the table and grabbed Tate, spinning his chair to face him. "If he dies, I'll see that you're charged with the murder of a cop. You'll do life at a minimum."

Shakespeare stared directly into Tate's eyes. But the eyes that stared back were cold, emotionless. And certainly not scared. *He doesn't care!* Shakespeare stood straight, one hand supporting the small of his back as his spine protested. *He's a psychopath!* He turned his attention to Tate's lawyer. "Tell your client if he doesn't want to die a quick death in prison, he better make sure we find our people before any of them die."

The door to the interrogation room burst open and Shakespeare spun around, his face flush with anger at the intrusion.

"There you are!" yelled an apparently equally irate Mrs. Tate. "What the hell have you gotten yourself into?"

"Get the hell out of here!" yelled Shakespeare.

She glared at him. "Didn't you learn your lesson last time? Unless you want another tongue lashing, this time from the Chief, you'll stay out of my way!" She turned her attention to her husband, Shakespeare apparently dealt with. "What the hell is going on?"

"Your husband is involved in the kidnapping of two of our people, and he knows where they are. We need to know their location immediately. One of them has already been shot."

Mrs. Tate looked at Shakespeare, then at her husband.

"Is this true?"

Tate said nothing, staring at the floor. She grabbed him by the hair and bent his head back, leaning over so her face was only inches away from his. "I said, is this true?"

His dead eyes stared back at her, but he nodded.

"Tell them what they need to know, now!" she screamed. "I won't have you ruining things with your little games."

Again, he said nothing, his cold eyes revealing no emotion. She let go of his hair, tossing his head backward. She raised her hand and swung it hard, smacking his cheek, the crack ringing through the room.

"Tell them!"

Tate's eyes continued to stare back, emotionless, but then they slowly turned to Shakespeare. "Get me my phone and take me to where you're watching the footage."

"Why?"

Tate's wife spun around. "Just do it!"

Shakespeare stared at her, then grabbed the back of Tate's shirt, hauling him to his feet. He opened the door and shoved him through, dragging him toward the squad room. "Get me his phone!" he yelled as he entered the room, everyone crowded around the display. He looked at the screen and saw Sarah raising the gun to her head. "Jesus Christ, get me Tate's phone, now!"

Trace looked back and her jaw dropped. She rushed to her desk and dumped out the contents of a manila envelope and grabbed the phone, tossing it over to Shakespeare who caught it then handed it to Tate. Tate dialed a number and spoke.

Sarah slowly squeezed the trigger, staring down at Frank, her tear filled eyes blurring his image. She sobbed as she realized she was about to add another sin to the long list that had already condemned her to this infernal place. *Suicide.* "I'm sorry, God," she whispered, and she made the final decision to squeeze.

"Stop!"

The roar of his voice startled her, and she almost fired the weapon. Her heart pounded against her ribcage at the shock of hearing his voice, especially now. She looked about the room. "Give me another chance!" she pleaded. "I can still convince him!"

The voice, deep and bestial, rumbled through the room. "Put down the weapon, your task is complete."

Complete? But I didn't succeed!

"But what happens to Frank?"

"Nothing."

"You mean he won't be tortured."

"No. Now put down the weapon."

She burst into tears as relief swept over her. She dropped the gun at her feet, and collapsed to the ground, crawling over to Frank's side and laying her head on his chest, her naked body lying on his. "You'll be okay now," she whispered.

The voice roared again, this time slightly different. "Frank, Sarah, this is Detective Shakespeare. We have your location and EMT is on the way."

What? That doesn't make any sense. She looked at Frank. "I don't understand."

He smiled at her. "It means we're going to be okay. Just rest for now."

She lowered her head again, and draped her arm across his chest, their sweat and body heat mixing together, feeling wonderful on her flesh, losing herself in the moment, not sure who was coming or how.

Shakespeare poked his head through the door and smiled. "Hey, room in here for two more?"

Frank looked up from his hospital bed and smiled, waving him and Trace in. Vinny was already there, along with a beaming Sarah who sat next to Frank, holding his hand. It had been three days since their rescue and she seemed none the worse for wear, and from all accounts, seemed more embarrassed about the entire detective squad seeing her naked than being convinced she was dead. Since she worked for the NYPD, she would be getting mandatory therapy for some time, but judging by the way she and Frank exchanged glances, Shakespeare had a feeling the 'tender loving care' would be more effective than the 'professional care'.

The officers arriving at the scene had initially arrested Sarah for shooting Frank, but both Shakespeare and Vinny had met with the DA and showed him the footage, and she was immediately released with no charges pending. Frank had been cleared as well, though he apparently had a stern lecture scheduled with the LT as soon as he was back on duty.

Shakespeare approached the bed and shook the kid's hand then leaned over and gave Sarah a kiss on the top of her head. He reached over and pulled Frank's bed sheet down, revealing his bare chest.

"What, no vest?"

Frank laughed then winced. Vinny roared. "Frank, they oughta keep you locked up. You're a bullet magnet!"

Trace gave him a pat on the forehead and hugged Sarah. "I'm just glad you two are still alive."

"You and me both," said Sarah. "So I hear Tate confessed?"

"Sort of," said Shakespeare, looking for a chair. Finding none, he was about to perch himself on the side of Frank's bed when Vinny jumped up.

"Take mine, old man, you're liable to kill the kid if your ass' aim is off."

Shakespeare chuckled and took the seat. "Here's what we know. He's been doing this for almost ten years. We found tons of video footage, audio recordings, notes and whatnot, all documenting what he was doing. It appears once a year he would choose a victim, kidnap them, then convince them they were in hell. He would torment them for days, weeks or months, some of them even years like St. Jean and Alders. The specialists who are looking into it seem to think he thought of himself as an amateur psychiatrist. He actually kept detailed notes, seemed to preplan everything to the last detail."

"The guy was basically psycho," proclaimed Vinny.

Shakespeare nodded. "No doubt about that. Through the files that you"—he nodded at Frank—"were able to hack, we found several addresses, all warehouses, all owned by various offshoots of his real estate empire, that contained the same setup of three shipping containers. One had the room that you guys were in, one had a room where he seemed to hold the other "players" as he called them, after he was done with them, and then the third was a control room, where he could sit and take notes, watch the tapes and interact over the speaker system with his victims."

"But where did he find the time?" asked Sarah. "Isn't this guy like uber rich?"

"Like I said, most of these originally seemed to be done over days, sometimes a few weeks. It wasn't until the last few years where he began holding people long term. The originals all appeared to be manipulated into suicides.

Sarah's head dropped. "Like me."

Shakespeare nodded. "Yes, exactly like you." He leaned forward in his chair. "Sarah, there's no shame in what happened. You were manipulated by a psychopath who was an expert in human behavior. He fed you everything you needed to hear to manipulate you into thinking you were dead. I don't think anybody in this room could honestly say they wouldn't have thought the same."

Sarah smiled gratefully at Shakespeare. "You know, the thing that had me convinced, is that I was never really hungry, and never had to go to the bathroom. I figured the only explanation was that I was dead. Otherwise I should be starving, I should have to use the bathroom."

"That was one of the more genius things about his plan. It appears about every twelve hours he would flood the room with gas, then—"

Trace held her hand up. "Shakes, I don't think Sarah will want to hear about this."

Shakespeare stopped and nodded. "Yeah, you're probably right."

"No!" exclaimed Sarah, whose head then dropped. "Sorry." She looked back at Shakespeare and Trace. "I need to know everything. If I'm going to come to terms with this, I need to know everything."

"Are you sure?" asked Frank.

Sarah looked over at him and nodded. "Yes."

Shakespeare took a deep breath. "Very well then. Every twelve hours he'd flood the room with a type of knock out gas. Odorless, so the victim would never notice. He'd then go in with a gurney, load the person on it, and take them out. What was done then we can only guess from the equipment we found, but it appears they were fed intravenously and through a tube, and then their bladder and bowels were emptied. Nails would be trimmed, hair cut, legs shaved. Whatever grooming that would be necessary to keep the appearance of time having stopped."

"But what about these long term ones?" asked Frank.

"From what we can tell, Alders had been held for three years, but based upon the notes, she was so well behaved, that he would regularly release her into public. She was so absolutely convinced she was serving her master, and that she was dead, she was able to attend school. He even had her set up as his mistress on the outside, and she had no clue it was him that had taken her captive."

Frank propped himself up on his elbows. "But why would she have set up the murder scene at the hotel?"

"*That* we're not sure of. It's not in the notes, but the thinking at the DA's office is that he did it as a test. We're pretty sure Angela Henwood, the first victim, was killed by Alders or Sandy. We're not sure why he was involved, but a powerful personality like Tate could manipulate someone who was weak or lacked self-confidence. But the masseuse, we're pretty sure she was killed by Alders. Perhaps it was a test to prove her continued loyalty.

"There's no doubt these women were manipulated by a pro. And they weren't the only victims. We've found almost two dozen bodies in the second containers. We're still trying to track down who these people are, but judging by the ones we know that were directly involved in your case, Sarah, he used amateur actors and actresses to play various roles in his experiments, then would kill them when he was finished. He even brought in a med student to tend to you when he was stuck in the hospital."

"And she's—"

"Dead, yes. We found her with the bodies of two NYU drama students."

"What about the Psyche Department? I thought things kept pointing there?" asked Frank.

"They did. The cameras, the email to the med student. Even the entire concept of these being set up as experiments screamed for it to be someone in the Psyche Department. Turns out, however, that Tate had someone set up a dummy email account at the department with an identical name to one of the department heads. Emails were sent from and cc'd to the dummy account, making them look legit, including an email that requested that when the cameras arrived, they be reshipped to the warehouse. It was really quite ingenious."

"This guy was basically one of the greatest serial killers in New York history," said Vinny.

Shakespeare nodded. "And I doubt he would see himself as that."

"There were four live feeds," said Frank. "Sarah's, and I assume St. Jean and Alders. Whose was the fourth?"

Shakespeare shook his head. "There was no data in that folder, just the live feed and a shell of the notes. Maybe he was setting up for his next victim, we don't know."

"But why did he choose us?" asked Sarah.

"Actually, he chose Frank."

"Me?"

"Yes. If you look at it, he was escalating. His first few years he appeared to kidnap someone, then manipulate them through speech into suicide, usually placing a gun in their chamber. Then he progressed to bringing in actors and others to play roles. This allowed him to do some of the killing himself, rather than just watch the suicides. With Alders he went a step further. He kept her long term, then eventually used her to do some of his dirty work, even had a relationship with her. St. Jean he held long term as well, and had just begun to use her for some of his dirty work.“

He seemed to be targeting women, so why Frank?” asked Sarah.

“Well, he targeted women for the chamber. It looks like this time he had cooked up an elaborate plan to see if he could get someone on the outside to believe they deserved to go to hell, and then commit suicide. We found a list of text messages he had planned on sending, including ones telling you to take some sort of pill to end it all.”

“What was the purpose of the text messages?” asked Frank. “Those things drove me nuts!”

“That's exactly it. According to the notes, they were designed to keep you on edge, to fear your phone, something you used constantly. He wanted you to panic, to make mistakes, and in the end, to kill yourself so it would all end.” Shakespeare sighed. “He had one hell of a lot of torment planned for you, kid. I don't think he counted on you figuring out the cameras.”

“Yeah, that was a pretty obvious mistake to make,” said Vinny.

“I think part of him was delusional enough to think he *was* the Devil, therefore him knowing any and all goings on would be natural. He made a mistake, because Trace getting suspicious of Frank was not in his plan. His judgment, clouded by his delusion, led to his error, then the discovery of the cameras, and then things began to unravel.”

“But why Frank?” asked Sarah.

“We found a lot of newspaper clippings about Frank after the shooting two weeks ago. I think he fixated on you, then planned to frame you for the murder of Angela Henwood. He had already killed her after she helped build the latest chamber along with the murdered drama students.”

“We found their fingerprints all over it,” explained Vinny.

“Sarah, you weren't part of the plan. With Henwood dead, timing was critical. Frank had to be taken that night, and since you were with him, you were taken too, and put into the chamber. I'm guessing he was going to take someone else that night, because the notes he had put together indicated someone was supposed to be in the chamber—he just got lucky with you.”

“Lucky's not the word I would have chosen,” said Sarah.

Shakespeare stood. "Well, you're safe. Frank got shot again and didn't die again. And the perp is in jail, awaiting trial." He approached the bed. "You two relax and recover. This case is over."

Tate sat down behind the glass and picked up the phone. It was his wife. He didn't care. He didn't care about anything anymore. His life as he knew it was over. He looked at her smiling face but didn't smile back. He didn't need to put on any pretenses anymore. He hated her, she hated him. No more hiding it.

"How are you, dear?"

It sounded artificial. A bullshit question to ask of a man looking at life in prison. A bullshit question that deserved a bullshit answer.

"Fine."

"Good, good. I talked to the lawyers and they said there was no chance of getting you out on bail."

He shrugged his shoulders.

"They're going to give you a psyche eval." She laughed. "I guess they think you're insane." He smiled. Just a small smile, but a smile nonetheless. "If only they knew."

His smile broadened. *I'm not insane. I did everything for a purpose.*

Her face became serious. "You know why you're being punished, don't you?"

He looked at her, puzzled. "What do you mean?"

"You shouldn't have fallen in love with her."

What was she talking about? How could she—?

"You were given one directive, one rule that couldn't be broken."

His mind reeled as he heard the words echo through his head. "Thou shalt not fall in love with this creature," he whispered.

"Precisely."

And then he knew. As his world came crashing down around him, he stared at her, his mouth agape as she glared at him. It all made sense, why he had been made to think Samantha was killed, and that he had killed her. Why so many events over the past few days had been out of control. It was punishment. Punishment for breaking the one rule.

He had fallen in love.

And it was forbidden.

Her glare was replaced by a smile. "I won't be able to see you anymore. Not until your return."

He snapped back to reality, and nodded, a new understanding of everything, of two decades of his life, a life that was being rapidly rewritten in his mind. "I understand. I understand everything, now."

She leaned toward the glass and placed her hand on it. He placed his hand over hers, aligning the fingers. He could almost feel her warmth through the glass. He knew it was his imagination, but it was a warmth he missed. The cold, damp prison he now occupied not at all to his liking. *I miss the heat.*

"I just want you to know one thing, before I leave."

He pressed the phone harder against his ear, just in case he might miss her final words to him.

"I'm very proud of you."

He smiled. Not a slight smile, but a broad one, his teeth almost breaking through, his eyes wide with happiness.

"Thank you, my master."

AFTERWORD

The idea for Tick Tock came from an intriguing phrase I heard almost two years ago, a phrase I now have no recollection of where I first heard it. That phrase was, "Hell is other people". Eventually I hit my "ideas" file, and researched this phrase. It came from a 1944 French play, Huis Clos, written by Jean-Paul Sartre, and has been performed in English under such names as No Exit, In Camera, No Way Out and Dead End, according to my trusty Hitchhiker's Guide to Earth, Wikipedia.

After reading a brief blurb on the play, the idea fascinated me, and I then made certain not to read the actual play, as I didn't want to be influenced by it. As I found out later, the play bears almost no resemblance to Tick Tock, instead acting merely as the spark for the central idea of someone believing they were in Hell.

On another note, after writing this book, and giving it a name that, after reading this book I am certain you, the reader, would agree fits, I discovered that James Patterson had recently released a book under the same title. A little bit of searching led me to find that another great, Dean Koontz, also wrote a book under the same name. As such, I apologize to Dean and James for any confusion this may cause. Perhaps people looking for this book will find yours instead, and your sales may improve.

With a mystery, things are usually held quite tightly to the chest, however several people did help me. I would like to thank my wife, Esperanza, my daughter, Niskha, my parents, Hugh & Bernice Kennedy, as well as Brent Richards (who I couldn't figure out how to kill off in this book, but maybe the next) and finally my friends for supporting me, and the tens of thousands of readers who have purchased, and hopefully enjoyed, my novels. You continue to have this author's humble gratitude.

ABOUT THE AUTHOR

J. Robert Kennedy wrote his first story when he was five.

Everyone in it died.

Things didn't get much better from there. After horrifying his teachers in creative writing classes he took an extended hiatus, returning to writing on a whim, haunted by the image of a woman standing in tall grass, the blades streaming through her fingers. The result was a short story, written in a single evening: *Does It Matter?*

And then he let it sit.

A couple of years later he let several friends read it and they encouraged him to try and get it published. He submitted it to *The Sink* and it was immediately accepted. Encouraged, he wrote a second story, *Loving the Ingredients*, and it too was accepted, along with a reprint of *Does It Matter?* by *The Writers Post Journal.*

With several publishing credits under his belt, he was ready for something bigger. A phone conversation with a best friend led to Robert writing his first novel, *The Protocol. Lachesis Publishing*, the first publisher he sent it to, agreed to publish it and cloud nine got a little more crowded.

This was followed by *Depraved Difference*, an international bestseller, and the re-release of *The Protocol*, and its sequels, *Brass Monkey* and *Broken Dove*, all international bestsellers. To date, all of Robert's books have been bestsellers in their categories.

Robert was born in Glace Bay, Nova Scotia, and grew up an Air Force brat, living in Halifax and Greenwood, Nova Scotia, Goose Bay, Labrador, Lahr and Baden, Germany, and finally Winnipeg and Portage la Prairie,

Manitoba. After a brief stint at the University of Waterloo, like Bill Gates, he went into business for himself and settled in Ottawa, Ontario. Robert has a wife and daughter, and is hard at work on his next novel.

Visit Robert's website at www.jrobertkennedy.com for the latest news and contact information.

The Protocol

A James Acton Thriller

Book #1

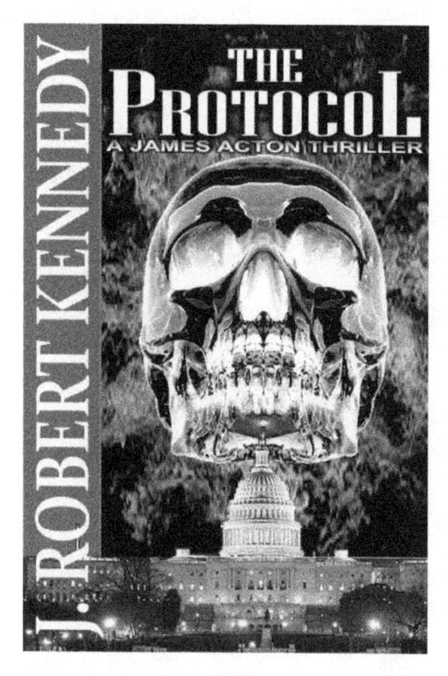

For two thousand years the Triarii have protected us, influencing history from the crusades to the discovery of America. Descendent from the Roman Empire, they pervade every level of society, and are now in a race with our own government to retrieve an ancient artifact thought to have been lost forever.

Caught in the middle is archaeology professor James Acton, relentlessly hunted by the elite Delta Force, under orders to stop at nothing to possess what he has found, and the Triarii, equally determined to prevent the discovery from falling into the wrong hands.

With his students and friends dying around him, Acton flees to find the one person who might be able to help him, but little does he know he may actually be racing directly into the hands of an organization he knows nothing about...

Brass Monkey

A James Acton Thriller

Book #2

A nuclear missile, lost during the Cold War, is now in play--the most public spy swap in history, with a gorgeous agent the center of international attention, triggers the end-game of a corrupt Soviet Colonel's twenty five year plan. Pursued across the globe by the Russian authorities, including a brutal Spetsnaz unit, those involved will stop at nothing to deliver their weapon, and ensure their pay day, regardless of the terrifying consequences.

When Laura Palmer confronts a UNICEF group for trespassing on her Egyptian archaeological dig site, she unwittingly stumbles upon the ultimate weapons deal, and becomes entangled in an international conspiracy that sends her lover, archeology Professor James Acton, racing to Egypt with the most unlikely of allies, not only to rescue her, but to prevent the start of a holy war that could result in Islam and Christianity wiping each other out.

From the bestselling author of Depraved Difference and The Protocol comes Brass Monkey, a thriller international in scope, certain to offend some, and stimulate debate in others. Brass Monkey pulls no punches in confronting the conflict between two of the world's most powerful, and divergent, religions, and the terrifying possibilities the future may hold if left unchecked.

Broken Dove

A James Acton Thriller

Book #3

With the Triarii in control of the Roman Catholic Church, an organization founded by Saint Peter himself takes action, murdering one of the new Pope's operatives. Detective Chaney, called in by the Pope to investigate, disappears, and, to the horror of the Papal staff sent to inform His Holiness, they find him missing too, the only clue a secret chest, presented to each new pope on the eve of their election, since the beginning of the Church.

Interpol Agent Reading, determined to find his friend, calls Professors James Acton and Laura Palmer to Rome to examine the chest and its forbidden contents, but before they can arrive, they are intercepted by an organization older than the Church, demanding the professors retrieve an item stolen in ancient Judea in exchange for the lives of their friends.

All of your favorite characters from The Protocol return to solve the most infamous kidnapping in history, against the backdrop of a two thousand year old battle pitting ancient foes with diametrically opposed agendas.

From the internationally bestselling author of Depraved Difference and The Protocol comes Broken Dove, the third entry in the smash hit James Acton Thrillers series, where J. Robert Kennedy reveals a secret concealed by the Church for almost 1200 years, and a fascinating interpretation of what the real reason behind the denials might be.

The Templar's Relic
A James Acton Thriller
Book #4

The Church Helped Destroy the Templars. Will a twist of fate let them get their revenge 700 years later?

The Vault must be sealed, but a construction accident leads to a miraculous discovery--an ancient tomb containing four Templar Knights, long forgotten, on the grounds of the Vatican. Not knowing who they can trust, the Vatican requests Professors James Acton and Laura Palmer examine the find, but what they discover, a precious Islamic relic, lost during the Crusades, triggers a set of events that shake the entire world, pitting the two greatest religions against each other.

Join Professors James Acton and Laura Palmer, INTERPOL Agent Hugh Reading, Scotland Yard DI Martin Chaney, and the Delta Force Bravo Team as they race against time to defuse a worldwide crisis that could quickly devolve into all-out war.

At risk is nothing less than the Vatican itself, and the rock upon which it was built.

From J. Robert Kennedy, the author of six international bestsellers including Depraved Difference and The Protocol, comes The Templar's Relic, the fourth entry in the smash hit James Acton Thrillers series, where once again Kennedy takes history and twists it to his own ends, resulting in a heart pounding thrill ride filled with action, suspense, humor and heartbreak.

The Turned

Zander Varga, Vampire Detective

Book #1

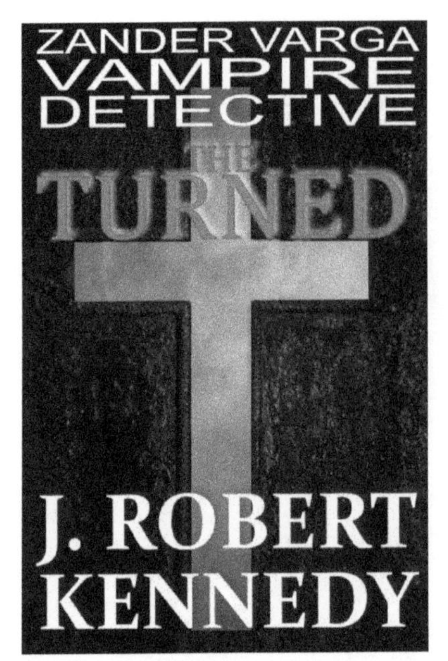

Zander has relived his wife's death at the hands of vampires every day for almost three hundred years, his perfect memory a curse of becoming one of The Turned—infecting him their final heinous act after her murder.

Nineteen year-old Sydney Winter knows Zander's secret, a secret preserved by the women in her family for four generations. But with her mother in a coma, she's thrust into the front lines, ahead of her time, to fight side-by-side with Zander.

And she wouldn't change a thing.

She loves the excitement, she loves the danger.

And she loves Zander.

But it's a love that will have to go unrequited, because Zander has only one thing on his mind. And it's been the same thing for over two hundred years.

Revenge.

But today, revenge will have to wait, because Zander Varga, Private Detective, has a new case. A woman's husband is missing. The police aren't interested. But Zander is. Something doesn't smell right, and he's determined to find out why.

From J. Robert Kennedy, the internationally bestselling author of The Protocol and Depraved Difference, comes his sixth novel, The Turned, a terrifying story that in true Kennedy fashion takes a completely new twist on the origin of vampires, tying it directly to a well-known moment in history. Told from the perspective of Zander Varga and his assistant, Sydney Winter, The Turned is loaded with action, humor, terror and a centuries long love that must eventually be let go.

Depraved Difference
A Detective Shakespeare Mystery
Book #1

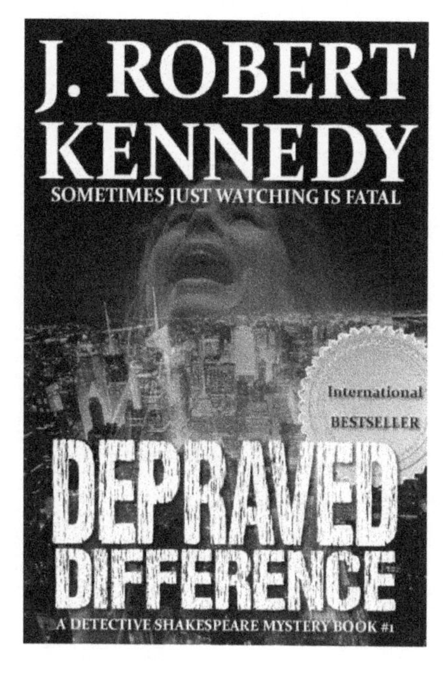

Would you help, would you run, or would you just watch?

When a young woman is brutally assaulted by two men on the subway, her cries for help fall on the deaf ears of onlookers too terrified to get involved, her misery ended with the crushing stomp of a steel-toed boot. A cellphone video of her vicious murder, callously released on the Internet, its popularity a testament to today's depraved society, serves as a trigger, pulled a year later, for a killer.

Emailed a video documenting the final moments of a woman's life, entertainment reporter Aynslee Kai, rather than ask why the killer chose her to tell the story, decides to capitalize on the opportunity to further her career. Assigned to the case is Hayden Eldridge, a detective left to learn the ropes by a disgraced partner, and as videos continue to follow victims, he discovers they were all witnesses to the vicious subway murder a year earlier, proving sometimes just watching is fatal.

From the author of The Protocol and Brass Monkey, Depraved Difference is a fast-paced murder suspense novel with enough laughs, heartbreak, terror and twists to keep you on the edge of your seat, then knock you flat on the floor with an ending so shocking, you'll read it again just to pick up the clues.

Tick Tock

A Detective Shakespeare Mystery

Book #2

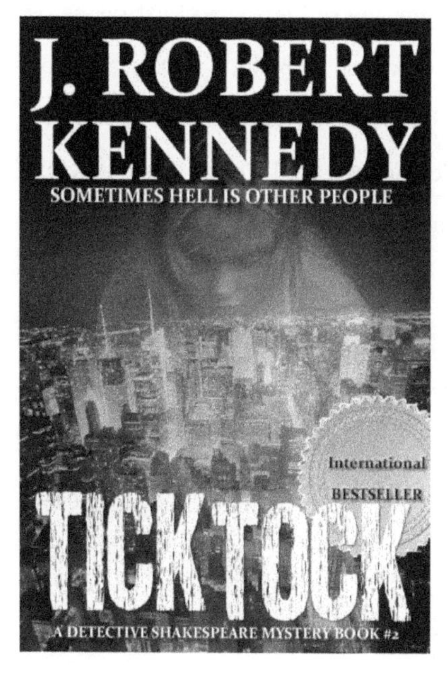

Crime Scene tech Frank Brata digs deep and finds the courage to ask his colleague, Sarah, out for coffee after work. Their good time turns into a nightmare when Frank wakes up the next morning covered in blood, with no recollection of what happened, and Sarah's body floating in the tub. Determined not to go to prison for a crime he's horrified he may have committed, he scrubs the crime scene clean, and, tormented by text messages from the real killer, begins a race against the clock to solve the murder before his own co-workers, his own friends, solve it first, and find him guilty.

Billionaire Richard Tate is the toast of the town, loved by everyone but his wife. His plans for a romantic weekend with his mistress ends in disaster, waking the next morning to find her murdered, floating in the tub. After fleeing in a panic, he returns to find the hotel room spotless, and no sign of the body. An envelope found at the scene contains not the expected blackmail note, but something far more sinister.

Two murders, with the same MO, targeting both the average working man, and the richest of society, sets a rejuvenated Detective Shakespeare, and his new reluctant partner, Amber Trace, after a murderer whose motivations are a mystery, and who appears to be aided by the very people they would least expect—their own.

Tick Tock, Book #2 in the internationally bestselling Detective Shakespeare Mysteries series, picks up right where Depraved Difference left off, and asks a simple question: What would you do? What would you do if you couldn't prove your innocence, but knew you weren't capable of murder? Would you hide the very evidence that might clear you, or would you turn yourself in and trust the system to work?

From the internationally bestselling author of The Protocol and Brass Monkey comes the highly anticipated sequel to the smash hit Depraved Difference, Tick Tock. Filled with heart pounding terror and suspense, along with a healthy dose of humor, Tick Tock's twists will keep you guessing right up to the terrifying end.

The Redeemer
A Detective Shakespeare Mystery
Book #3

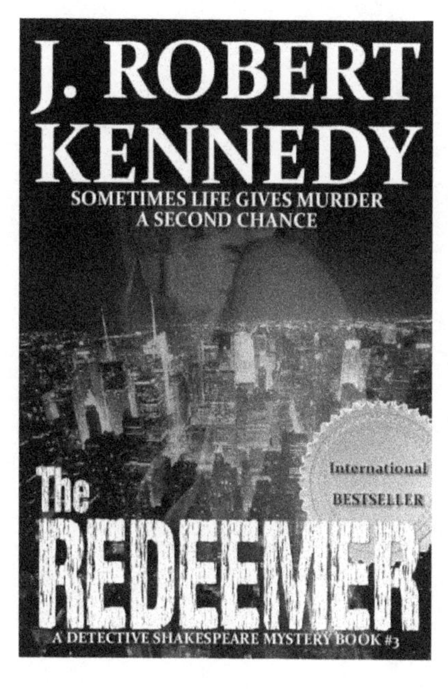

Sometimes Life Gives Murder a Second Chance

It was the case that destroyed Detective Justin Shakespeare's career, beginning a downward spiral of self-loathing and self-destruction lasting half a decade. And today things are only going to get worse. The Widow Rapist is free on a technicality, and it is up to Detective Shakespeare and his partner Amber Trace to find the evidence, five years cold, to put him back in prison before he strikes again.

But Shakespeare and Trace aren't alone in their desire for justice. The Seven are the survivors, avowed to not let the memories of their loved ones be forgotten. And with the release of the Widow Rapist, they are determined to take justice into their own hands, restoring balance to a flawed system.

At stake is a second chance, a chance at redemption, a chance to salvage a career destroyed, a reputation tarnished, and a life diminished.

A chance brought to Detective Shakespeare whether he wants it or not.

A chance brought to him by The Redeemer.

From J. Robert Kennedy, the author of seven international bestsellers including Depraved Difference and The Protocol, comes the third entry in the acclaimed Detective Shakespeare Mysteries series, The Redeemer, a dark tale exploring the psyches of the serial killer, the victim, and the police, as they all try to achieve the same goals.

Balance. And redemption.

CPSIA information can be obtained
at www.ICGtesting.com
Printed in the USA
BVHW031841191119
564291BV00001B/48/P